The Silent Sound of Darkness

A NOVEL

Sue Skalicky

PLOTLINE

BISMARCK, NORTH DAKOTA

Sue Skalicky/Plotline
1108 Hillside Terrace
Bismarck, ND 58501
https://lifeplotline.com/

Publisher's Note: This is a work of fiction. Names, characters, places, and incidents are a product of the author's imagination. Locales and public names are sometimes used for atmospheric purposes. Any resemblance to actual people, living or dead, or to companies, events, institutions, or locales is completely coincidental.

Book Layout ©2017 BookDesignTemplates.com

Cover Design Bre Cain

Ordering Information:
Quantity sales. Special discounts are available on quantity purchases by corporations, associations, and others. For details, contact the "Special Sales Department" at the address above.

The Silent Sound of Darkness/ Sue Skalicky. -- 1st ed.
ISBN 978-0-5785345-5-8

Contents

To my younger self

And yours

Prologue

Oblivious to what was happening, her young soul began to shrink deeper and deeper within her. When she was only nine years old, Jaclyn had wandered away from safety, lured by the attention and charisma of Damien Langley, one of her father's employees. Although she welcomed his thoughtfulness at first, it wasn't long before his charm had turned to lust and, by the time she was ten, his body began to do most of the talking. His reminders to hurt her father and brother if she ever uttered any word of their times together shredded her innocence. Fear became her constant companion.

She drew her knees closer to her chest and tried to shrink flat against the living room wall as her father screamed into the phone. His anger was her fault, and she feared the worst. Why did she have to cry when her father mentioned the company picnic the next day? She was finding it more and more difficult to pretend when Damien was nearby. Her father had questioned her growing aversion to helping at his plant and tree nursery, the largest and most profitable in Denver.

A week ago she'd heard her father talking to his sister, her aunt Lacey, on the phone. They discussed Damien. He told his sister he didn't trust Damien, and Jaclyn's behavior worried him. He even pondered the possibility of a connection between Damien's absences from work and Jaclyn's quietness. His sister listened and agreed that something wasn't right.

"Three times this week you were nowhere around when I needed your help moving some trees." Jaclyn's father's neck was turning a darker shade of red and a large vein bulged just above his shirt collar.

"If you knew how to run a business you wouldn't need to be looking for me," Damien screamed so loudly Jaclyn could hear as she sat a half a room away.

Jaclyn's heart beat so fast that pain pulsed in her temples. She held both hands to her head willing the phone conversation to end. But, her father continued to reprimand Damien for being late and taking long late-afternoon breaks. Then finally he turned and looked into Jaclyn's eyes. As he softened his expression to give a slight smile to his young daughter, her tear-filled eyes crested and uncontrollably wet her cheeks. She quickly grasped her knees and held them tightly to her chest as her body began to shake.

"That's it! You're fired. Don't bother coming in today. I'll have your final check processed today." With Damien's voice spewing profanities her father hung up the phone.

Since Jaclyn's mom died two years ago, they had just pretended to be a family. She knew her dad meant well, but he was so busy grieving and trying to take care of them, she often waited for him to tuck her in at night and he never came. When she snuck out of bed and looked into the living room, she saw her father fast asleep on the couch. She didn't blame him. He worked hard. But, she felt so lonely. She longed to tell him what had happened between her and Damien, but Damien had threatened to kill him and her brother if she uttered a word of the abuse.

Her father set the phone down on the table and walked over to Jaclyn. He quietly slid his back down the wall and sat next to her. She leaned into his embrace and began to weep. What had she done? She didn't want her father to die. As she tired from crying and her father carried her to the couch, her soul slid into a dark abyss in her heart and she went numb.

• CHAPTER 1 •

She longed to feel fully alive. To experience confidence and joy. To freely love and receive love from another. Even the wet, cold wind whipping Jaclyn Friedman's hair against her cheeks and stabbing her eyes felt dull. She lowered her head and bent her body into the wind as she jogged across the daycare parking lot. Once in her slate gray Jeep, she dug for tissues in her purse and then wiped the rain from her face and blew her nose. But, as soon as she dried her face, warm tears found easy paths down her cheeks and cascaded into her lap. She dug for more tissues but found none. Being alone was torture for she wept almost every time. Yet, being with others was bondage no one seemed to understand. But, she didn't blame them. She didn't understand it herself. All she knew was she couldn't bring herself to rely on anyone. She had the constant urge to dictate what was going on around her. All the time. She needed the peace of knowing everything would turn out right. And that she and her family could enjoy life without dangers. On one hand, she realized it was ridiculous and unnecessary, but she couldn't ever seem to let her guard down. Whenever she would even get close to trusting or depending on someone else, fear would grip her and she would panic. Over her adult years, she had tried plenty of anti-anxiety medications and was faithful to a yoga routine for almost six months once, but peace never came. The idea of peace had become only a fantasy. Something, she had accepted, would never happen. Even her dreams, filled with romance and goals being realized, would end in violence brought on by darkness and evil. She could never escape the fear, night or day. And control had become her only ally.

Jaclyn drove away from the daycare, her three-year-old daughter Anya with her favorite preschool teacher Miss Meaghan. She tried to always drop off her three oldest daughters, Mandy, 10, Mackenzie, 8, and Jenae, 6, before Anya, so they could play on the playground before the bell rang. Then, whenever she had the time, she would say goodbye to the girls, circle around the block, and watch them play on the playground from a parking spot across the street. Anya would allow the delay for a short time if she had her pink tablet with her learning games and songs. Jaclyn loved to watch the girls play and laugh, innocent and uninhibited. She grasped at and treasured every moment of living vicariously through her girls, willing the joy she felt to push back the fear planted in her when she was a young girl.

But, this morning Jaclyn hadn't had the time. She had scheduled an interview for a story she was writing with a deadline of Wednesday before Thanksgiving, only six days away. Before the interview, she needed to prepare some questions and do a little background research on the company to find a good angle. Her editor, Mark Geobani, was a seasoned journalist who had taken the editor position at the Cliff Creek Courier only three months after he had retired from a large newspaper in Chicago. Divorced, lonely, and still grieving the death of his only daughter, he had moved to Cliff Creek, Colorado, to get away from the memories and try to feel alive again. He and Jaclyn hit it off right away when she started work at the Courier eleven years ago. His loss and her need for fatherly guidance brought them into a relationship deeper than boss and employee.

Jaclyn saw little of her own father who still lived in Denver, where he and her brother ran the family nursery. It was always difficult for them to get away from the nursery to visit Jaclyn and Jaclyn avoided traveling far from her home. She feared to leave her home and the boundaries of her daily life. She felt out of control in unfamiliar territory, even though her father still lived in the family home where he raised her and her brother. The home where she had grown up had been her safe place, but it had also been her prison. She had no desire to spend the night there again. Grant suggested they stay with his mom, but Jaclyn said it was too small and the girls would end up breaking something. During the few trips they had made to Denver to see both of their families, Jaclyn had insisted that they stay in a hotel. She said it was so the girls could swim. Grant hated the idea, but Jaclyn always won.

So, Mark filled the gap of a meddling father, aggravating Jaclyn only on rare occasions. She craved his wisdom and hung on every word, even though her body language and aggressive tone made him think she didn't need his help. But, with work, Mark ran a tight ship. He demanded accuracy, integrity, and no missed deadlines. Jaclyn knew she was one of his favorites on staff, and she never wanted to compromise their special relationship.

Since she had several hours before the interview, Jaclyn headed for home. She pulled into the driveway of their two-story Dutch Colonial home, still unable to stop the tears. She put the Jeep in park and turned off the engine. The din of rain and branches hitting the car's roof matched her heart rate. How many times had she asked her husband Grant to get his construction tools and lumber out of their garage so they could park the cars in there before cold weather hit?

His construction company had a whole warehouse and shop in Pine Ridge, only thirteen miles from their home, but he kept unloading more and more into their garage, always promising to move it once he had the room in his truck to do so. Sometimes Jaclyn would stack all of his supplies on one side so she could at least get her car in the garage, but, she hadn't had the time before the weather turned. Cliff Creek experienced far more beautiful days than cruddy days, but when bad weather hit, it came in with a vengeance. And today was one of those days.

Jaclyn sat in the car, working to regain her composure before venturing inside. Out of the blue, her thoughts turned to how she and Grant had met. She had interviewed the young, handsome Grant Friedman for a story she was writing for the university's daily newspaper. He was majoring in Business Administration and had signed up to be part of a research study that was a first in the School of Business. His baby blue eyes and messy mop of dark wavy hair and a sexy day's growth of beard had instantly captivated her. But, what caused her heart to stir was the deep calmness of his voice. It wasn't what he said, but how he said it that mesmerized her. Twice during the interview, he had to ask her if she had any more questions because she was just staring at him. And then he had laughed. Her heart jumped, and she felt hope for the first time in her young adult life, but then she instantly scrambled to shut that door. She had become nervous and dropped her recorder. While picking it up she spilled her purse, some of its contents scattering under the oversized chair in the campus coffee shop. He stooped down to help her and she swatted his hand away and began to cry. But, he grabbed her hand, told her it would be okay, and asked if they could meet that night for dinner to finish the interview. She said yes, then instantly regretted her decision.

But, she pulled herself together and made it to the restaurant on time. She had refused Grant's offer of picking her up. That night they ended up not talking about the story at all. He was funny and easygoing, and she enjoyed that he didn't pry into her life. In response to his questions about her family, she recounted that her mother had died of a brain aneurysm when she was only eight years old, so her dad had raised her and her brother alone. Grant said he was sorry for her loss, then asked how she handled that at such a young age. Jaclyn's answer was direct and strong, showing no hint of grief. Naively, this impressed Grant.

She came across strong and confident as she talked about how her family had just worked together and took one day at a time. Jaclyn listened as Grant talked about growing up in Denver. They discovered they had gone to rival high schools and laughed about their memories of certain football games that each team had won and lost. In a pregnant pause in the conversation, Jaclyn became nervous and blurted out she had to be going and that she would text him her remaining questions. He again grabbed her hand and lied that he didn't text. Then he smiled and asked, "Breakfast?"

Twelve years of marriage and four beautiful, spunky daughters later, Grant could still captivate her with his eyes and calming voice. But, she could never relax into his strength and love and trust him. In fact, she purposely turned everything into a fight. When things didn't go her way, she would spend endless time and energy lecturing him and the girls about how to do whatever it was right, and why doing so were so important. The fight would give her the emotional space that made her feel safe. During the first few months of their marriage, Grant still had the ability to grab her hands, just like when they were dating, and calm her down. She would pull away from his hold, but then realize her overreaction, and they would laugh it off. Or at least she pretended to concede.

Only a month into their marriage Jaclyn had been watching Grant mingling with their friends at a local bar and she withdrew from the crowd and sipped her rum and Coke at a corner table. Grant caught her gazing at him, smiled and made his way to her, pulling the stool next to her so close that his thigh rested against hers. She stood, moved her stool several inches away from him, sat down, and looked away. Grant lost it. He demanded to know what was wrong. She couldn't talk. Her eyes welled with tears. Grant stood up and stormed out of the bar. He was angry, but not surprised. This wasn't abnormal behavior for Jaclyn. While they dated she had been more affectionate, but Grant could always sense her holding back. He hoped when they married she would relax and they would be inseparable. He longed for them to grow closer, not farther apart. But, marriage had only seemed to make things worse

But, as a few months became years, Jaclyn's defenses just grew stronger. Grant's eyes started to lose their luster with her constant attacks. She continued to cringe when he touched her and he felt it. They rarely fought in front of the kids, but behind closed doors, Grant would beg Jaclyn to tell him what he had done for her to treat him this way. She would cry and say it wasn't him, it was her, but there was never any resolution because Jaclyn wouldn't talk about it. The strength and confidence that Grant had fallen in love with, was now what stood between them. Those qualities had become a wall between them that grew thicker every day. Grant asked to go to counseling, but she said they were too busy. To cope, they both poured themselves into their work, she was a journalist, and Grant the owner and primary contractor of his own construction business Integrity Homes.

During college, Jaclyn had won many awards for her investigative journalism, her top honor being the Golden Journalism Award for outstanding reporting on social justice and human rights. The Cliff Creek Courier had also awarded her awards every year at their annual awards banquet. She thrived on understanding injustice and giving a voice to the voiceless. But, she seemed to bury the injustice she endured as a child deeper every year. She was mute to her own broken heart. But, she liked to believe she was giving to others what she couldn't have for herself: justice, safety, and peace.

Grant talked to everyone. He managed his construction company with fairness and enjoyed getting to know his employees and their families. He was so easygoing she ached with envy when she watched him enjoying others. His first impulse was to trust others, hers was to find out what was wrong with them. Jaclyn knew her compulsive need to control everything weighed on Grant, but, she couldn't bring herself to stop. Her priority was to keep her daughters safe. She needed to protect them from anyone who may harm them. The thought of her girls falling prey to a man like Damien made her physically sick.

Jaclyn's phone vibrated and jostled her mind back into the present. She glanced at the screen. Grant. His timing was always terrible. She didn't want to talk, but she answered so he couldn't say she was ignoring him. She forced out, "Hey."

"Hey, Jack! How are you?"

He had called her Jack since their first official date, a name she loved because he was the only one who called her that. But, today it grated on her nerves.

"Good. What's up?"

"I need you to get the girls from school today."

"What?! You said you could get them. I told you I have an interview at three."

"I know. I'm so sorry. But, I just connected with a new business and I need to meet with the owner and see if we can work together on my new home in Spindrift. He can only meet today at three. I'll make it up to you, Jack. I promise."

"Whatever. I'll reschedule. Again."

"Babe, I'm sorry."

Click.

Fury instantly dried her tears. Once again life was screaming at Jaclyn that she didn't matter. And that she never would. It seemed like the more she tried to be successful, the more life threw at her. Was it even worth it to try? Damien had often whispered to her that pleasing men is what she was made to do. He said it was all she would ever be good at and it would be the only way she would ever find love. Well, it seemed like that is all Grant wanted from her. But what was love? She thought she had found it when she met Grant, but his messages to her were often confusing. He said he loved her, but he also craved her body. His needs haunted her, and she feared to be intimate. In the dark, it wasn't Grant making love to her. It was Damien taking from her. Sucking more life out of her already depleted soul. After making love with Grant she couldn't stop the tears. She tried to hide them from him, but he always knew. He would want to talk, his needs fulfilled and her body and emotions racked with pain. She wanted to let him know it wasn't his fault, that it was hers. Damien had broken her. He was whole. But, the words never came. She was powerless against the fear that kept her from uttering a word. She cried for Grant. He deserved more than what she could give him. And she cried for herself. She felt dead inside. She begged God to have mercy on her. But, there was only a frightening silence.

Jaclyn got out of the Jeep and ran through the driving rain and wind. She fumbled with her keys, cursing the weather while she struggled to unlock the front door. Once inside, she plopped down on the couch by the fireplace near the kitchen. Every bit of her was soaked, but she didn't care. Her body hit the couch, and she clicked on the flame and reached for her laptop, hoping that doing research for her story would help to calm her anger. Her searching led her to the All's Quiet website. The soundproofing business originated in Calgary, Alberta, Canada, fifteen years ago. But, the new Cliff Creek store was the first in the United States. The Canadian-based stores carry a complete inventory of all things quiet: soundproofing for walls, silencers for guns, dog training collars, headphones, drum shields, doors, wall panels, etc. However, the new store in Cliff Creek only specialized in commercial, home, and studio soundproofing.

Jaclyn yawned and threw her laptop to the side. Why did Mark give her this story? He knew she hated this kind of writing. It was public relations. Simple advertising. Yes, people needed to know what was new in town, but her talent was investigative journalism. Mark did a great job of keeping her busy, even in this small Colorado community. It was still the Wild West, just gunfights on Main Street have turned into drive-by shootings in dark alleys. It even surprised her to uncover money laundering in the Cliff Creek valley. But, a new store? One that keeps things quiet? Boring. She needed to be working on her ongoing coverage of the Moorman trial. Peter Moorman was being tried for the murder of four college students in Arizona and New Mexico, and the attempted murder of a Cliff Creek College student who had survived his attack. They had postponed the trial while the young girl recovered.

Her hospitalization lasted seven weeks, two of those weeks spent in the intensive care unit. He had raped her, then broke both of her arms and legs. He cracked her skull with a hammer and then raped her again while she was unconscious. The girl's roommate had found her, soon after Moorman fled the scene, and called for help. They arrested Moorman ten days later in Nevada at a sleazy motel where he had used the young girl's credit card to pay for the room. Jaclyn had an interview scheduled with the victim for the Monday after Thanksgiving. Giving a voice to those who violated and abused was what breathed life into her. She thrived on others attaining the justice they deserved, feeling fulfilled through informing the world of the truth behind the abusers, thieves, and criminals' actions. But, Mark had insisted she cover this story. But, she found it to be meaningless. It was a huge waste of her time and talent.

Frustrated, she pressed her Facebook app on her phone and began to scroll, seeking something to get her mind off her marriage, her job, everything. Jaclyn rarely posted anything on Facebook because she felt like it was all a lie. Behind every innocent photo of joy, accomplishment, achievement, or humorous event, was pain. At least for her. She took lots of photos of their girls but kept them to herself. She feared predators finding her girls from photos posted on Facebook, so she didn't do it. Grant did. And they had big arguments about it. He told Jaclyn that she was overreacting and that he did it so his family could see photos of the girls. Once, he posted a photo she had allowed him to take of the two of them hiking in the canyon lands of southern Utah. They were both tan and fit. The photo was almost perfect. Jaclyn smiled big and had her arm around Grant. It was a photo of everything Jaclyn wanted in life but knew she couldn't ever have. Grant loved it for the hope it offered and Jaclyn hated it for the same reason. After Jaclyn fell apart and locked him out of their bedroom for three nights, Grant took it off his profile. Instead, he just texted photos to his family. He enlarged the photo Jaclyn hated and hung it in his office. He needed the hope it offered and Jaclyn rarely visited his office, so it didn't matter if it was there.

Jaclyn continued to scroll through her profile, envious and appalled at what people posted. Nothing was what it seemed, and it made her sick. Her friend Angela made life look like a fairy tale. She talked about her faith on Facebook like God was a fairy godmother. This morning she had posted a verse and made the assumption that God had given it to her because she had needed to hear those words today. What a joke. Jaclyn loved Angela like a sister and craved a faith like Angela's, but today it made her sick. She hated herself for being so critical of others, but she couldn't stop herself. She kept scrolling but didn't know what she was looking for. It all made her more frustrated. She clicked on her brother's profile and looked at photos of her niece and nephew. She smiled remembering their last visit when their youngest was only six months. That had been three years ago. She could still feel her niece's chubby arms and legs and how her heart had warmed when the baby fell asleep in her arms. She missed her family. They were only two hundred fifty miles apart, but they rarely saw each other. She just couldn't get past her fears of venturing far from the safety of her home.

Jaclyn realized that looking at Facebook had been a bad idea. She just felt worse. Just as she was going to close the app, a new friend request notification popped up. Hardly anyone ever communicated with her because she was so inactive. She clicked on it anyway, just to get rid of the annoying red icon. Her breath caught in her throat. She sat up, horror filling her eyes as she stared at the screen in disbelief. The phone dropped from her hand as she screamed.

• CHAPTER 2 •

Grant heard the click, glanced at his phone and exhaled a heavy sigh. What was he doing wrong? He had always admired Jaclyn's strength and confidence, but her behavior was ridiculous. She was constantly on the defense, ready to fight or flee. She had seemed happy to move to Cliff Creek twelve years ago, and they both thought it more than a coincidence when Angela Brixton, the real estate agent who had sold them their home, became a family friend and a mentor and confidant for Jaclyn. But, her excitement for new opportunities and the joy of their growing family seemed to wane every year they were in the Cliff Creek valley. Grant went back and forth between compassion for Jaclyn and anger for her behavior. He knew to lose her mom at such a young age must have been horrible, and he didn't blame her for feeling the need to take charge of her family in her mom's absence. But, that was a long time ago. Their family now was whole. They needed each other. But, they didn't need a dictator ruling everything they did. Grant had gone to counseling for several months early on. Jaclyn had refused to go, so he had gone alone. He learned a lot, but nothing seemed to help once he got home. After several years of trying to talk and work things out, he had settled into a pattern of letting things unfold and dealing with them as they came. And every day seemed like it was a new battle.

He loved Jaclyn, and always would, but he didn't know where she had gone. All he saw of the Jaclyn he had met in college was a beautiful woman with a towering, thick wall around her heart. Most days he felt sad for her, but today he was angry.

Grant only had five hours before he needed to meet the subcontractor and over five hours of work to do. He put his truck in gear and hopped on the interstate and headed east to Pine Ridge to his shop. He needed to order and organize supplies and make sure his employees were on task.

On the drive, he asked Siri to call his friend Davis Markle. Davis and Grant went way back to high school. They had played both football and baseball together and, although they went to different colleges, they stayed as close as brothers. Davis and his family were now living in Omaha, but he and Grant tried to connect every month. During his senior year, Grant's father had left him, his younger brother, and their mom for another woman whom Grant still has never met, even though he heard that they are still together. Having to take on the role of the man of the house at seventeen, Grant recognized the benefit of hanging out with Davis and his family, learning a lot from Davis' dad about what being a real man means. Davis' dad was a pastor of a small congregation in Littleton and he modeled to Grant what it looked like to love his wife and children and to live a life of faith.

"Hey, Grant, how are you, buddy?"

"Hey, Davis. Well, I wish I could say great."

"What's up, bro?"

"You know, everything is going pretty well. My business will hopefully turn a profit this year, if I'm lucky, and the girls are doing awesome in school. But, Jaclyn...."

"No better?"

"Worse."

"Oh, man. So, sorry, Grant. She still won't go to counseling?"

"Absolutely not! I just don't get it. I go out of my way to help her when she's in a bind with her job, but if I ask for her to change her schedule, I get the cold shoulder. Hell, I get the cold shoulder even when I ask nothing of her. I love her, man. I do! But, I don't know how much longer I can live like this. She corrects everything I do. Everything. I can't parent right, vacuum right, sleep right."

"I wish I had some great advice, but all I can offer is what my dad always said to me when Amy and I would struggle, 'Man up, son, and love your wife. It was never her job to make you happy. But, it is your job to love her as God loves you.'"

"Oh, Jesus, Davis! Please, enough with the God stuff. I need a buddy, not some rote philosophy that makes my ninety-two-year-old grandma feel like she has a purpose."

"I'm just letting you know what has always helped me. Listen, Amy and I also have our rough moments. Often. But, the more we learn to give each other grace and accept each other's quirks, the better life is around our house. Maybe you are just being too hard on Jaclyn. Give her some space, Grant."

"Yep. Thanks, Davis. I should go."

"Grant, wait a minute..."

"Talk soon."

Grant hit the end call button on his dash with a vengeance, then he took a deep breath and let out a sigh. He cranked up the speed of his windshield wipers as the rain came at him like a flood of angry accusations. What was he becoming? Even when his father had had an affair, he hadn't felt this angry. Or had he? Grant prided himself on how he had handled his parents' divorce. Being the oldest he stepped up. He remembered being angry back then, but not about the divorce. His mom had deserved better. What he was furious about was how others didn't respect him enough to give him credit for holding the family together. Everyone tried to tell him to ease up on managing everything and just be a kid. Even his mom and brother were more apt to criticize him than thank him. But, his confidence didn't waiver through the end of high school or throughout college. He was determined to show everyone who he could become. He paid for school with scholarship money and by working two jobs, leaving him with no student loans after graduation. He had also developed a relationship with a small construction company owner in Cliff Creek the summer between his freshman and sophomore year while interning with him for ten weeks. Grant came back the next two summers as a full-time carpenter and would occasionally take the time to drive some custom doors or other unique items up from Denver-based manufacturers. The owner, Darren Archer, could have just ordered online and had the items shipped, but he enjoyed seeing Grant and mentoring him about running a small business. He saw so much potential in him.

In fact, Darren attended Grant's college graduation and, that day, offered him a job with his company, Integrity Construction. Five years later Darren retired and offered Grant his business. By then Grant and Jaclyn had been together close to five years, marrying during the summer after graduation. They had a three-year-old and an almost one-year-old and seemed to navigate their early marriage the way most young couples did, with plenty of arguments and growing pains. Grant renamed the business Integrity Homes and decided to only specialize in new home construction. Jaclyn worked for the Cliff Creek Courier, arranging interviews around Grant's schedule so they didn't have to rely on too many sitters.

But, as the years passed and they added two more daughters to their craziness, the tension between him and Jaclyn didn't let up. Grant stopped sharing anything about work with Jaclyn early in their marriage because she couldn't give him any credit for his successes. All she seemed to see was the bottom line. Darren had warned him, that although he was taking over an established business, he would have to not get discouraged the first few years if he didn't hit the profits he had hoped for. Darren focused on remodels and an occasional new home, but Grant wanted more. He wanted to be the most successful home builder on the Western Slope. He knew he would get there, but it seemed every year Jaclyn exploded at their growing debt and accused him of driving them to bankruptcy. He had a solid plan, and it irked him she couldn't see his progress. So, he stopped talking to her about it. He made sure that the family had what they needed, and he never said no to a purchase Jaclyn wanted to make because he didn't want to fight.

But, he, too, had become concerned about the business. Last year, he had rushed building a home so he could enter it into the Parade of Homes, but some work was sloppy and he was sure people saw it as they walked through it. No one said anything, but his profits this year showed it. His current hope of making it to the next level was the home he was building for a local oncologist right outside of Spindrift. And that is why he needed to pull out all the stops and make this home his best.

Standing water jolted Grant from his introspection as his tires hydroplaned. He gripped the wheel tighter and lifted his foot from the accelerator, slowing without spinning out of control. He canceled the cruise control, a stupid move on his part to even put it on in this kind of weather. He slammed his hand against the steering wheel and took a deep breath. He let it out with a shudder. He turned off at the next exit and made his way to his shop. Calling it a shop was an understatement. The Integrity Homes shop was massive - 50,000 square feet massive. Grant had been expanding the size of his shop over the years so that crews could build parts for the homes off-site and deliver them when ready. This way he could also hire a night shift that worked while he slept.

Grant turned his thoughts from Jaclyn to the day ahead. He was excited to meet with the owner of the new soundproofing business in town. Making this connection may just give him what he needed to turn the corner in his business. He had hated to back out of picking up kids and causing Jaclyn to miss her interview, but connecting with the owner of this business could prove to be his ticket to starring in the Parade of Homes.

The owner of All's Quiet, Evin Wolfe, had contacted Grant, and he had liked what he heard. Wolfe offered all things quiet for homes and studios: sound barrier materials, isolation hardware, and acoustical door seals. Grant had pitched an in-home theater to the owner of the Spindrift home, and it had been well-received. The doctor's only concern is he didn't want the noise in the theater to cause noise anywhere else in the home. He and his wife already had three children and were hoping to get pregnant with their fourth soon, so waking up babies was a big issue for them. Grant promised that there would be no sound leakage. He had no experience with soundproofing and had researched companies when out of the blue, Wolfe had called his cell phone. Today at three had been the only option to meet, so Grant agreed and took his chances on breaking his promise with Jaclyn. He had expected her anger, and she didn't disappoint.

Now that Grant was at the shop, he had less than five hours before their meeting. He made his way through the building to his office, stopping often to talk with several employees. Grant prided himself on the good relationships he had with every man and woman who worked for him. He demanded respect, but he always tried to see his employees' efforts and acknowledge them both privately and publicly. He had even set up an annual awards banquet for his team and every year, he gave everyone some kind of award. Grant knew that he thrived best when someone recognized his efforts and he would do nothing less than that for those who worked for him.

Grant made it to his office, shut the door, and began to work. He tried to focus on punch lists for his project managers for the next week, but couldn't focus. He'd received an email from his accountant asking for a projected financial statement for the end of the year. The bottom line worried him. The numbers would not add up. He should make more profit every year, but he wasn't. Had he jumped too soon on specializing in new homes? He knew it was the right move, but all he could hear in his head was Jaclyn's criticism. Before he knew it, it was time to go meet with Evin Wolfe at All's Quiet. He handed his secretary what he had finished on the punch lists and told her he would email her with any additions so she could get them printed by tomorrow.

The weather outside had not improved in the least. The wind had knocked down several branches from the trees surrounding the shop, causing him to zig-zag his way out of the parking lot. As he drove he tried calling Jaclyn, but she didn't pick up. He had expected her normal blast of texts throughout the day making sure he was where he said he was going to be and doing what she needed him to do. But, since she hung up on him this morning, his phone had been quiet. She was mad at him. He turned off the radio and just listened to the rain and wind as he drove to All's Quiet. The new store was across the street from the Cliff Creek Courier where Jaclyn worked. He looked for her car but then realized she would already be on her way to the school to pick up the kids. Which, of course, was his fault.

With eyes downcast and his body twisted against the driving rain, Grant navigated his way to the front door of All's Quiet. He grasped the slippery handle and yanked hard. It didn't give. "Damn!" Grant huddled closer to the building and knocked with impatience. He let his frustration get the best of him, swore under his breath, and set off jogging back to his truck. As he reached for the handle, a loud whistle caused his neck to turn into the downpour and squint at the dark figure standing in the doorway, motioning him to come in. He sprinted back, now soaked. Evin Wolfe held the door but blocked the entrance until he had introduced himself. Grant had to somewhat forcibly make his way past Evin and into the store.

"Sorry, Mr. Wolfe, I'm just soaked to the bone."

"Come in," Evin said evenly. He turned and locked the door.

"Are you closed today?"

"I just want to give you my full attention. Let's look at your plans for the in-home theater."

"Okay, well… I'm Grant Friedman," Grant said, reaching out his hand to shake Evin's.

Evin turned and took a seat on one side of a work table and motioned for Grant to sit next to him. Grant dropped his hand, rubbed it against his wet jeans, and took a seat. He opened his briefcase, hoping the plans weren't too wet. Fortunately, they were dry enough to spread them across the table in front of him and Evin.

"Looks simple enough," Evin said dryly.

Grant paused and looked at Evin. "Listen, I'm not getting a good vibe from you. Do you want my business?"

Evin looked at Grant and stared silently for an uncomfortably long time. Finally, he smiled. "Oh, I definitely want your business. And I will do a great job for you. Sorry, I just moved to town and have a lot on my mind with getting everything set up."

Grant continued confused. "No worries. Okay, so my end goal is to impress at next year's Parade of Homes. I will invest a little extra to make that happen, but money is definitely tight."

"You're fine."

"Excuse me?"

"Oh, I'm just saying you're fine because all contractors seem to live on the edge financially. But, in reality, they are fine. It is quite a business, isn't it? How are your investments doing?"

Grant sat back at the sudden change in conversation. "What? Yes, I have investments, but they are far from being mature."

"Maybe I can help. Where have you invested your money?"

"Um, stocks right now. My employees are all shareholders."

Evin laughed rudely. "My first bit of advice would be to not think of your employees so much this early in the game. You need to keep yourself and your family at the forefront of all your financial decisions. Are you married? Have children?"

"Yes, my wife Jaclyn is a journalist here in town and we have four daughters." Grant's anger returned, and he felt uneasy about this conversation.

"What is your net worth right now?"

Grant looked up and searched Evin's eyes. Something just didn't seem right. "Hey, sorry we've gotten off track talking about my personal life. We should plan a day and time for you to come to see the property so you can get started on the theater. The crew will finish sheetrock by the end of the day today. I'm assuming you don't want us to do much more until you install some materials."

"Uh, yes, that's for sure," Evin sighed, clearly upset with the turn in the conversation. "For the best results, we will need to install a sound barrier to the walls, acoustical caulk, floor underlayment, and sound diffusers."

For the next hour, Grant and Evin poured over the plans and discussed several approaches until they both agreed on one, both for the cost savings and meeting the homebuilder's requirements.

Evin banged his large hand on the table and determined their meeting was over. "How does your day look tomorrow? I need to come look at the property to take some measurements. Then I will shoot you an estimate and I can get going early next week. Does this same time work?"

"Sure! I'll text you the address right now."

"Great!"

"But, before I leave, can I have your business license number and credentials?"

"I'm a sole proprietorship, so I don't have a business license."

Grant took a breath in the awkward silence. "How about your employer identification number? I could get a contract drawn up so we can both sign it when we meet tomorrow."

Evin stared at Grant while appearing to plan an answer for longer than necessary. Grant began to sweat. Then Evin grabbed his business card, checked some records on his phone and jotted down his EIN.

"Here. Giving you this information shouldn't be a problem in the long run," Evin said then stood.

Evin's behavior and comment confused Grant, but he took the card and thanked him, anyway. Evin towered a good six inches above Grant as they finally shook hands.

Grant said goodbye, pushed open the door and pulled up his hood against the sleet that was now replacing the rain. As he dashed to his truck, he thought he heard Evin yell at him. Once he got the truck door open, he turned towards the storefront and yelled, "Excuse me?!" But, Evin had retreated behind the door, darkened by raindrops and window film.

He shrugged, shut the truck door and turned the engine over. As the cab warmed Grant glanced through his phone. Still no messages from Jaclyn. He sighed and rubbed his face with the palms of his hands. Maybe Davis was right, he needed to give her more grace. Maybe they could get away for the weekend. Even one night. They could just have Angela come watch the kids and they could stay at the Avalanche Lodge at the small ski resort near town. Since they didn't have much snow yet, he was sure he could get a good deal.

There was a text from Davis. Grant felt bad for hanging up on him earlier and expected a rebuke. He clicked on the text and breathed a sigh of relief by the grace Davis offered.

"Grant, take it one day at a time. Praying for you. Love you, bro!"

Tears stung Grant's eyes. He took a deep breath and put the truck in gear. He hopped on the highway leading to Spindrift to check on progress at the job site before heading home. It had been a long time since he had even thought about God as anything but a cosmic gamer, using him to attain some goal at his expense. But, he trusted his friend Davis, and always marveled at his calm demeanor. He and his wife Amy had lost a baby to SIDS three years ago and Grant never heard them once blame God. A year and a half later they had healthy twins:

a boy and a girl. Yet, they continued to celebrate the birthdays of the child they lost, praising God for the day he would reunite them. Grant didn't understand their joy. He was angry for them.

Grant turned up the music and tried to relax. He needed to not think about anything. Classic rock filled his cab, and he tapped his left foot to the beat. Soon, his heart rate decreased, and he relaxed. He mentally looked at the theater in the Spindrift home, dreaming about what it would look like during the Parade of Homes. He had a lot of work to get done. His phone buzzed on the seat next to him, but he didn't feel it. A message popped up on the screen from Jaclyn.

"I don't expect you to understand but need you to know that i'm canceling all our plans for the weekend. Mandy will be upset but i will try to make it up to her."

•   C H A P T E R   3   •

Jaclyn put her hand to her heart and sat upright. Her breathing increased, and she felt dizzy. It must be some sick joke. She took several deep breaths and tried to calm herself down. He was dead. It couldn't be him. Maybe it just looked like his name. Her heart raced and her hands shook as she bent down and picked up her phone, turned it over, and touched the screen to bring it to life. Her hands were shaking so much that she kept getting her passcode wrong. Finally, she set the phone on the coffee table, rubbed her hands together to stop the shaking and kept taking deep breaths. The last thing she needed was the phone to lock her out. When she felt steady enough to try again, she attempted to sign in, this time keeping the phone on the table and tapping each number gently with her index finger. The screen lit up and there it was. His name: Damien Langley. She clicked on his profile, being careful to not accept his request. The limited profile came to life, and she scoured every detail of what was available to those who were not his friends. His last profile picture update was only two weeks ago. It was him. She will never forget the look in those dark eyes. He looked twenty years older, but it was definitely him. He didn't add a location to the photo, so she copied the image address and searched on Google Images. She sat back and brought her hands to cover her mouth. He posted it from

Cliff Creek! She felt lightheaded again. Then she noticed that she had been holding her breath. She released her breath in bursts, beginning to hyperventilate. She dropped her head between her knees and panted. After forcing herself to take several deep tremulous breaths, she felt like she could finally sit with her head up without passing out. How could he be here? He was dead.

Three days after Jaclyn's dad had fired Damien Langley, when she was only ten years old, someone had reported him missing. Witnesses said he was drunk on a boat in Lone Mesa Reservoir, about 200 miles southwest of Denver. A park ranger found the boat, damaged and bouncing against a rocky shore up a narrow gorge on the north end of the reservoir. Sheriff's deputies, park rangers, and search crews looked for Damien until dark on the first day. The next morning, they changed the effort from a rescue to a recovery mission and the teams hunted for Damien's body for the next five days. The final ruling, based on the accounts of witnesses, Langley not returning to his home, and the over 300-foot depth of the water in the gorge where they found his boat, was that Damien Langley was dead.

Jaclyn remembered her father reading about the accident and the pronouncement that Damien was dead. He had called his sister Lacey and sighed, "That son-of-a-bitch is finally gone for good. Thank God." Jaclyn had known that her father suspected something had gone on between her and Damien, but he never brought it up and she had never braved the silence to tell him. But, she knew that they were both relieved that Damien was dead, and he was no longer a threat.

But, now was he? Jaclyn still couldn't wrap her mind around the idea that Damien was still alive. It couldn't be possible. But, they had never found his body. And how did he even find her on Facebook? He didn't know her married name. She stood up and locked all the doors and windows. Then she put on a pot of coffee. While the coffee brewed, she sat on a stool and searched for any news of Damien's death online. After an hour, the lack of information almost convinced her that the Facebook request came from someone pretending to be Damien. Then, right when she was about to give up, she came across a small article in the Denver Post, eighteen months after Damien's alleged death. Someone had claimed to see him in Sioux Falls, South Dakota. Damien's face had been a match on the police database for a shoplifting incident at a local convenience store. The article contained information about him being declared dead eighteen months earlier and about the memorial service held by his mother. It explained that he had been in their system because they had previously arrested him for several DUIs, assault with a deadly weapon, and tax evasion over the previous ten years. Why had her father even hired him?

Jaclyn got up and poured herself a steaming mug of coffee. She leaned against the counter and took a long sip. She had only been eleven and a half years old when this article was written. Had her dad read it when it came out? She couldn't remember him and her aunt having any conversation mentioning anything about a news article about Damien. And she eavesdropped every time he called her. Deep down she knew her dad and his sister hated Damien for more than just being a poor employee. All Jaclyn remembered about her dad after they declared Damien dead was that he buried himself in work. Now, as an adult, she could understand that that had been his way of grieving. And, if he had read the article, and it scared him, wouldn't he have been overprotective of her?

She topped off her coffee and returned to the couch. There had been no follow-up articles about the Sioux Falls police finding Damien, so she began to look into his police records. Her journalistic instincts kicked into high gear as she set out to piece Damien's story together. She needed the facts. And, soon. If she didn't figure out what he was doing in town and what he's been doing all these years, her life could be in danger. She shuddered as she remembered the threats Damien had made when she was still a young girl. Putting her head in her hands she wondered if her family was now in danger, too.

Jaclyn grabbed her phone and dialed her dad before she even knew what she was going to say to him. She just needed to know that he was okay.

"Stone Plant and Tree Nursery, this is Bill, can I help you?"

"Hey, dad! I'm so glad you picked up."

"Hey, sweetie! How are you?"

"Good. Good. Listen, I just wanted to see if you remembered that Mandy's tenth birthday is coming up."

"Yep. Wrote it on the calendar. So sorry I won't be able to drive over. The holidays keep us hopping with all the winter flowers, wreaths, and trees."

"No problem, dad. Just making sure you call on the right day."

Jaclyn could hear a lot of commotion in the background and the beep of a forklift backing up.

"Well, dad, I can let you go."

"What is that, Jaclyn? I have a forklift in my ear."

"I just said I love you. Talk again soon!"

"Love you, too, honey. Give the kids a hug from grandpa!"

Jaclyn breathed a sigh of relief then returned to her laptop and continued her search. Nothing. How could someone just up and vanish? If, in fact, that happened. Was his body still at the bottom of the reservoir and the whole sighting in South Dakota a mistake? But, he had been in the police system and the face on the security footage pinged a match. Jaclyn toggled back over to Facebook and again scoured his page. Nothing much available except that profile photo with his dark gaze drilling into her wounded soul through the screen.

Jaclyn knew that she couldn't tell anyone. She had gone twenty-three years not telling anyone about the abuse she suffered at the hands of Damien Langley, and she would not start now. And, just like then, she wasn't about to put anyone else in danger. She would sort this out and, if she needed to, she would meet with Damien and confront him alone.

She turned her attention back to her laptop, trying to find evidence of Damien living in Cliff Creek. If he had rented a place or bought a house, his name and address would pop up if she paid a couple of bucks to get the information. But, no luck. Nothing. Frustrated, she closed her laptop and walked through the house. She paused at each of the girls' bedrooms and whispered an awkward prayer, "Please God, let no one hurt my babies." Jaclyn and her family had all gone to church every week and she and her brother had gone to youth group on Wednesdays until their mom died. The aneurysm had taken their mom without warning and gave no one the chance to save her. Or, to even say goodbye to her. After the funeral was over, and extended family and friends traveled back home, not one of them went to church again. In fact, no one even talked about church or God. The pastor tried calling their dad, but he brushed him off a couple of times and then stopped answering. The youth pastor saw Jaclyn and her brother at several sporting events and tried to understand why they weren't at youth group anymore. They just smiled and lied they would try. They just didn't go. It was like they had never gone. It wasn't like they were angry and yelling at God. They simply never talked about him or to him ever again.

But, now, as she stood at the doorway to Jenae and Anya's room, staring at the converted crib toddler bed tucked next to the twin bed, she couldn't help but think about God. Her thoughts were filled with doubt. She demanded the meaning behind these cruel events. She knew that life is hard for everyone, even those who seem like they have everything and never suffer. And, she believed that there is someone or something bigger than their puny minds and physical abilities. But, what was this higher power doing? What was the purpose of her mother's death and the abuse she endured? Why did someone she thought was dead and buried now return unexpectedly, bringing her to her knees again? She didn't understand any of it, but as she continued to each of the girls' doorways she chose to whisper a plea of protection to a God she didn't fully trust.

At a loss, she descended the stairs, glanced at her laptop, and kept walking to the kitchen to refill her coffee mug. She leaned back against the counter, sipping on her coffee when she felt the familiar tug on her instincts to enter whatever battle lies ahead between her and Damien. Jaclyn knew this feeling well. She had always referred to it as simply putting on her big girl panties and controlling the outcome of the situation so the results were in her favor. Fear and doubt sunk back deep inside her as her brain launched into militant protective mode. This was no time to worry about what Grant and the girls would think. It would be up to her to protect them. Just like she had protected her dad and brother when she was a child. She returned to the couch, grabbed a pad of paper and pen and began to make a plan.

"Damn!" Jaclyn blurted out loud when she realized that it was nearly two o'clock and she hadn't rescheduled her three o'clock interview. "Damn, you, Grant! I just need to get this stupid interview out of the way. I don't have time for this."

She set the paper and pen down and looked for the number for Pete Black, the manager of the local All's Quiet store. She dialed the number and waited impatiently. Her fury about Mark assigning her this story in the first place resurfaced and raged each time the phone rang without being answered. When the call went to voicemail, she banged her fist on the counter then waited to leave a message.

"Good afternoon, Mr. Black, my name is Jaclyn Friedman from the Cliff Creek Courier. I apologize but need to reschedule our three o'clock appointment. Please call me at your earliest convenience so we can get this done. Thank you."

Jaclyn knew she had sounded curt, even aggressive. She felt bad for taking her anger out on this poor innocent guy, but she couldn't let that affect her focus on what to do about Damien and protecting her family.

She returned to the paper and pen and began to write a list of immediate actions that she needed to take: Cancel Mandy's sleepover Friday night, she needed to keep all the girls close; Get Grant to install the security system he purchased over three months ago; Call Mark and try to get someone else to write the story about the new business. That would do it for now. It was a start.

She dialed Mark, and he answered before she even heard a ring.

"Hey, world changer! How are you doing?"

"Hey, Mark. Well, I've been better. Grant and I have run into some issues with the girls and I'm wondering if you could cut me some slack and assign someone else to this All's Quiet business story."

There was a long pause before Mark answered. "I wish I could, Jaclyn. I know it really isn't your cup of tea. But, the owner of the business specifically asked for you. Normally, I wouldn't assign someone just from a request, but Della and Ryan are up to their eyeballs in public records for the upcoming story on the Mayor, and Russ is in the hospital with pneumonia."

"Ughhh! Whatever. I will do it." Tears burned Jaclyn's eyes, and she bit her lip.

"Listen, Jaclyn, I'm sorry to hear about your troubles at home. Is there anything I can do?"

"Yes, take me off this story!"

Click.

Jaclyn hung up on Mark as her tears crested and ran down her face. She knew the tears were from the stress of her current situation, but they were also from hurting Mark. Mark had always been a faithful mentor and friend. He was fatherly when she needed it, but deep down she has always treasured him as her very own Yoda. He hadn't so much taught her about journalism as he has taught her about people. She'd accused Mark of seeing the good in so many people that he could tell her something good about Hitler. Mark had responded that yes, there was something down deep in Hitler that was good, for God created him. He left it at that. Jaclyn admired Mark's ability to keep firm boundaries with unsafe people at the same time as offering them grace and forgiveness. But, today it irritated her. All along she knew that if Mark knew what Damien had done to her he would be angry, but he would also try to understand what was going on in Damien's heart that would cause this violence. And, anyone offering Damien grace would send her over the edge. Just one more reason she couldn't tell anyone. Ever.

But, now what? There were already too many dead ends in her effort to track Damien. She glanced at her phone and sighed when she saw it was time to go get the girls. Further investigation would have to wait until tonight.

Once again, she cursed Grant as she braced herself and turned her back against the driving rain as she locked the front door. The garage needed to be available to park in. This was ridiculous. As she ran towards her Jeep, she kicked up rain and mud and nearly tripped on a downed branch behind her car. Angrily, she booted the branch out of the way, unlocked the car and jumped in.

Jaclyn's phone rang as soon as she put the car in reverse. She punched connect on the dash and answered.

"Hello, this is Jaclyn."

"Mrs. Friedman?"

"Yes."

"This is Pete Black, manager at All's Quiet. I just arrived for our meeting. I guess I should have given you my cell number instead of the store number. Are you sure you can't swing by this afternoon?"

"So sorry, Pete. I really can't. Family emergency. Are you available in the morning tomorrow?"

"Well, I guess, if I live through driving in this here hurricane. Who ever heard of weather like this in the mountains?"

"I agree with you, sir. What is the earliest time you could meet tomorrow? I have a packed schedule."

"Well then, come on down to the store about seven and I will have the coffee on."

Jaclyn worried about getting kids to school, but Grant would just have to rearrange his schedule this time and get them there. And a seven o'clock interview would mean she would have most of the day to do more research on Damien.

"That sounds great, Mr. Black. See you at seven."

"Just call me Pete, Ma'am. Goodbye."

"Goodbye, Pete."

Jaclyn hung up the phone and turned her thoughts toward her girls. She couldn't believe Mandy was going to be ten soon. Jaclyn had been ten when no one knew she was being abused. She tried to put herself in Mandy's shoes. Would Mandy tell her if she was being abused? Jaclyn hadn't told her dad because Damien said he would kill him if she did. What if someone threatened Mandy the same way? Or one of the other girls? How much did Damien know about her and her family? Could he know where they went to school? She sped up. She needed to see her girls now.

"Damn it!" Jaclyn swore when she realized she had just missed the turn to the school. She moved into the right lane so she could turn at the next street and circle back. Her phone rang. This time it was her friend Angela. Jaclyn just let it ring. She didn't want to talk. As she pulled into the pickup lane, she glanced at her phone and saw that Angela had left a voicemail. That would have to wait, too. As she inched forward, she could see her girls all together, bouncing up and down and laughing, waiting for her to get closer so that the pickup lane monitor wouldn't reprimand them. Soon enough, they were climbing in the car and all vying for her attention about their day. The car was a buzz of conversation and giggles and bickering that soothed Jaclyn's soul. She needed her girls. They centered her. They gave her a purpose. And, now, they gave her a reason to fight Damien. As she pulled up to the daycare to get Anya, Mandy told her mom how excited she was for her sleepover Friday night. Jaclyn cringed and asked all the girls to come with her to get Anya.

"Noooooo, mom! It's too wainy," said Jenae with as much pitch as she could muster as a fairly new six-year-old.

"Mom, you always let us wait in the car because it is easier," Mandy said, always the logical one.

"Let's go!" Mackenzie said as she was halfway out the door, letting rain blow all over her sisters.

"Get out now!" demanded Jaclyn. "This is no time to disobey me!"

There was no way Jaclyn was going to leave the girls alone with Damien so close by. They all trudged into the daycare, retrieved Anya, and plodded back to the Jeep. By the time they reached the car, Jenae was in tears because Mackenzie had let the daycare door slam in her face.

"You're selfish!" Jenae yelled through her tears.

"You're too slow!" Mackenzie fought back. "Next time hurry!"

"All of you! SHUT UP!" Jaclyn screamed. This wasn't like her. She knew she was out of control, but the girls needed to listen to her so they didn't get hurt. But, she couldn't tell them why. Instantly regretting yelling at the girls, she apologized.

The rest of the way home there was silence, except for an occasional sniff from Jenae. Jaclyn turned into the driveway and put the car in park.

"Girls, listen. When you go inside change into dry clothes and grab a snack. I will get supper going. And, if you're quick I'll even let you watch an episode on Netflix."

"Yay!" the girls shouted in unison and jumped out of the car.

Jaclyn unlocked and opened the front door for the girls then walked to the kitchen while the girls changed. She stood by the island and sent Grant a text: "I don't expect you to understand but need you to know that i'm canceling all our plans for the weekend. Mandy will be upset but i will try to make it up to her." Jaclyn knew that tonight would be a battle. With Grant and the girls. But, she had to fight, and she had to win. Nothing or no one was going to hurt her family. She hoped that she was overreacting, but her gut told her she couldn't let her guard down. Not even for a minute.

Mandy ran across the living room towards the kitchen holding a pair of her favorite pajamas. "Mom! Can I bring these to my sleepover tomorrow?"

• CHAPTER 4 •

Angela hung up the phone after leaving a message for Jaclyn. She knew tomorrow morning they were having coffee at eight o'clock after Jaclyn dropped the kids off at school, but she was dying to tell her about the man she just met online. By the time Angela had turned forty, she had accepted the fact she, more than likely, wouldn't marry. Instead of continuing to actively look for a mate, she invested much of her time into the small church she attended, leading a small group of women, serving on a couple of committees, and building her real estate business. Dating had always seemed to elude her. She rationalized her lack of dates on the fact she didn't really have many ways of meeting men her age. The median age of those attending her church being sixty and most of her real estate clients were families. But, lately, she kept thinking how nice it would be to meet someone she could spend the rest of her life with. The last time she and Jaclyn had met for coffee Angela had even asked for advice on navigating the online dating scene. Jaclyn had shrugged. She didn't offer Angela much support, simply just said that if she felt like she needed a man, then she should go for it. It wasn't much help, but then Jaclyn had told her what to look for to assure the guy wasn't some scum looking for a one-night hookup. Her list included: make sure he has a decent job, look for evidence of whom he admires (especially his mom), and never meet him the first time in a secluded place.

After reminding Jaclyn of their coffee date in the morning on the voicemail, she baited her with hints of someone new and exciting in her life. She asked Jaclyn to call her back before her date came to pick her up at six-thirty. She was nervous and needed to have her best friend talk her down a little.

Angela admired Jaclyn for her strong-willed nature. Nothing seemed to bother her. Angela, however, was afraid of everything. This online dating scene definitely topped the list of her greatest fears. What was she doing? She could just cancel and spend the night in front of the fire watching some reality TV show. Again. She had seen all seasons of at least eight shows. More than once. She would never admit that to anyone, but the characters made her laugh.. She even felt like her favorite character when she stepped outside her comfort zone. Everyone else seemed to make life look easy, but she had so much social anxiety. She constantly released her fears to God in her morning prayer time, knowing for as long as she could remember that all things were possible with Him. But, it definitely didn't calm her nerves.

While deciding what to wear, Angela had to sit down because her stomach hurt so bad. She scanned her clothing from the end of her bed and her eyes were drawn to a black form-fitting dress that rested uncomfortably high above her knees. As long as she was jumping outside her comfort zone, why not jump with style? A couple of months ago, Jaclyn had talked her into buying the dress. It was marked fifty percent off; it was her size, and, when she tried it on, Jaclyn had told her it made her look strong, confident, and in charge. With the lack of confidence building in her belly, Angela knew she needed some extra help tonight and grabbed the dress. She put it on, gave herself a pep talk out loud while looking in the mirror, and began to feel better almost instantly. She glanced at her phone and felt a surge of adrenaline as she saw it was already six-twenty. She tried calling Jaclyn one more time, but it went straight to voicemail. Angela took a deep breath, closed her eyes, and focused on the fact that in a few hours she would be back home and the date would be over. She tried to channel Jaclyn's courage as she walked to the bathroom to check her makeup. She would surely have a lot to share with Jaclyn tomorrow morning at coffee.

At exactly six-thirty, a strong knock on the front door jolted Angela from the final touches on her makeup. She smoothed her hands on her thighs, pushing her dress downward hoping to extend the length of the fabric just a little. As she reached the door, she took a deep breath, said a silent prayer and opened the door.

He stood under the overhang of the roof, his broad shoulders set against the wind and rain. The natural elements seemed to obey his confident stance, and he seemed unaffected by the horrible conditions. She met his dark eyes and became speechless. After several seconds of awkward silence, he finally stepped forward and asked to come in out of the rain. Angela flew back, flustered at her lack of manners and apologized. Her date again was unfazed. He cleared his throat and Angela stopped talking mid-sentence.

"Angela, I'm Jason. It is so nice to meet you." He extended his hand and accepted hers warmly and gently.

"Nice to meet you, Jason. I'm Angela." She blushed at the thought she shared her name when he already knew it, and at how warm his hand was in hers.

"It is nice to finally meet you, Angela."

Angela blushed and looked down. "You, too."

Jason laughed and suggested they continue the conversation at the restaurant. "We have reservations at the Stampede Bar and Grill at seven. Have you been before?"

"No, I can't wait." Angela grabbed her floral raincoat and keys. "Shall we go?"

As they stood on the front porch, Jason hovered over Angela while she locked the deadbolt on her front door. His six-foot-five-inch frame shielded her against nature's tantrum until she was safely in the front seat of his oversized black truck. As they drove to the restaurant, their conversation became easier, more natural, and Angela felt herself relax. Jason talked about his career and he asked about hers. He seemed genuinely interested in real estate and she felt safe in the hands of an undercover police officer.

Once seated inside the restaurant, Angela retreated to the restroom to check on the damage done to her makeup and hair by the wicked storm. Jason glanced at his watch. He turned the waiter away opting to order together instead of assuming her tastes in alcohol and food. Angela returned to the table, smiled at Jason and sat down. Jason looked into her eyes, making her blush, and simply said in a whisper, "Thank you for choosing me tonight."

She broke eye contact and fidgeted with her purse and chair not knowing how to respond except by blabbering on and on about there not being a whole lot to choose from. She instantly regretted her choice of words and began spewing her apologies.

"I am so sorry, Jason. That came out so wrong. I love this place so far! I guess I'm used to too many choices at McDonald's." Angela laughed uncomfortably.

Jason just kept looking her in the eyes as a sexy smile spread across his strong jaw.

Just then, the waiter reappeared and Jason asked Angela what she would like to drink. Angela knew the safest thing to do would be to order a beer because of the lower alcohol percentage, but that choice seemed substandard in Jason's presence. He appeared to be more refined than a beer drinker. Instead, she asked for some Merlot. Jason ordered the same.

"May I suggest some appetizers with your choice of wine?" the waiter offered.

"Yes, please," Angela said, not taking her eyes away from Jason's.

"The spinach and artichoke dip and fresh crusty bread are delightful, and would be enriched by the Merlot."

Jason raised his eyebrows to suggest to Angela that she decides.

"Sounds wonderful. Thank you," she whispered.

The waiter left to put in the order. Angela realized that they had been looking at one another for a long time. She fidgeted, but he sat still, not flinching. Her natural impulse was to turn the conversation to get to know one another. She keenly knew of how attracted she was to Jason and shared about her involvement with her church to calm herself down and keep her boundaries intact. Jason didn't seem the least bit affected by her talk about how much she enjoyed her pastor's sermons and how she couldn't live without the closeness and accountability of her small group of women that met each Tuesday night. After taking the risk to talk about her spirituality, she felt brave enough to let Jason know that she would love to see where their relationship may go from tonight forward. After one more pause, she told Jason she didn't believe in sex before marriage.

Jason reached for her hands and reassured her of his willingness to honor her every way he could as they moved into the days ahead together. Then he hung his head and asked if he could share something really personal.

"Of course." Angela's heart pounded as she waited for him to share.

After a long pause of gathering his thoughts, Jason looked into Angela's eyes and began to reveal his heart. "Well, I am not a virgin. I was married for ten years to a woman I would have taken a bullet for. She was strong and beautiful and the most intelligent human being I had ever met. We tried having children for years with no success. So, we went the long, expensive route and had all the tests done. But, we didn't end up with any children. All we ended up with was my wife's diagnosis of cervical cancer."

Angela couldn't find any words that fit his revelation. Finally, she whispered, "I am so, so sorry, Jason."

"It's okay. I've healed in so many ways. Counseling has been a godsend and my wife's last words to me were to move on and remarry. She was so selfless and gracious. I miss her every day. But, it has been thirteen years since her death and I don't want to grow old alone. I long to share my days with someone, but I reassure you that sharing the nights can wait."

The waiter returned with two glasses of Merlot, interrupting the moment. Before they lost the mood, Angela tucked this moment away, eager to share it with Jaclyn tomorrow. Could this guy be the one? Or, is he too good to be true?

Jason broke into her thoughts. "Are you ready to order?"

Angela and Jason looked at each other, then both burst out laughing.

"So sorry, sir," Jason said. "We haven't even looked at the menu. Please give us a few more minutes."

The waiter backed away from the table to give them privacy. Angela and Jason again laughed together. They each grabbed a menu, and both mentioned that the Cowboy Ribeye Steak looked delicious.

"Two it is," smiled Jason.

"Yes, two it is," Angela agreed.

After placing their order they eased back into the conversation. Angela was feeling much more relaxed having drunk her whole glass of wine. She glanced at Jason's glass and instantly felt embarrassed. He had only taken a few sips. She really needed to get out more. He was so refined, and she was just so awkward. Jason stopped talking when he noticed the change in Angela's expression. He looked from her to her empty glass. Then with a big smile summoned the waiter. "Two more glasses of Merlot, please."

The waiter left to retrieve the drinks.

"But, you've hardly touched yours." Angela blushed.

Jason tipped his glass back and downed the wine in a few big gulps. "Not very classy, but I don't want to fall behind you, beautiful lady."

Jason read her like a book. It was like he knew her thoughts before she shared them. And he kept putting her at ease. She had never been this comfortable around any of the men she had dated in the past. With half of their second glasses of wine gone, the steaks, potatoes, and steamed fresh vegetables arrived.

While they ate, Jason talked about close calls he had experienced during his last ten years as an undercover police officer. Angela hung on every word.

"How do you sleep at night? Are you ever scared?" Angela said, admiration filling her gaze, and the wine warming her skin and relaxing her nerves.

Jason laughed away her questions and simply said, "It's all in a day's work."

Then Jason asked her to share more about her life. What makes her happy? Who are her closest friends? What's her favorite part of her job?

"Well, I am happy right this moment, so that should answer that question," Angela smiled. "As far as closest friends, I really only have one. I know many people, but I attract older ladies."

They both laughed at the image in their minds.

Angela tried to explain. "Seriously! I must be an old soul or something. But, my best friend, Jaclyn, is who I go to for advice and to vent when I need to. Those old ladies don't have the advice I'm looking for."

Jason smiled at her last comment and prodded her to continue about Jaclyn, "What is it about Jaclyn that allowed her into your inner circle?"

"Well, we have little in common. Maybe that makes it work. She is married and has four beautiful daughters. All her girls call me Auntie Angel. I absolutely love it!"

"Now that you say that, I thought I saw a glimmer above your head."

"Oh, stop, now! They are my family here in Colorado. I was an only child and my parents have both passed away. So, I really am an Aunt to them."

"Okay, okay! Relax Auntie Angel. Go on." Jason grinned, urging her to continue.

"Well, we also differ spiritually. My faith is my constant. It keeps me stable. Well, most days. But, Jaclyn? She seems mad at God, but I don't know why. I've asked, but she won't give me anything. Every time I invite her to my small group she declines. She blames it on not enough time because of her husband Grant and the girls. I guess I don't know what that is like, so I can't judge."

"Okay, well, all you've told me about your best friend is what you don't have in common. Why are you even friends with her?"

Angela chuckled and shook her head. "Honestly, some days I don't know. But, I love her inquisitive brain. She's a journalist for the Cliff Creek Courier and she's super smart. She's also a great mom. She adores her girls. We've toyed around with the idea that she and I could start a business together. We just can't agree on what that business would be. I enjoy being with her, though. She is much braver than me and I kind of live vicariously through her at times. But, what I really want is to live an adventure of my own. I don't know. I think I'm just too scared to make it happen."

"Well, you are sitting here with me, aren't you?

Angela pondered that thought as she watched Jason chew the tender ribeye.

"Yes. Yes, I am. Thank you."

The rest of the evening flew by as they continued to share about themselves. When the first pregnant pause occurred, Angela suggested that it was getting late. She needed to go home since she had an early appointment the next day. Jason paid for the meal and escorted Angela to the front door.

"Please, stay here. I will go get the truck."

Angela smiled the few minutes it took him to pull the truck up to the entrance of the restaurant. She couldn't believe what a blessing tonight had been. Maybe she wouldn't be alone for the rest of her life.

Jason pulled up and parked at the curb. Then he jumped out and ran around the truck to meet Angela at the restaurant door. He used his broad shoulders to protect her from the rain and helped her walk to the truck and get into the cab. Back in the driver's seat, Jason hesitated before putting the truck in drive.

"Listen, I couldn't help but notice that feeling safe is important to you. I know where you live, but if you show me where your best friend lives and where their girls go to school, I will make sure I add those locations to my patrol. Most days aren't very exciting and I have lots of time on my hands. Besides, any friend of yours is a friend of mine."

"That is so kind. Thank you. Just take North First Street to Central. I'll show you the rest of the way from there."

Angela was more chatty than usual with three glasses of wine in her bloodstream and Jason seemed to enjoy it. The smile never left his face as he followed her directions.

"Tell me, why are you and Jaclyn such good friends if you have little in common? I'm still a little confused."

"I guess it's because we offer each other different perspectives. We are also like family. Like I told you earlier, I'm the kids' auntie and I love that. I really don't think so much of just Jaclyn and I being friends, but I'm friends with the whole family. We are all family. I'm the auntie and Jaclyn and Grant are like my big sister and brother. Except I'm older. Hhhhhm? Maybe that analogy doesn't work. Let's see..."

"I get it," Jason laughed. "Anything I should know about them or their home since I'm adding them to my rounds?"

"Well, Jaclyn is religious about locking all the doors, but Grant is constantly leaving them unlocked. Jaclyn gets on him all the time about that, but he still does it. I worry about it, too. I feel safe in our community, but I still believe we shouldn't take any chances."

"Well, you are right. There is a level of crime in this valley that most citizens don't even know exists."

"Take a right at the next street, then another right, then a left. They are the gray house on the left with the large deck out front."

"This street is so secluded. They must enjoy that with all the kids. Not much traffic because it's not a thru street. But it is also a perfect set-up for a burglary. Tell Jaclyn to keep after Grant to lock those doors."

His words rendered Angela speechless. Jason smiled and looked into her eyes with a gaze that reached her soul. He had pulled the truck to the curb in front of Jaclyn's house and put it in park. She felt her heart pounding and her body felt like it was on fire. She needed to throw some cold water on this moment so she blurted out, "Let's go get ice cream!"

Jason laughed again, put the truck in drive and pulled away from the curb. "Your wish is my command, my lady."

Angela smiled at the realization that he respected her boundaries. This relationship might just work.

"Is there any ice cream near the kids' school? I would like to patrol that area, too. Any nieces of yours are worthy for me to protect."

Angela smiled. "Take a right on Central then go about a mile down the road. It will be on the left. I will point it out. But, we are not stopping! Remember, we are on a mission for ice cream."

"Yes, ma'am!" Jason smiled back.

The ice cream turned into a nightcap at a dive bar downtown. By this time Angela didn't care where they were. The cold drink had no effect on the warmth that flooded her whole body. She knew she was falling in love. But, she couldn't stop yawning. Finally, Jason suggested he take her home.

"Sorry I've kept you out so late. You probably need to be at work in the morning."

"It's totally fine. Practically every day is a work day when you are in real estate. I'm definitely not yawning because I'm bored," she smiled. "But, I am tired." Then, with a burst of confidence, she asked, "Will I see you again soon?"

"Of course," Jason smiled. "But, I'm working all weekend. Would Tuesday work?"

"Yes, Tuesday would work great." Angela looked at Jason's strong jaw as they neared her home. He was staring straight ahead watching the road with intensity. Finally, as if sensing Angela's gaze, he reached over the console and grabbed her hand gently. She smiled. "Jason, thank you for a wonderful night."

Jason pulled up to the curb in front of Angela's small home, put the truck in park, and turned to face Angela. "You are more than welcome, pretty lady. I had a wonderful time myself."

Jason squeezed her hand, then got out and walked around to open her door. She wobbled when she got out and he reached for her hand with amazing quickness. The rain had stopped, but the wind bit as the temperature had dropped. But, Jason's hand was warm. She thanked him, reluctantly took her hand back, and swept her hair out of her eyes. "I've got it from here," she said while trying to navigate all the fallen branches on her front walk.

Jason stood by the truck and smiled. "Okay, pretty lady, you look like you've got this. See you on Tuesday." He watched Angela stumbling forward wondering if he should try to help.

"Yep, Tuesday," she shouted at the ground, afraid to look up or she would trip. When she finally reached her front door, Jason was already seated back in his truck laughing. She smiled, waved him off with her hand, and unlocked the door. She could hear his truck pull away as she locked the deadbolt.

Angela pressed her back up against the door and fought with her alcohol clouded mixed emotions. First, she was ashamed that she had drunk so much. That wasn't like her at all. But, every time Jason asked if he could get her another drink, she couldn't resist. But she felt proud of herself that she had kept her physical boundaries. If they continued to see each other, that part was going to become more difficult. In the future, she would have to watch how much she drank so she wouldn't compromise her convictions. She really needed to talk to Jaclyn. She crawled in bed, sent a quick text to Jaclyn, and passed out.

• CHAPTER 5 •

Grant came home late Thursday evening and walked through the door with a grin and the same excuse he always used, that he had to check on a job site and there had been problems to take care of before coming home. Jaclyn looked up when Grant walked in but just kept eating and monitoring the girls' manners, avoiding any eye contact with him. Grant took off his coat, hung it up and joined the girls at the table.

"Looks great, Jack!" Grant smiled at Jaclyn, but she didn't return the connection. He knew he had upset her and she may not even talk to him for days. He knew her pattern. And he didn't like it. He turned his attention toward the girls. When there was a break in the conversation, Grant jumped in, telling the girls about an old board game he found at the job site. His story entranced the girls as he described what the box and the board looked like. They all kept asking questions and Grant stayed up with their inquiries, but Mandy called him out when he said that he had heard drums pounding in the distance.

"Daddy! That's Jumanji, you silly." Mandy, Mackenzie, and Grant all laughed because they had seen the movie. But, the two youngest girls, who had not seen it, wanted him to keep telling them about the game.

"Did you bring the game home, daddy?" Jenae asked.

"I wanna play?" Anya whined.

"It's not a real game. Daddy's just making it up." Mandy laughed at her sisters' ignorance.

"How do you know that I didn't find a game? Come over here and I'll show you." Mandy got up and walked meandered towards Grant's chair. She giggled more with every step she took toward him. He held his hands behind his back, grinning and laughing a maniacal laugh. When Mandy got close enough, he grabbed her sides and tickled her. She shouted with glee and tried to wiggle free. "That will teach you to doubt your father. I found the tickle game! These hands are ancient tickle hands and no one can escape their power of stealing giggles from little girls."

Jaclyn didn't even crack a smile during the chaos Grant was stirring up at the dinner table. She just wanted to get girls ready for bed so she could do more research on Damien.

"All right, girls! Enough fun and games. Everyone go get your jammies and meet me in the bathroom." The girls kept giggling and tempting Grant to tickle them by getting close to his chair. Instead of stopping, Grant just kept tickling.

"Stop! All of you!" They all looked at Jaclyn, quiet. Anya started to cry.

"Whoa, there Jack. How about if I assist with baths and jammies tonight so you can kick back? I can even read bedtime stories." The girls all shouted with glee.

Jaclyn tried her best to smile at Grant and said, "Thank you." But, before she retreated to her home office, she tapped Mandy on the shoulder and asked to talk with her for a moment. Mandy stayed back while Grant and the other girls raced for the bedrooms to get jammies.

"Hey, honey, I know you will not understand why I'm doing this, but please do your best to trust me. I cannot let you go to Mia's sleepover tomorrow night."

"Mom!!! Why? I will be the only one not there. Please, mom, please!!!"

Jaclyn reached out and touched Mandy's shoulder, but Mandy jerked her body away from her touch. "Mandy, I will make it up to you, I promise. Please just try to understand. I think we should have a family weekend. We can do some fun stuff like watch movies, bake cooki...."

"You're mean!" Mandy shouted over Jaclyn and ran crying to her room.

Jaclyn's hands started shaking again. This would be much harder than she thought. Without being able to explain what she needed to do, no one would give her any grace. She sighed and walked upstairs to her office. On the way, she overheard Grant say to Mandy, "I'm not sure why either, baby girl, but I will talk with mommy. No promises, but I will try."

"You're the best, daddy!"

Jaclyn grimaced. Why did Grant offer her any hope of going to the sleepover? He could never just agree with her one hundred percent. Instead, he was like putty in their hands and an obstacle for her. He was the good guy for saying he would check with her, and she was the bad guy for saying no again. She shut the door to her office a little harder than necessary and sat down at her desk.

Her office had been a surprise from Grant. When she went to a three-day conference in Denver, he had moved Anya in with Jenae and turned the nursery into an office for her. He had covered one entire wall in barn wood and built floor-to-ceiling, wall-to-wall bookshelves on two more walls. The fourth wall had a large window that overlooked the backyard trees, a pond, and lots of laughter when the girls were out on the trampoline or playing on the tree swings. He had reasoned that Jaclyn could get some work done while also being able to see what the girls were up to. When the girls were in school, she would have a place she could get away from the laundry and other chores that could distract her. It had thrilled her, and she hugged and kissed him with a passion he hadn't experienced in years.

But, when Grant heard Jaclyn slam the door, he regretted ever creating a place for her to retreat from him. She had always retreated emotionally, but now she wasn't even physically near him. Once the girls were in bed, he knocked on her office door and then poked his head in. Jaclyn seemed flustered and slammed her laptop shut as she turned her chair to face Grant.

"Don't scare me like that, Grant!" Jaclyn's eyes flashed with anger.

"Sorry, babe. I just wanted to see how you are doing. You seemed pretty frustrated earlier."

"Well, why wouldn't I be frustrated, Grant? I have a busy schedule, just like you, but I seem to be the one that always has to reschedule my appointments. Now my interview is at seven tomorrow morning. I hope you can get girls to school because I can't take them."

"No worries, Jack. I've got it. Hey, what was all that about with Mandy and the sleepover? She's pretty upset."

"You won't understand that either. Why can't you just be on my team and honor what I say to the girls, instead of giving them false hope that I will change my mind? Grant, you make me the bad guy over and over and I'm tired of it. She can't go to the sleepover and that's that. Either support me or give me the space to be a single parent."

"What? You can't be serious. You want me to be your bitch and just do what you say with no explanation? Hell no! Jack, what has gotten into you?"

"What has gotten into me? Who made you lord and master of our home that you can dictate what happens with our family?!"

"Jack, Jack, please..." Grant said, softening his tone. "What are we even fighting about? I'm so confused. I want to support you, but you won't share everything me. What is your reason for not wanting Mandy to go to the sleepover? And what was your text about? The one that said you are canceling all of our plans for the weekend? Care to give me some reason behind that decision?"

Jaclyn took a deep breath and realized she needed to lighten up or she wouldn't be able to do what she needed to do to find Damien.

"I'm sorry. I'm really sorry, Grant. Work has been crazy and Mark gave me a stupid entry-level story that is just bullshit. I don't have time for it, but I will do it for Mark. He always has my back. Sorry I jumped all over you. Thank you for getting the girls in bed."

"No problem, babe. What can I do to help?"

"Just give me a little room to tie up some loose ends and trust me even when I make little sense."

"I can try, Jack. But, seriously, if Mandy goes to the sleepover we will have one less kid to wrangle."

Jaclyn forced a smile and countered, "I would love to let her go, Grant. But, I'm working on another story that I can't say anything about that scares me a little. Until I feel that this threat in our community is under control, I just feel safer keeping everyone I love under one roof."

"Okay, then. That I can stand behind. I don't need to know everything." Grant reached for her hand with his own. "You are one fierce mama bear, you know that?"

Jaclyn pulled her hand from Grant's. "Oh, there is something you could do for all of us."

"You name it!"

"Please install the security system you bought months ago. It does no one any good sitting in the box."

"How about I install it Saturday morning, then we ask Angela to come watch the kids for a night and you and I go to the Avalanche Lodge? Just you and me. One night. What do you say?"

Jaclyn sighed with defeat. Had he not just heard her say she didn't feel safe? Grant would never understand her. The last thing she wanted to do was leave her girls for a night. She needed to protect them. And she didn't feel safe alone with Grant either. "Sorry, Grant, I just can't. Not with what I know about the story I'm working on. I wish I could tell you more, but I can't. You are just going to have to trust me on this one."

Grant nodded then kissed her on the forehead. "Going to bed soon?"

"Unfortunately, no. I have a lot of research to do before morning. You go ahead. Good night."

Grant sighed and attempted a smile, but Jaclyn knew she disappointed him again. Some days she felt sorry for Grant. He deserved more than her and her damaged self. He deserved a wife to love him: body, soul, and spirit. She just couldn't do it. Damien had stolen that which made it possible. And now he was back in her life. What more did she have that could be taken away? She knew in her gut it was her girls. He wanted her girls. And she would do anything to make sure that didn't happen.

Once the house fell quiet, she made her way downstairs to make a cup of tea. She filled the water kettle and turned it on. As she waited for it to boil she jotted down ideas for finding out more about Damien. She knew nothing personal about him, but she wondered if she might find information about his family. If he had any. Could he be reaching out to her to make amends? Maybe his apparent death was all a mistake. What if he had amnesia and wandered for years not knowing his name? Did his parents or a sibling know the full story?

The kettle was at full boil. Several scalding drops hit Jaclyn's hand, and she jumped back and cursed. She turned the kettle off, poured the water over the two tea bags in her mug, and rubbed her palms against her eyes while the tea steeped. What was she thinking? She couldn't give him the benefit of the doubt with no evidence. She needed to be militant and not let her guard down. Her very life and the lives of her family could depend on it.

She made her way back upstairs to her office, shut the door, and settled in at her desk. She pulled up Damien's Facebook account again to study the few photos she could see. What was he doing in Cliff Creek? What was he doing alive? She started searching for Langleys in the Denver area. Several popped up and she paid the few dollars with her Courier account to get more information about each one, including public and court records. Hours later she had come up with nothing except a handful of shots in the dark. Tomorrow she would reach out after her interview. She stretched and then laid her head on her folded arms for just a few minutes.

Jaclyn awoke to Grant rubbing her shoulders. She started and pushed away from him. Still trying to figure out where she was and what was happening, she rubbed her eyes then looked around. She was still in her office.

"What time is it?"

"Six-thirty, Jack. I just woke up and noticed you never came to bed."

"Shit! I need to be at my interview in thirty minutes!" She pushed Grant away and ran to their bedroom to change her clothes. She threw on some clean jeans and an oversized sweater then looked at herself in the mirror. She grimaced and rinsed her face with cold water. She dried her face in a towel and applied some eyeliner and mascara. She slapped her cheeks several times to bring out some color, pulled her hair back in a clip and ran downstairs for her jacket and laptop. Grant met her near the garage door with a travel mug of coffee and a banana.

"Go get 'em, tiger!" He grinned.

"Thank you!" Jaclyn grunted out as she clicked the car starter on her key chain. "Uggghhh! Still raining?"

"Here you go," Grant said as he presented her with an umbrella.

She took a breath and gave Grant a quick kiss. "Thank you, again!"

Jaclyn took the turn at the end of their cul-de-sac fast and fishtailed into the field on the left side of the road. The rain had turned to sleet and was coating everything with a hazardous layer of ice. She put the Jeep in four-wheel drive and climbed back on the road. As she inched her way to All's Quiet, she called Pete Black to let him know she would be a few minutes late because of the road conditions. She got no answer. She hoped Pete would not cancel the interview. She just needed to get this story out of the way so she could focus on Damien. She left a message and trudged on. Sleet piled up on the sides of the road and slush formed everywhere on the windshield that the wipers didn't touch. Jaclyn's shoulders ached, and a knot was forming under her right shoulder blade. Her head pounded with the stress she held in her muscles. As she navigated the last few turns to All's Quiet, she focused on breathing deeply and exhaling fully. The thought of seeing Damien caused acid to pool in her stomach and burn with each shaky breath. She cursed the weakness of her flesh.

As Jaclyn pulled into the parking lot of the store, Pete pulled up beside her. She waited until he had unlocked the door to the store before leaving her car.

"Good morning!" Pete called out as he held the door open.

Jaclyn ran from her car to the store and thanked Pete on the way past him as she entered the store. "This weather is getting ridiculous. So sorry to make you come out on such a nasty day."

"Not a problem, hun. We are open in an hour, anyway. Where should we start?"

"Should we have a seat?"

"No can do," Pete said with his back to her. "If I don't get my butt in gear, I will not be able to meet the boss man's expectations for the Grand Opening on Black Friday."

"No worries. I will just ask questions and follow you around. Is that okay?"

"Yep. That'll work great."

"I will record the interview."

"Go for it, young lady. Shoot!"

Jaclyn went through her list of questions while following Pete in and out of the back room. At one point he said he had to head out into the warehouse and she might want to throw a coat on because the heater had stopped working the day before and no one could come to fix it until Monday. She threw on her coat and followed Pete into the warehouse. All sorts of materials filled the large metal building. Sheeting and large rolls of soundproofing lined the walls. There were boxes stacked everywhere and Jaclyn agreed that Pete needed to get his butt in gear if this were to be presentable in less than a week. "Can you tell me how you see All's Quiet making a positive impact in the Cliff Creek Valley?"

"For this one let's go sit for a few minutes. I promised you coffee, remember?"

Jaclyn laughed but looked at her watch. This interview was taking way too long. She needed today to dig something up on Damien before everyone was home for the weekend.

Pete led her into a room next to the office. It had a small kitchenette, and she had to admit that the coffee smelled fantastic. Jaclyn sat at the table and set up her recorder. She accepted the steaming cup and Pete informed her that the coffee was Highlander Grog, his favorite. He sat, took a couple of sips, closed his eyes then cleared his throat.

"To be honest, Miss, this is just a job for me. I've been with the company for fifteen years and I'm trying to stick it out another five so I can purchase an RV and head back home to Calgary and spend time with my sons. They are both working and taking care of the family home. Their mom, my wife, died a year and a half ago. When the boss offered me a significant bonus to move down here for a few years to get this new store up and running and then manage it, I jumped on it. It feels good to be away from daily reminders of my wife being gone, but I miss it, too. It's like I left a big part of me at home. So, I'm not the best person to ask about the mission and the vision of the company. I have a single focus on what's best for me and my sons. I put in my hours and then go home, watch a little TV, garden if the weather is good, and talk with my grandkids back home."

Jaclyn wanted to be more empathetic but instead drew the interview to a close. "I'm so sorry, Pete. Listen, I need to get going so I can work on another story. Do you have any printed material about the history of the business? That would help me."

Pete sighed and stood up. "Yep, let me look over here." He reached behind the front desk and took a box off a big stack that lined the wall. "I need to get this front part of the office set up today, anyway."

Jaclyn asked Pete a few follow-up questions about his own personal history with the company while he looked for the printed material. As Pete answered he kept rummaging. He opened one box that had signs to go on the window and walls in the front office. Two of the items were framed. One was a framed dollar bill, the first made in the first store in Canada. Pete explained that it had become a tradition to hang this particular dollar in each new store until another new store opened. Then the dollar would move to the newest store. The other one was a framed photo of a small group of people, all smiling, and one cutting the ribbon in front of what Jaclyn assumed was the first store. She asked if she could see it. Pete nodded and moved closer to tell her who was who. It drew Jaclyn to the tall, dark-haired man in the middle who was bent over cutting the ribbon. It must have been a cold day because everyone had big parkas on with hoods drawn up around their faces. Why did the man in the middle look familiar?

"Who is the man cutting the ribbon?" Jaclyn asked.

"Oh, that is the owner of All's Quiet."

"Do you have another photo of him?"

"Yep! Right here." Pete produced an eight by ten inch framed photo of the owner.

Jaclyn sucked in her breath. She gripped the photo and her knuckles turned white.

"Hey, Miss, where are you going? Are we done?"

Jaclyn had dropped the photo on the table, grabbed her coat and headed out the door without saying a word to Pete. She ran to her Jeep, threw her coat on the passenger seat and turned the engine over. She took a deep breath and looked at her phone. There were three missed calls, a text, and another voicemail from Angela. She couldn't worry about that now. She searched in her notebook for Pete's number, dialed, put the Jeep in gear, and started driving towards home.

"Well, hello, Miss! Did I say something to offen…."

"No, no, no, of course not. Hey, Pete, I really need to schedule an interview with the owner."

"Well, he has me meeting with a couple of customers throughout the day tomorrow, but he said he would be here working with the inventory. How does one o'clock sound? I could call him and let him know."

"That sounds great, Pete. And, also, what is the owner's name?"

"He would be Evin Wolfe," Pete said. Then under his breath uttered, "A fitting name for a sorry sonofabitch."

"Excuse me?"

"Oh, nothing important, Miss. Don't hesitate to call back if I can be of any other help."

"Thanks, Pete! Sorry about rushing out. I didn't realize how late it was."

"No problem, Miss."

"Thanks! Bye."

Jaclyn hung up and knew instantly that she had to prepare for this interview differently than all the others she has done. As she drove home, she tried to remember the last time she had seen Grant's gun cabinet. And where she last saw the keys.

• CHAPTER 6 •

Grant shook his head as he watched Jaclyn back out of the driveway and speed off down the cul-de-sac. He offered more of a plea than a prayer for her to make it to her interview, then he turned back into the kitchen to refill his mug with coffee. The girls were all up and fighting over the last of the marshmallow cereal. Mandy was still stewing about her sleepover being canceled. And he didn't blame her. It made little sense to him either. Jaclyn's reasoning was weak. There was more to what she was offering him, but he couldn't get her to share it. Her stubbornness aggravated him to where he tossed and turned all night. He had hoped that she would come to bed so he could encourage her and see if she would talk. But, she never came into the bedroom. And, now she was late. A sure indicator that the rest of her day would not go well. He grabbed the box of cereal out of Mandy's outstretched hand before rainbows and unicorns were strewn all over the kitchen.

"Hey, hey, hey, Mandy! It's okay. I can make some eggs if there isn't enough cereal."

"But, I want marshmallow cereal!" she wailed with tears running down her face.

Grant grabbed her in a bear hug and just held onto her, rubbing her back. He had learned pretty quickly that when girls are being overly emotional, he shouldn't tell them that. Jaclyn had drilled that into him early in their marriage. He tried to bite his tongue with Jaclyn but was definitely more successful with the girls. He didn't say a word, just held her close. When Mandy finally wiped her tears and gave into Grant's hug, he bent down, gently placed his weathered hands on either side of her face, looked into her eyes and asked if she wanted some hot chocolate with mini marshmallows. She smiled, nodded her head and hugged his neck.

"Thank you, daddy. But, I still want marshmallow cereal."

Grant smiled at her then let everyone know that they would all be eating eggs and drinking hot chocolate with mini marshmallows. The girls cheered and Mandy smiled, satisfied that no one would get to eat the cereal. While the girls were getting dressed for school, Grant called his secretary for an update on all his crews and to see if he had any messages. She convinced him that everything was going smoothly so far and that he didn't need to stop in if he had other work to do. He thanked her and hung up.

Anya came out in the living room dressed in Mackenzie's clothes. Grant laughed and talked her into at least changing the pants to ones she wouldn't trip over. Once everyone passed Grant's assessment of readiness, they all ran to his truck, Grant holding Anya in his arms. He buckled her in her car seat, gave the command for everyone else to buckle up, and started his truck.

Mandy waited until Grant had buckled and then said in her best kind and respectful voice, "Daddy, can you talk to mommy again today? I really, really, really want to go to the sleepover."

"Awww, honey. I know. And I'm so sorry. Mama and I talked last night and she and I need to stick together on decisions that involve all of you rascals. So, how about if we talk to mama about planning a sleepover at our house soon?"

Mandy crossed her arms, sat back against the seat, and pouted. Grant looked at her in the rearview mirror and smiled.

"It will be okay, honey. Let's play some of your favorite games tonight."

Mandy kept looking down. But, when they got to the elementary school, she hugged Grant's neck and whispered, "I love you, daddy."

"I love you, too! Try to have a super good day today, okay?"

"Okay."

Mackenzie and Jenae gave Grant hugs and ran after Mandy into the building. No morning recess because of the weather. Again. Grant knew that part of the girls being argumentative and whiny was from not having enough time outdoors to run and play. Hopefully, this storm would move through fast.

After taking Anya to daycare, he hopped in his truck and headed towards Spindrift. The gentle, steady flow of rain hitting the cab and hood of Grant's truck pulled him into a thoughtful trance. He stared out his side window, not looking beyond to the drenched neighborhood, but focused much more closely, drawn into the swirls of earthy colors absorbed by the drops captured on the glass. Then his thoughts turned to his meeting with Evin Wolfe. Why did his stomach constrict and his senses heighten when he met him? There was nothing obvious that was sketchy about his business, but the man himself was different. Guarded. Grant had sensed he had been withholding something. But he couldn't put a finger on it. Evin had seemed more interested in Grant's family than in working for him. Maybe he was working on his customer relations? But, his personality needed a little refining to work well with people. And, what was up with the silent treatment when he had asked Evin for his business license number and EIN? And, more than that, why did that silence make Grant nervous? He was not one to be intimidated. He learned as a kid that he had to love himself and believe in himself, especially when he believed no one else did. His dad had made sure that Grant wouldn't depend on anyone the day he walked away and didn't come back. After that, he had let no one stand in the way of his goals of earning a college degree and owning his own business. Yet, here he sat feeling so unsettled. His thoughts swirled aimlessly in his mind, all finally falling on the same question: Why did Evin Wolfe make him sweat?

Grant grabbed his phone and tapped it against his thigh. He needed to get a grip and move on with his day. He scrolled through his contacts then hit send.

"Well, I wasn't sure if you would ever call me back after we talked yesterday."

"Hey, Davis. Sorry about that. I thought about what you said and you're right. I just need to love Jack unconditionally. Maybe one day, because of it, she will trust me."

"Glad to hear you talking sense today, buddy. Just think of the rough edges in you that are being smoothed out by being patient."

"More like jackhammered out. It's not easy man."

"Never said it was."

"Well, hey, I am wondering if you could help me out with something."

"Shoot."

"I am trying to draw up a contract with a business owner who will do some work on a home I'm building. We met yesterday and, I don't know, it just felt weird."

"Weird? Like crazy weird?"

"No. More like he wasn't being upfront with me about who he is and about his company. I mean, it all looks legit, but his behavior was weird."

"Grant, I'm a criminal investigator, not a counselor. Can you have a third party meet with you so there are no misunderstandings?"

"It's not that, Davis. I'm not sure what it is. But, I got his EIN, and I wondered if you knew of anyone who could run it and find out if this guy and his company check out."

"Better Business Bureau?"

"I need more than that. I need to know that this guy isn't some criminal."

"Grant, what needs to happen before an investigator gets involved is someone needs to file a police report. Why don't you call the police and then a local investigator can look into his background?"

"Davis, I can't do that because he really has done nothing to report. Please, can't you find out personal information about him once you have access to his social security number? Criminal records? Stuff like that? Please? I have never felt this way about anyone before. He genuinely creeps me out."

"Listen, I can't go too far into it, and I can't share any personal details, but I could give you an all clear or a heads up. Will that work?"

"That's a start. I think I will feel better about it if I know he is clean. Thanks, bro!"

"Okay. Give me a few days. It can take a little time to get the results. Nothing is easy with investigating someone. But, I will see what I can find. Text me everything you know about him: name, address, company name, EIN. The more information the better the results will be."

"I really appreciate it, Davis."

"Should we schedule a call for tomorrow or do you think you can make it all day on your own?" Davis started laughing.

Grant joined in on the laughter. "Let me see if I can make it. I always know you're there if I need you."

The call ended and Grant took a deep breath. He was overreacting, but he wanted nothing to prevent his home in Spindrift from doing well in the Parade of Homes. This coming year would make him or break him. He promised himself he would do everything he could to make life a little easier for his family. Maybe Jaclyn would settle down and be more at peace if they didn't have so many financial worries. Before getting on the highway to Spindrift he looked at the time and swung by home to grab some tarps from the garage. Another load of sheetrock was being delivered to the Spindrift house today, and he wanted to make sure this drenching rain wouldn't ruin it.

As soon as he turned onto the cul-de-sac, he could see that Jaclyn was also home. Instead of going into the garage for the tarp, he parked in the driveway and went in the front door.

"Hey, Jack!" Grant shouted as he took his boots off in the entryway. But, there was no answer. He walked into the kitchen, but Jaclyn wasn't in there either. He backtracked through the living room and ran up the stairs to her office. The door was closed, so he knocked. "Hey, Jack!"

Nothing. He ran back downstairs at a loss of where to look for Jaclyn. The bathrooms were empty. He checked her car to see if she was still in it, but she wasn't. She couldn't have gone for a walk because of the rain. He tried calling her, but the call went right to her voicemail. Trying not to panic, he fought against the thought that maybe she had left him. Back inside, he ran up to their bedroom to see if she had packed anything. Everything was where they had both left it this morning. He sat down on the bed and put his head in his hands. What had gotten into him lately? Why was he so paranoid about everything? He stood to walk out and Jaclyn came barreling into the bedroom. She ran right into Grant and screamed. Grant put his hands up and tried to reassure her she was safe.

"Hey, hey, hey, honey, it's okay. It's just me."

"Grant! What are you doing home?" Jaclyn yelled while she walked backward toward the door. "I thought you had work in Spindrift."

Grant didn't answer. He was staring at her right hand. Jaclyn self-consciously tried to move her right hand behind her back.

"Jack, what are you doing with my gun?"

She raised the gun and placed it flat in her left palm.

Grant searched her eyes.

Jaclyn stared him down.

"Well?" asked Grant.

Jaclyn turned her countenance from surprise to anger. "What are you accusing me of, Grant?"

"Um, Jack, you are the one holding the gun. I'm not the one who should answer questions."

Jaclyn took a few uneven breaths and lowered the gun and placed it on top of the dresser by the door.

"Thank you for putting the gun down. Now, why do you have it?"

"Why do you instantly jump to the conclusion that I'm in the wrong here? You don't even give me a chance to explain myself."

"Oh my God, Jack, that's exactly what I'm doing. I'm giving you a chance to explain yourself. So....?"

"It's for work, okay?"

"When did journalists start carrying guns?"

"Stop being a jerk, Grant! It is for the story I told you about that makes me worried for our safety. I was checking to see if this was the same gun one of my sources described as being the gun involved in the crime."

"Okay. So, why do you need it to be in our bedroom? Seriously, Jack, this makes me nervous."

"I just had to use the bathroom and then I was going to take it into my office and compare it with my notes. Are you happy now?"

"Are you happy, Jack?"

Jaclyn glared at him, grabbed the gun and turned toward her office.

"I thought you had to use the bathroom!" Grant yelled.

Jaclyn slammed her office door, locked it, sat at her desk, and wept.

Grant took a deep breath, sat on the bed, and cursed. After a few minutes, he got up and headed to the garage to get the tarps. Once in the garage, he glanced over at the gun cabinet which sat behind stacks of boxes and tools. Jaclyn had made a path to the cabinet, but how did she open it? He carried the key on his key ring. He walked towards the cabinet and, even before he got there, he could tell she had pried back the side panel to get into it. Why couldn't she have just asked him? Now his kids would not be protected from the other guns. What kind of desperation would cause her to go to these lengths just to validate the make of a gun? Couldn't she have gone to a gun store? He opened the cabinet and took out his two hunting rifles and his Beretta 92FS. Jaclyn had his Walther P99, but he would figure out how to get that back later. He took a hammer and tried the best that he could to close the hole in the side panel. Then he put the guns in the cab of his truck and went back for the tarps. Before leaving he poked his head in the door leading into the kitchen.

"Jack! Are you okay?"

There was no answer. He shut the door and headed to his truck. "God, help her," he breathed out with a long sigh. Because he now had the guns in the truck, he decided to go to the shop first and put them in a locked cabinet before heading to Spindrift. As he drove, Grant wracked his brain trying to process what would lead to Jaclyn obliterating his gun cabinet just to verify a weapon involved in a crime. He thought about it from every angle and couldn't come up with anything that validated such aggressive behavior. Maybe Jaclyn was bipolar. One of his supervisors had just told him the other day that his wife had finally gone to a doctor for her manic mood swings. She had been just as shocked as her husband when she found out she was bipolar, but she started taking some medication to ease the symptoms. Jaclyn would probably resist the medication, even if, by some miracle, he could figure out a way to get her to a doctor. But, this behavior with the gun was over the top. He would have to think of a way to get her to concede to a physical and mental examination. It was too much to think about right now. He focused on the road and turned up the music, willing himself to relax.

Once he walked into the shop, Grant was hit with several fires that needed his advice. His secretary apologized and told him it really had been quiet when he called earlier. He reassured her he had several hours before he had to meet Evin at the Spindrift house and could tackle the problems. But, first, he retrieved the guns, emptied a cabinet of miscellaneous parts, and locked them up.

Grant worked with his supervisors through lunch and before he knew it, it was two o'clock. He wrapped up what he could, grabbed a couple of stale donuts and a bottle of water and headed out the door.

On the drive to Spindrift, he tried to rationalize his paranoia about Evin and calm his fears about what was happening with Jaclyn. But, the more he thought through each situation the more acid he felt rising in his throat. He reached into the console and felt for the bottle of Tums and popped two in his mouth. He tried to focus on the rest of his day, but the thought of meeting with Evin just made him feel worse.

Finally, Grant forced himself to look around and be present right where he was at. He pictured himself high above his truck where he could look down and see the bigger picture of his day. He had learned this technique from a psychology class he had taken in college, and he tried to use it when he felt anxious. He meditated on looking down through the parting clouds as his truck meandered down the state highway to Spindrift. He began to see shafts of the sun hit the nearby hills. He rolled down his window part way and noticed the smell of the drenched earth. He focused on his breathing and grew increasingly thankful for his good health. He became aware that the days of battering winds and driving rains had passed by and the sun was slowly finding its way into full view, if even for a few seconds at a time. The clouds were still heavy and dark in their bellies, but they rose high and majestic and white near the heavens. He felt hope rise within him as he continued to breathe the fresh, fragrant air.

Grant turned onto the long dirt driveway that curved a full quarter of a mile to the job site. He rolled up his window and focused on a plan for the afternoon. He didn't expect the All's Quiet owner Evin Wolfe for another thirty minutes, but as he approached, he saw a big black truck that he didn't recognize. He grabbed his tool belt and entered the house. Right away he could tell there was work happening in the walk-out basement. He descended the stairs where he saw two of his workers laughing with Evin.

"Hey, Grant! Hope you don't mind that I let myself in. I had a little extra time and wanted to get a feel for the project before you got here. Your guys have been more than hospitable."

Grant noticed right away that, like the weather, Evin seemed more relaxed and warm. "No worries. Glad you all got to meet each other. So, what do you think about the project?"

"This will be fun. I love spending other people's money," Evin laughed.

Grant had never thought about his job that way, but Evin was right, they were spending someone else's money. He laughed along with Evin and continued, "So, do you have a good idea on a timeline, what supplies we'll need, and an estimate for a final cost?"

"Not yet, let's work on that together."

"It's a deal, let's do it!" Grant smiled at Evin as they shook hands.

By five o'clock, Grant and Evin had put together a contract, a supply list, and an aggressive timeline. Then they and the two other workers finished preparing the in-home theater so Evin and his workers could begin installing the soundproofing Monday morning.

"Hey, Grant, before we leave, I'm curious why there is a half door opening in the wall behind the bar."

"Yeah, I tried to talk the homeowner out of it, but his wife didn't want supplies for the bar cluttering up the area. She plans to store kegs, wine, popcorn, and more in there. There isn't much room in there, and it just has a cement floor, but she plans to keep it locked so their kids can't get into any of it."

"Well, to each his own. How about the lighting? It doesn't affect my work, I'm just wondering when you think they'll have lights installed in the theater."

"They were supposed to have lights up and running last week. But, like everyone seems to be, they are behind."

"No worries. Can I just use your work lights?"

"Absolutely!"

"Great! I'll be here on Monday morning to start. Will there be someone here or can I have a key?"

"I'll make sure someone is here." Grant locked eyes with Evin, feeling better about him, but not a hundred percent sure.

"No problem. Have a good weekend."

"You, too!"

Grant watched Evin walk to his oversized truck. His gait was confident, even a tad too arrogant. Grant knew the type. For some reason, some guys need to fluff up their feathers and showcase what they've got. Grant's pursuit of earning others' respect came from what he could prove by his actions than how he looked and acted. As Grant turned to gather his tools, he heard Evin rev his engine before retreating down the driveway.

"What the heck," Grant chuckled to his workers. "I guess every guy has something to prove."

They all laughed and continued to pack up.

Grant jumped in his truck and sat for a few minutes. He looked at his phone and noticed two missed calls from the school about three fifteen. What was happening at home? He decided not to find out until he got there. He put on his favorite country station and noticed that the stars were out for the first time in a while. He popped a couple more Tums and took a long drink of water. He would face whatever it is he needed to face. He loved Jaclyn. And he would do anything for their girls. Anything. He finally put the truck in gear, but, before taking his foot off the brake, he revved the engine. Pathetic compared to Evin's truck. He laughed at himself out loud. He needed a good night's sleep. He drove down the driveway and headed towards home.

CHAPTER 7

Jaclyn took several deep, shaky breaths and wiped the tears off her cheeks. Why did she have to always lose it with Grant? She stared at the locked doorknob, waiting to see if Grant would come back and try to open it. Deep down she really wanted him to check on her. She wanted to share everything with him. The abuse, the news that Damien was still alive, that he was right here in Cliff Creek. She longed to face it all together. But, she knew that wasn't possible. She couldn't face herself reflected in his eyes, in his judgment of her. How could he love her if he knew how much she had lied to him and withheld from him. Even if by some remote chance he would have any compassion for her, she knew they could never restore the divide between them. For the girls' sake, she had to keep the facade intact. She knew there would always be a distance between her and Grant, but she could pull it together enough to give the girls a loving home and protective parents. And, Grant deserved so much more in a wife. Being kind to him would be a start.

She waited several more minutes, staring at the door, hoping Grant would come to check on her. But, why would he? Now Grant was suspicious of her. Why would he believe anything she said ever again? She knew she looked guilty the second she had run into him in their bedroom doorway. She hadn't been able to pull herself together fast enough and now he would question everything she said or did. She had been a fool. And now she would pay the price.

Finally, Jaclyn heard Grant descend the stairs and go out the garage door. He didn't even hesitate before heading downstairs. She felt defeated and embarrassed. Her explanation about why she had the gun had been pathetic. She wouldn't have believed herself either. But, he didn't seem to even want to hear her explanation. He acted like he already knew he wouldn't believe it or agree with it. She couldn't imagine what he would do when he saw how she had to get the gun out of the cabinet. He was going to flip out. Why had she been so impulsive? She should have just waited and asked him for the key, but she had felt so desperate when she first got home. She still felt desperate.

Turning away from the locked door, Jaclyn glanced at the skimpy notes on her desk she had written about Damien. Every lead a dead end. There was so little information that she already had it memorized. She ripped off the top sheet of the notepad, wadded it up, and tossed it in the wastebasket next to her desk. She had to figure out why he was here in Cliff Creek and what he wanted. But, how could she get answers? And, if she didn't get any answers, how would she protect her family from Damien? She could not trust him at all. That she knew for sure.

Then an eerie calm came over her. She grabbed a nearby pen and wrote across the top of a notepad: Why I need to fight back. Under the heading, she wrote out the names of each one of their daughters: Mandy, Mackenzie, Jenae, Anya. She hesitated then squeezed Grant's name above Mandy's. He should come first in her life, but she had never placed him there. The girls were her flesh and blood. She saw herself in each one of them. In their eyes, their attitudes, and their joy,

Jaclyn saw good memories of when she was a young child. But, Grant? He was not her flesh and blood. And, he was a man. Damien had stolen her appreciation for men. For the beauty of men and women together. Jaclyn could only offer him her shell of flesh and blood. She had always hoped that that would be enough. But, she knew it wasn't. True intimacy had to involve the heart. She grieved for what she couldn't bring herself to give him. But, they had never talked about it. Grant had been asking her to go to counseling for years, but she refused. She belittled him for even asking. And then she had cried when she was alone, berating herself for her cruelty to him. She had very little hope for her being able to confide in Grant, but the little bit of hope she held onto gave her a temporary reprieve from her guilt. And now was definitely not the time to test that hope. She would need to face Damien alone.

Jaclyn was used to it, though. She thrived on being independent and preferred to conquer tasks and difficulties alone. It had been this way her whole life. Well, almost her whole life. There had been a time when she had never wanted to do anything alone. Before her mom died, Jaclyn would copy everything she did. At just six years old she had begged her mom to show her how to cook, and from that point on, they cooked together almost every day until the day she died. She loved running errands with her mom and even dressed up in her mom's clothes when she could get away with it. Her dad used to call them twins. He joked that Jaclyn could never live on her own without her mama. Then that day came. And it came way too soon.

At first, after her mother's funeral, Jaclyn spent time with her dad at the nursery and began to fall in love with learning about all the plants and flowers. She didn't enjoy being alone. She loved being with those who loved her and she thrived when she was with family nearby. But, then Damien cast a long dark shadow across her heart and she began to retreat. The more she withdrew, the more independent she became to her family and friends. Then one day she stopped sharing the details of her life with her dad and her brother, wrapping her pain deep inside of her and refusing to let it show. And when her relationship with Damien became abusive she learned how to shut off her emotions. By the time Damien went missing, Jaclyn was a shell of a girl with only a brief living history. She didn't cause any problems at home or school and everyone just assumed she was being brave. She eventually figured out everything on her own and found a sense of peace in knowing that she didn't have to depend on anyone. With Damien gone and having learned to function on her own, she even accepted her dad's offer of an after-school job at the nursery, but only so she could save up money to take care of herself. She loved her dad and her brother and felt guilty for putting so much distance between herself and them. She had to do something when Damien threatened to kill her dad and brother if she said anything about the abuse. Then when Damien was declared dead, she regretfully kept that distance, believing she was now just being an independent teenager, which was completely normal.

But, here she was, thirty-three years old and feeling just as isolated. She had never been completely honest with Grant about anything personal. Early in their marriage, he had tried to get to know her likes and dislikes and figure out her love language, but his efforts always proved fruitless. She willfully resisted his efforts until the thickness of the wall between them made her feel safe. But, now that wall seemed impenetrable. Total honesty would be the only thing that could bring it down. She longed to share her secrets, fears, and desires but didn't know how. Or, even if their marriage would survive such a blow.

Jaclyn locked the gun in a file cabinet and then stayed in her office for the rest of the morning, trying to focus enough to get some work done for the Courier. She knew Mark would be on her case if she didn't. But, thoughts of Damien and her plans of attack kept swirling around in her mind. Twice she had typed Damien's name instead of her source's name in the news briefs she was catching up on.

Finally, at about twelve-thirty, she made her way to the kitchen to see if there was anything that looked good to eat. She searched the kitchen island with a far fetched hope that maybe Grant had left her a note of encouragement. He used to do that all the time. Deep down she knew she needed his kind words. They kept that ember of hope deep inside of her lukewarm. But, she had never returned the favor. She had heard that people love others how they feel most loved. But, in her reclusive state, she could only nag him about what he was doing wrong. She hated herself for it, but at the moment, when she felt vulnerable, she drew her sword and thoughtlessly cut him to bits with her words. Now, as she stood in the empty kitchen, she was overcome with sorrow for so much of her life lost to her fears. Would she ever feel alive? Would she ever freely laugh with her family and cry uninhibited? She couldn't even imagine it.

Jaclyn grabbed some leftover noodles and sauce and put them in the microwave. While she waited, she searched Damien's Facebook profile again. How could so much evil be packed into those dark eyes? To her, he was the embodiment of the devil himself. She tried to remember all his threats to her when she was a child, but her heart started beating out of control. The microwave dinged and she jumped. As she lowered the warm bowl to the counter she placed her other hand on her heart and willed it to slow down. She convinced herself that it didn't matter what his threats used to be. It was the threat of his presence near her and her family today that mattered. She had to get a grip.

Jaclyn turned on the TV and Paula Deen appeared cutting vegetables with what looked like magician's hands. Tired from sleeping at her desk the night before, she laid her head back on the couch and closed her eyes. She focused on her breathing, and with each breath felt more confident. The rhythm calmed her. Then her stomach started growling. She turned on her side and stretched long on the couch. Slowly she opened her eyes and stretched. Paula Deen was gone and Emeril filled the screen, laughing, and his eyes sparkling. Jaclyn yawned and sat up, grabbed her phone off her lap, and looked to see the time.

"Shit!" She had fallen asleep. She had three missed calls from the school and a voicemail. She looked at the time and stared in disbelief at the numbers: three forty-three. In one fluid movement, she jumped off the couch, grabbed her keys and rushed out the front door. Once she was on her way she called the school and apologized. The secretary was annoyed but kind.

As Jaclyn pulled up to the curb, she could see the girls right inside the glass doors. She got out of her car and ran to the doors to meet them. Jenae and Mackenzie ran to her and hugged her, but Mandy hung back. Not only was it the day of the sleepover that she wouldn't be going to, but now her mom forgot her at school and she had to listen to the secretary complain about parents who do this all the time. Mackenzie and Jenae ran to the car and got in their seats, but Mandy sat on the bench near the secretary's desk. Jaclyn bent down to eye level and touched Mandy's shoulder. Mandy drew it back away from her hand.

"I'm sorry, baby girl. Work got crazy, and...."

Mandy stood up and walked out the door and towards the car.

Jaclyn sighed and cursed as she followed her. About halfway to pick up Anya, Jaclyn had an idea. "Girls, I am so, so sorry I was late. I was catching up on work and lost track of the time. Listen, I'm yours for the evening. What do you want for dinner? It is your choice. Anything!"

"Pizza!" cried Mackenzie.

"Waffles!" yelled Jenae.

"How about you, Mandy? What would you like for dinner?"

"Whatever."

"Mandy, I'm so sorry about the whole sleepover thing. Let's pick up a pizza, and make waffles, and how about you pick the movie on Amazon and I will buy it?"

"Kay."

Jaclyn knew that getting even that one word out of Mandy was a victory. After picking up Anya, they stopped at the grocery store. Then they all arrived home about an hour later with pizza, syrup and waffle mix, and four swirled lollipops. Jaclyn carried the groceries into the kitchen. She had just started unpacking the bags when she heard Mandy yell from the living room.

"The TV is on, mom! You weren't working, you were watching TV! You lied!" Mandy started balling and Jaclyn pounded her fist on the counter.

Jaclyn walked out to the living room to smooth things over with Mandy. But, Mandy folded her arms and held them tightly to her chest, refusing to even look at Jaclyn.

Just then Grant walked through the front door and the three youngest girls all screamed in unison, "Daddy! Daddy!"

Jaclyn avoided Grant's eyes and mumbled that she had to get the pizza in the oven and left the room.

Grant hugged the three girls, tickling them and kissing them. After several minutes, he could see Mandy's anger. Again. She was definitely her mother's daughter. When all the giggling subsided and the younger girls got interested in the blanket fort they were trying to make, Grant sat gently next to Mandy on the couch. Once again, he just wrapped his arm around her, sat back, and pulled her close to him. And after a few minutes, Mandy settled in under his arm and rested her head on his chest.

"What's going on, kiddo?"

"Mom was watching TV and forgot us at school."

Grant flinched and rubbed his eyes with his free hand. "Well, honey, sometimes adults make mistakes. Your mom didn't mean to hurt you, I'm sure of it.

"Yes, she did. She always does. She doesn't want me to have any fun. I don't like her!"

"Hey, hey, now that's a little harsh. Your mama does a lot just for you. Who got you signed up for riding lessons last summer and rearranged her schedule so just you and she could go out to the stables once a week? Who helped you decorate your room just how you wanted it and made sure that you had special things in your room that only the oldest kid in our family could have? Who lets you stay up a little later on the weekends? Who lets you...."

"Okay, dad! I get it! But, she left us all at school. What kind of mom does that?"

"One who is busy trying to make a living, just like me, so we can provide everything you and your sisters need. That's who. Enough with being hard on your mom. How about picking out an episode for you and your sisters and I'll go see mom in the kitchen and find out what happened?"

"Kay."

Grant got the episode running then walked in the kitchen and smiled empathetically at Jaclyn. "Hey, Jack. You okay?"

"Why wouldn't I be?" Jaclyn kept stirring the waffle mix.

"Mandy is pretty upset."

"When is Mandy not upset these days?"

Grant took a deep breath and sighed. "Okay. What can I do to help with dinner?"

"Nothing. I've got it. Just go watch TV with the girls. Maybe help Mandy pick a movie on Amazon. I told her we would buy one for tonight."

Grant knew when it wasn't worth trying to get anything out of Jaclyn. "Got it." He retreated into the living room, shrugged his shoulders at Mandy who had been watching him, and sat down next to her again. The other girls piled on the couch and they started their search for a movie.

After dinner, they all sat in the living room and watched the new release that Mandy had been begging to see.

Jaclyn sat in the big, overstuffed chair next to the couch while Grant settled in on the couch with all of the girls. He searched Jaclyn's face in the blue glow from her phone. What could be so important that she couldn't take an hour and a half to watch a movie with him and the girls? He willed her to look his way so he could plead with his eyes for her to put the phone down. But, she was unaware, completely engrossed in whatever was on her screen. Mandy looked at her dad looking at her mom and elbowed him.

"Dad, watch!"

Jaclyn looked up and caught Mandy's eyes. Mandy looked away and grabbed onto Grant's arm, hugging it to her chest. Jaclyn sighed and left the room. She retreated to her office and locked the door. She knew it would raise Grant's suspicions but not as much as if he walked in on her unannounced. She unlocked the cabinet and gently pulled the gun from the drawer. Grant had always wanted to teach her how to shoot, but she had said she had no interest. Now she regretted her stubbornness. She placed the gun on her desk and Googled "how to shoot a handgun." She chose "How To Fire a Handgun Safely and Correctly / The Manly Man." The title irked her, but she began reading every word. She checked to make sure the gun wasn't loaded and she practiced holding the gun with her trigger finger not on the trigger, but at the ready for when her target came into view. She also practiced holding the gun with two hands, a must for beginners, so the article emphasized.

After about forty-five minutes she stored the gun away again and checked her phone. She saw the two voicemails and remembered she had missed several calls from Angela that morning and the night before. Without listening to the messages, Jaclyn leaned back in her desk chair and called Angela.

"Well, hello stranger!" Angela shouted a little too loudly.

"Hey, friend. Listen, I'm so sorry I didn't catch any of your calls. Work has been crazy."

"It must have been. Drinking coffee alone this morning was a real bummer, too."

Jaclyn slapped her hand on her forehead. "What?! Oh, Angela, I am so sorry. We had a coffee date today didn't we? Ugh! I am a pathetic friend."

"Yep, you are." Angela laughed nervously at her own harsh comment, not used to being so direct with Jaclyn.

"Thanks a lot."

Angela changed her tone and backpedaled. "You are. But, I also forgive you. Tell me, what exciting story are you working on that has you so scattered?"

"It's all confidential at this point. I could tell you, but then I would have to kill you."

"Do you have a gun?"

Jaclyn felt adrenalin pierce her heart and she stood. "What?!"

"Just kidding. Forget it. I have some exciting news!"

Glad to change the subject, Jaclyn asked, "Who is it now?"

"You make it sound like I go through men like water." Angela sounded genuinely offended.

"Just kidding! Who is it?"

"He is a police officer here in town. We met online and had our first date last night. Jaclyn, he is too good to be true."

"Good for you!" Jaclyn sat back down, weirdly dejected by Angela's good news. Why couldn't she be happy for others? She was tired of herself. She couldn't even imagine how tired Angela and Grant were of her.

Angela talked non-stop for nearly an hour. Jaclyn offered a few words here and there, but mostly just listened. Finally, after Jaclyn could tell that the movie was over and Grant was orchestrating bath time, she told Angela she needed to go.

"Okay, no problem. So, when are we going to get together? I miss you!"

"I miss you, too, friend. By Thanksgiving, I should have some breathing room. You are coming over, right?"

"Of course! And I'm bringing the turkey, remember?"

"Thank you!! I will take care of the rest of the food"

"If things are still going well, can I bring my new friend?"

"Absolutely. What was his name again?"

"Jason. I never found out his last name." Angela laughed at herself.

"Well, we will see you and Jason in a few days. I'm happy for you, friend." Jaclyn cringed at her insincerity.

"Thank you. See you then!"

Jaclyn hung up, but instead of going to help Grant with the girls, she made a solid plan for her interview tomorrow afternoon. Since it was Saturday, she would have to make sure that Grant hadn't also made plans. She needed him to stay with the girls. She wrote down a few questions, surprised at how few she had that she needed answered. Then she pushed the pad of paper aside and took the gun out again. She felt its coldness. She felt its weight. It matched her own heart. Would she be able to use it if the situation called for it? As she turned the gun over in her hands doubt filled her mind.

Soon, the house was quiet. Again, she waited for Grant to come to check on her. But, he never even tried the doorknob. She felt the heaviness of her loneliness. She told herself that she was safe there. And so were those she loved. Eventually, she left her office and found Grant snoring on his side of their bed. She quietly slid under the covers but kept her distance from him so she wouldn't wake him up. Her last conscious thought was that she would finally meet Damien Langley face to face tomorrow at All's Quiet. Then she drifted off into a fitful sleep.

• CHAPTER 8 •

A ray of sunshine snuck through the crack in the curtains and landed on Jaclyn's face. She rolled on her right side and stretched. She breathed evenly as her mind slowly drifted into consciousness. Her first thoughts were about food. She was so hungry and couldn't figure out why. Had she been dreaming about food? With a big yawn, she rolled to her other side and pulled the covers tight under her chin. After several minutes of clinging to the warmth and safety of her bed, she forced her eyes open to look at Grant. But, when she did, all she saw was his empty pillow. She rubbed her eyes, stretched, and tried to remember what day it was. Then reality came in like a nightmare and jarred her awake. It was Saturday and she would meet Damien today. What would she say first? Would he be civil? What should she wear? She didn't dare give him an opportunity to imagine her body. She was thankful it was nearly winter and she could wear layers.

Suddenly, Jaclyn wasn't hungry anymore. She sat up, grabbed her phone and was shocked that it was almost nine-thirty in the morning. She had finally slept a little. But, she still felt tired. The last forty-eight hours seemed like a blur. Only two days ago she had still believed that Damien was dead. How could that be possible? She was living a nightmare.

There was screaming coming from downstairs and Jaclyn started, adrenalin reaching her gut. She grabbed her robe and sprinted to the landing of the stairs to see what was going on. With a sigh of relief, she smiled when she saw Grant filling each of the girls' open mouths with whipped cream. He was such a good dad. And he always had been. She was beyond thankful that she had married him. But, the growing sadness in his eyes haunted her. She stayed on the landing for several minutes, enjoying the joy the girls all exuded. Finally, she walked down the stairs and quietly crossed the living room. Not one of them noticed Jaclyn come into the kitchen until she clanked her coffee cup against another trying to get it out of the cupboard.

When Grant saw Jaclyn, his smile instantly left his face. "Good morning, Jack."

"Hey." Jaclyn took a sip of her coffee then shared a shadow of a smile with him.

Grant smiled back and took a risk. "Can we find some time to talk today?"

"I've got an important interview at one o'clock today. How about after?"

He stood his ground. "Why not now?"

They stared at each other until they were both uncomfortable.

Jaclyn broke the silence. "Because I need to stay focused on my interview and the story I'm writing."

"Really? Why does this story have you acting so defensively? Just tell me. Please." Grant cringed at the sarcasm that slipped out. He didn't want to come across that way.

Jaclyn stiffened and replied dryly. "I told you, I can't."

Grant worked hard to soften his tone. "It's me, Jack. Have I ever given you a reason to not trust me?"

Grant seemed genuine, but his comment hurt because Jaclyn knew that he had no reason to trust her. She had made sure of it.

"After, Grant. Or, not at all." She bit her lip and stared at him until he finally looked away.

Grant looked away and finished the last few bites of his eggs and pancakes. He rinsed his dishes and put them in the dishwasher, all without looking at Jaclyn again. Jaclyn watched him head for the front door. Right when she thought he was going to walk out, he grabbed the box with the security system off the shelf in the front closet. She let out her breath that she had been holding. They didn't say another word to each other for the rest of the morning. Jaclyn turned and fixed a plate of food and sat at the table with Anya, who had been staring at her and Grant while they were talking. Anya licked all the syrup off her plate then grinned and gave Jaclyn a sticky kiss.

"Mommy, dinosaur movie. Please!"

Jaclyn couldn't resist Anya and tickled her with an energetic, "Yes, baby, dinosaur movie it is."

After breakfast was over and Jaclyn had cleaned up the kitchen, they snuggled on the couch under a big, soft blanket. The other girls had taken off to Mandy's room to play school, so Grant was the only other person in the great room, besides her and Anya. Jaclyn watched his face as he worked. He looked deep in concentration as he bent over the security system installation instructions. As Jaclyn watched him work, she realized just how much she appreciated his abilities to do things like this around their house. Angela only had herself, and other friends of hers had husbands who didn't lift a finger when it came to handyman type work. She was proud of him, but rarely had the courage to praise him. She had an aversion to letting him know she was doing okay because he seemed to take that as it was a good day to be intimate. She felt safer around him when she was aggravated. And she knew that kind of thinking was wrong. She longed to be honest. She demanded honesty from others and if she caught someone lying to her, she was vicious in her attack on their character. But, her whole marriage to Grant was a lie. And she was responsible. Deep down she hated herself. And, deep down, she knew that healing would never come until she could be honest with Grant.

Maybe, when she could put this whole thing with Damien behind her, she would thank Grant. She needed to do it. She must do it. He deserved it. Maybe they could get away for a night or two just by themselves. But, not as long as Damien was a threat. But, who was she fooling? Ironically, Damien had threatened her marriage even when she thought he was dead. Why would it be any different this time? But, it had to be different. It just had to be. Jaclyn closed her eyes and willed herself to settle the argument in her mind and stand firm on the belief that one day their marriage would be a joyful one. She just didn't know when that one day would come. But she had to believe that it would. She closed her eyes and started naming everything for which she was grateful about Grant, her kids, her job. One thing led to another. She was thankful for Mandy, which led her to be thankful for Mandy's strong-willed nature, which led her to be thankful that Mandy protected her sisters at school. Which led her to be thankful for each one of the other girls, and their teachers, and their health. Her breathing eased as she kept the gratitude snowball going. All the girls were making a huge snowman and Jaclyn was helping them. Everyone was laughing and rolling in the snow. Then Jaclyn felt someone poking her in the nose. She opened her eyes, not realizing what was happening, and saw Anya grinning at her.

"Mama! You were snoring! Watch da movie, mama!"

"Okay, baby. So sorry. Mama must be tired." She grinned at Anya and hugged her tightly. She turned to check on Grant, but he was gone. The security panel showed a small green light. Which she assumed was a good sign. Soon enough the other girls appeared, running into the living room arguing. Jaclyn sat up and tried to listen to each girl's passionate case, but it all seemed so trivial compared to what she faced today. Her patience grew thin quickly, and she announced that the court was adjourned for a lunch break and they could discuss the matter once she fed everyone. It was only eleven o'clock, but she had to be at All's Quiet by one and needed to pack.

The girls all had seconds and their moods improved greatly. By the time the girls were done eating, Jaclyn still hadn't seen Grant. His truck was in the driveway and when she glanced in the garage, she didn't see him. Once the girls were busy playing, she ran upstairs and saw that their bedroom door was closed. She could hear Grant talking, but it was too soft to make out exact words. She leaned her ear as close to the door as she could without being heard and listened. She picked up only a couple of words when Grant emphasized them, but not enough to make any sense. Then the talking stopped. Before he could catch her she tiptoed across the hall to her office and gently shut the door without a sound. She locked the door and started to pack her backpack. She quietly unlocked the cabinet, put a 15-round magazine in the gun, set the trigger guard, and wrapped it in a hand towel. Her heart pounded as she cautiously lowered the gun into her backpack. What was she doing? She told herself that she would only retrieve the gun if she felt threatened by Damien. She was an adult now and had convinced herself that she could handle him with her words. But, just in case, she wanted him to know that she wasn't a little girl anymore and she could take care of herself. This would all end today. After she met with Damien, she would know where they both stood. She was probably making this into a bigger thing that it really was. Maybe he was just trying to reinvent himself. He was in his fifties now and probably having some kind of identity crisis. Changing his name would make sense. But, what are the chances that he would end up in the same small community as she was?

She slung her backpack over both shoulders and headed downstairs. Grant was making something to eat.

"Hey, I already fed the girls. Where are they?"

"Oh, that would have been nice to know." Grant threw the two empty boxes of macaroni and cheese in the garbage can. The noodles boiled on the stove as he turned back to her. "What's in the backpack?"

"Just my notebook and recorder and stuff. Why?"

"Where's the gun?"

Jaclyn glared at him. "Locked in the cabinet in my office. I'm not stupid, Grant! Where are the girls?"

Grant rolled his eyes then looked down. "In Mandy's room playing."

"I should be back in a couple of hours."

Grant turned back to stir the boiling noodles and didn't answer.

Jaclyn sighed and left. As she walked to her Jeep, the wind playfully lifted her hair away from her face. She noticed the sun peeking through the clouds and hoped the weatherman had been wrong about a bigger storm than the last one coming in before Thanksgiving. Glad that the weather had taken a turn for the better, she cracked her car window while she drove and tried to breathe in the cool, crisp air as she made her way to All's Quiet.

When she was in sight of the store her heart started pounding in her ears. She felt light-headed and nauseated, and everything in her wanted to run and hide. It was only twelve forty-five, so she backed her

Jeep into a parking spot that faced the front door and waited. She took several deep breaths and thought of who she was protecting. Her girls. She had to be brave. She had to face this challenge for them. She had to quit hiding. She turned off the radio but kept the heater on low to take the edge off of the somewhat cold outside temperature. Glancing at the clock on her dash made time seem to stand still, and she tried not to look, but its pull was stronger than her will. At one o'clock she checked to see if the door was locked. Maybe he had parked out back. She grabbed her backpack and keys, locked the Jeep and approached the door. The film on the door reflected her image as she walked closer. She looked old. And scared. She took a deep breath, shook her hair loose from her coat, and held her head high. The door was locked. She knocked and stepped back, her hand tightly gripping her keys, each key tucked between two fingers in case she needed a weapon quickly. There was no response.

Jaclyn got back in her Jeep and drove around to the back of the store to see if there was another entrance. There were no cars in back, but she jumped out to try the back door. Also locked. She drove back to the front, parked, and tried to call Pete. But, it went directly to his voicemail. She sat there for another twenty minutes hoping Damien would show up. Why had she not asked Pete for Damie..., Evin's number? Finally, she wrote a note and stuck it in the door's crack.

By the time Jaclyn left All's Quiet, it was close to two. She drove home quickly trying to fight off a terrible gut feeling that her girls were in danger. It made little sense because they were with Grant, but the feeling made her sick. She didn't like the fact that Damien had not shown up for their meeting. She needed to see her girls. As she pulled in the driveway, she noticed Grant's truck was missing. She put the Jeep in park, grabbed her backpack and walked towards the front door. The wind kept blowing her hair in front of her eyes, but when she swept it away, she stopped dead in her tracks. The front door was slightly ajar. Grant was terrible about locking doors, but he always at least shut them. She took off her backpack, reached inside for the gun and held it with two hands, just like the website had suggested. She kept the trigger guard on because her hands were shaking so badly, and she didn't want to shoot her family on accident if they by chance were there. When she worked the door open with her foot her eyes zeroed in on a laminated newspaper article lying on the entry floor. She kept the gun raised and searched every part of the great room. Keeping the gun raised, but bending her knees, she reached for the article and stood up. It was the same article she had found on the Internet about Damien possibly being seen in South Dakota. Her breath caught in her throat and she dropped the paper. Her eyes darted around the room again and she shouted, "Where are you, you bastard?!" There was no response. She closed and locked the door then walked from room to room. She kept the gun raised while she dialed Grant on her phone. It went directly to voicemail.

"Where is my family, you son of a bitch?!"

She checked every room, every closet, every bathroom. Nothing. She stopped in the last bathroom and threw up in the toilet. She started to cry. "Stop it! Stop it! Stop it!" She yelled at herself. She had to get a grip. Grant had said nothing about going anywhere. She tried calling him again, but she just got his voicemail. Returning to the entryway, she bent down and picked up the article again. She turned it over and written across the back in red permanent marker were the words, "Can't wait to see you again. D." It was Damien! He had been in her home. She fell to the floor, unable to stand. Where were her girls? What had he done with them? Couldn't Grant fight him off? She screamed, and the tears flowed, dripping on the floor.

Just then she heard laughter. She quickly stood up and turned around just as Mandy burst through the door.

"Mommy!" Mandy shouted happily, but then saw the gun in Jaclyn's hand and ran back outside, running right into Mackenzie, knocking her flat on her back. Mackenzie yelled and started to cry. Grant looked up from searching for his phone in the cab of his truck and saw Mandy beelining it for him. He caught her in his arms and tried to get her to calm down enough to understand her. But, when he heard Mandy sob the word "gun" he reassured her he would be right back and took off running.

"Stay outside girls! I'll be right back!"

"But, daddy, Mandy pushe...."

"I said to stay outside!!!" Grant had never spoken like that before and Mackenzie retreated, grabbing the hands of Jenae and Anya on her way to where Mandy was standing by the truck.

"Jaclyn!" Grant yelled from the entryway. "Where are you?!"

Jaclyn had fled up the stairs and into her office to put the gun away. She had locked the office door, but she couldn't get the key in the cabinet because of her shaking hands. Grant tried the office door and then pounded with his fist. "Unlock this door right now! Enough is enough, Jaclyn!"

"Just a minute."

"No! This ends now, Jaclyn! Now!"

"I said just a minute," she raised her voice a little. The key fit and she unlocked the drawer, threw the gun and the article in and re-locked the drawer. She walked to the door and unlocked it. Grant came barreling in.

"What the hell, Jack?!"

"I'm so sorry. I was analyzing the gun and some notes in the living room and didn't expect Mandy to walk in. Where have you been?"

"You cannot have that gun anywhere in the house, but right here in a locked room. I don't want any of the girls to think they can walk around carelessly with guns like their mother."

"Stop! I'm not a criminal. I'm a journalist. And, where were you and the girls? I was worried sick."

"Well, start acting like one! I left you a note on the island in the kitchen like I always do." Grant turned and went back out to reassure the girls it was okay to come in.

Jaclyn made her way to the kitchen and searched for the note. Nothing. Soon the girls ran in and hugged her.

"I'm so sorry I worried you, Mandy."

"It's okay. Daddy said you made a mistake."

"Yes, mommy did and I am so, so sorry. I never want to scare you like that. Mommy was just doing her job. Anyone want a snack?"

"Daddy bought us ice cream for being good while he shopped at the hardware store!"

Grant walked into the kitchen and announced he had finally found his phone.

"Hey, sorry, Jack, I see you tried to call me several times. I couldn't find my phone the whole time we were out. It had slipped between the seats."

"That's okay. Why didn't you tell me you had to run errands? You could have gone when I got back?"

"I was going to, but my new subcontractor needed me to meet his manager at the hardware store right at one so he could buy the materials for a job they are starting for me in Spindrift on Monday. Sorry we worried you."

Jaclyn accepted Grant's hug, glad for the security it offered. Jaclyn could also see the relief in Mandy's eyes watching them. She stayed in his embrace longer, not for herself, but for Mandy. Somehow, she needed to model a loving marriage to her girls. She didn't want any of them to suffer as she had. They shouldn't be afraid of men. They should be able to be vulnerable. She envied their futures.

"Hey, Grant, did you set the security system when you left?"

"Nope. Sorry. It will take some getting used to. You know me, it's difficult for me to remember to lock the doors." Grant chuckled.

"Yeah, I know," Jaclyn whispered, overwhelmed with the thought of Damien being in their home. And what was with his note? He was playing with her. She felt an all too familiar fear growing stronger within her. Would he harm her family? She couldn't let that happen.

"Lighten up, Jack. Your job has you paranoid. It's safe here."

"Not really, Grant. You do not understand."

"Okay, tell me why we are not safe."

"Not until the story runs. You can read it for yourself."

"Jack, come on...."

"Please stop asking!" Jaclyn raised her voice more than she had intended. Mandy looked her direction and frowned. Jaclyn sighed and gave Grant another hug.

"Whoa, what's this for? Aren't we fighting?"

"Yes," she whispered in his ear. "But, I need you."

Grant held Jaclyn and didn't say a word. Since they had met, she had never come close to being so vulnerable as saying she needed him. What was going on with her? Was she dying and just not telling him and the girls? Was the gun for her to end her life before the disease got too painful?

Jaclyn could feel Grant's heart speed up and she held him a little tighter.

Grant whispered in her ear. "Jack, are you doing okay? I mean physically? Is there something going on with you that you're not telling me?"

Jaclyn pushed away and reached for her phone. "I'm fine, Grant."

Grant's breath was uneven as he exaggerated a long exhale. He didn't believe her, but he let the subject drop.

Jaclyn weighed her options. She could retreat or stay engaged. She needed him to trust her somewhat. Because she needed the freedom to handle Damien. "Can you show me how to set the security system?"

Grant looked deeply into her eyes, but still saw a vast void of connection. Where had she gone? He had to fight to get her back.

"Sure. Follow me." Grant grabbed Jaclyn's hand, and they walked to the panel by the front door. He patiently explained the system and the app, helping her download it and sign up for an account.

When they were done, Jaclyn tried it out and locked the front door and set the alarm.

"It's only four-thirty, Jack." Grant laughed.

But, Jaclyn was serious. "I feel safer if it's on. Can we just stay in tonight?"

"I don't think I will ever understand you, Jack." He smiled and Jaclyn tried to smile back.

•   CHAPTER 9   •

The sun set a few minutes before five, darkness filling in the space between the long shadows. Jaclyn bathed the girls early and retreated to her bedroom to put on her pajamas. The night was young, but Jaclyn was exhausted. She laid down on the bed and shut her eyes for a few moments. The heat kicked on and the sound of the warm air pushing through the slotted vents helped her relax, easing the tension she had been carrying in her shoulders. In the silence, she was reminded of a prayer her mother had often said. She reached deep in her memory for the right words. She whispered it out loud, with her arms relaxed at her sides, palms up.

"God, grant me the...." Jaclyn stopped. She couldn't think of the word that her mom had said. It had begun with an S, that she knew for sure. "Sanity?" She laughed at her version. She could definitely use some sanity. But, she was confident that she knew the rest. "To accept the things I cannot change, the courage to change the things I can, and the wisdom to know the difference." It felt good to ask for help, even if she really didn't know who she was asking. Her mother's savior. When her mom was alive, Jaclyn really believed in the God she talked about and prayed to. But, that had been a child's faith, and it had been shattered when her mom had passed away. Jaclyn took a few deep breaths and allowed herself to relax even more. This coming year, she would be the same age her mom was when she died. Wasn't it time that she discovered a faith of her own? Her mom hadn't relied on anyone else's faith, but her own. At least that is what Jaclyn assumed. She wished she had had more time with her mom to learn from her. She would have told her mom that Damien was abusing her. Right? She had to believe she would have confided in her mom. Because she needed her own daughters to confide in her if they ran into trouble. These thoughts stirred in her mind as she listened to the heat fill the room.

Then, suddenly, she heard a door slam and opened her eyes. The bedroom window was open, and the wind blew the curtains against the wall. Jaclyn's heart pounded. Her eyes darted about the room trying to get used to the low light. Then she heard footsteps ascending the stairs. Diving for cover she hit the floor and rolled under the bed. The footsteps got closer, and she scooted farther from the edge of the bed. The door creaked open and, in the light from the hallway, she could see large work boots. Somehow she knew they weren't Grant's. She closed her eyes and pleaded with God to save her. There was only silence. She looked, and the boots were gone. She scooted back farther and her back found the wall. Then, in one swift movement, the bed lifted off of her and landed on the other side of the room. In an instant, his body covered hers completely. She began to gasp for air, batting her hands against his head and upper back. It was no use. He didn't move. His weight was overwhelming. She struggled to breathe, but, when she could inhale, her lungs flooded with the acrid smell of death. He still didn't move and she couldn't move beneath him. Jaclyn screamed, but little sound escaped, her shallow lungs struggling to push enough air past her vocal cords. She stopped trying. Giving in to the inevitable, she relaxed her body and his body pushed hers closer to the ground. She tried one more time to take a breath, but her chest couldn't move enough to draw any air. She opened her eyes and his eyes flashed open, an intense evil flooded her soul. She screamed into the silent sound of darkness.

Jaclyn sat straight up drenched in sweat. She struggled to her feet and backed herself into the corner of the room. She screamed uncontrollably, her eyes scouring every inch of the room. Footsteps pounded up the stairs quickly and the bedroom door flew open. Grant ran to Jaclyn and tried to grab her shoulders. She swung and hit him hard in the jaw. He lunged forward and grabbed her in a bearhug. She kicked and screamed, but he held on.

"Jack! It's me, Grant!"

Jaclyn just screamed louder and kicked wildly.

"Jack. Shh." Grant began to whisper in her ear as he gripped her arms.

Slowly, she calmed down and began to sob.

"Honey, what is going on?"

"A dream. An awful dream. I'm so sorry. I'm good." She struggled to get out from within his grasp. She awkwardly dried her tears and avoided Grant's empathetic gaze.

"Jack, you scared me. What was your dream about?"

"Nothing. I can't remember it. I just know it was upsetting. Whew! I feel like I already worked out. That's a plus." She tried to laugh.

"This isn't funny, Jack. What is going on in your life that this kind of nightmare would haunt your dreams? It's not right."

"Can't I have a scary dream now and then? Quit criticizing me, Grant!"

"I'm not criticizing you, Jack! I'm trying to show you I care."

"If you really care, you would just laugh it off with me. What time is it?"

"Almost ten-thirty. The girls have been in bed for an hour. I peeked in on you earlier and you seemed to be sleeping peacefully, so I left you alone."

"Thank you. I guess I haven't been getting the sleep I need. Well, now I'm wide awake. I might read a bit in my office."

"Jack, just come to bed. Please."

"I want to wait a bit, maybe read something lighthearted. I just don't want to dream again right now. I'll come to bed soon. I promise." Jaclyn gave Grant a quick hug and left him in the bedroom.

On the way to her office, she stopped in the guest bathroom, locked the door, and threw up as quietly as she could. What was that dream all about? Who had been on top of her in the dream? She only remembered feeling that scared one other time in her life. With Damien. She flushed the toilet and washed her face. She didn't dare go back in their bedroom, so she rinsed her mouth and scrubbed her teeth with the girls' bubblegum toothpaste using her finger.

Once in her office, she locked the door. It had become a habit. She sat in her desk chair and stared at the cabinet that held the gun. Would she really need to use it? Her thoughts turned to the security system. Had Grant set it? He seemed to forget to do all the important things. She quietly opened the office door and tiptoed down the stairs. The light was yellow. Not set. "Damn it, Grant," she whispered. "You want to help me? Then set the damn alarm."

She couldn't set the alarm without her phone. She slipped back upstairs to grab it, but couldn't find it in her office. She must have left it in the bedroom. Waiting to set the alarm wasn't an option for her so she tried to sneak into their bedroom to find her phone. The light was on and Grant appeared to still be awake, although he was sitting in bed with his head in his hands, elbows on his bent knees. He didn't move. She saw her phone on the nightstand and grabbed it. Before she could turn to leave, Grant looked up and their eyes met. His eyes were moist with tears. Jaclyn quickly looked away and walked out of the room.

By the time she locked the door to her office again, she had tears streaming down her face. She knew she was hurting Grant, but she felt incapable of stopping. She had to keep her guard up. Grant could never know what she went through as a child. No one needed to know. She would deal with Damien and then get her marriage together. Her life together. If any of that was even possible.

Her phone vibrated. It was a text from Angela. "Hi, friend! I miss you. When can we meet for coffee? I can't wait until you can meet Jason. I think you will love him!"

Jason must be the man she had met online. She didn't remember Angela mentioning his name when they talked the other night. But, it had to be him. A pang of jealousy hit Jaclyn's stomach. He sounded like a good man. But, why did she always feel jealous of Angela? Grant was a good man, too. Then she looked at the string of texts from Angela, at least ten, with no responses from herself. She canceled out of the text, again without responding. She had nothing to say to her right now. She found the security system app and redirected her energies towards trying to remember what Grant had shown her about how to set it. Once it appeared she was successful, she traipsed down the stairs again to see if it worked. The green light was lit. She breathed a short sigh of relief and grabbed a snack before returning to her office. She turned on the light and rummaged through the refrigerator. A Tupperware of green fuzz caught her eye. "Gross," she whispered to herself. The garbage was almost full so she lifted the lid and went to dump the smelly contents into the trash. A crumpled piece of paper caught her eye. She reached in and grabbed it.

"Jack, had to run to the hardware store. Be back soon. Love, Grant."

What? Why was this in the garbage? Grant had said he had left a note, but there had not been one on the counter when she had arrived home. She shuddered in the cool kitchen. What kind of maniac was she up against? She tossed the note back in the bag, dumped the food, and threw the tied bag in the garage. After putting a new bag in, she settled on some milk and Oreos. She sat at the island eating and rummaging through the mail that littered the countertop. A contract stood out amongst the mail. In Grant's handwriting the words "All's Quiet" were scrawled on the top line and Evin Wolfe had signed the bottom line. She dropped the Oreo into the milk and began to read the whole contract. Her husband and Damien were working together? No! This couldn't be happening. Jaclyn paced around the island with the contract in her shaking hand. If so, then Damien was the one Grant needed to meet Thursday when she had to reschedule her interview with Pete Black. Damien had already met her husband. A deep chill ran up her spine. Damien had also been in her home. Fear hit her heart with a jolt.

She was glad that it was Sunday tomorrow, so she had more time to think of what to do. She glanced at the clock. It was actually Sunday now. She placed the contract back on the counter and went up to their bedroom. Grant breathed heavily as she slid between the sheets and got close enough to feel his warmth. Unable to sleep, she rolled over and faced the bedroom door. She stared at the doorknob and pondered whether she should lock it. She closed her eyes, but she could instantly see the door open and a large figure fill the doorframe. Her eyes shot open, and she again stared at the door. Over forty-five minutes later, her eyelids grew too heavy to keep open, and she rolled onto her back and finally gave in to sleep.

Jaclyn woke before Grant and made her way into the kitchen to make coffee. She stood in the dark kitchen, comforted only by the noise of the coffee maker and the dark roasted smell of hazelnut. The contract stared back at her from the counter upon which she had left it only a few hours ago. She reached into the cupboard for her favorite coffee mug, "I Write Like a Mother" printed on one side in typewriter font. Grant had found it online years ago and Mackenzie had begged him to let her give it to Jaclyn for her birthday. She filled the mug and walked into the living room, grabbed the plush gray blanket off the couch, and settled into the overstuffed chair by the fireplace. She opened her Facebook app and searched her friend requests for Damien's. It was gone! She looked all over and couldn't find his name. She sat up a little straighter and typed his name in the search bar to find his profile. Gone. A handful of people shared his name, but none matched. Where could it have gone? Why was he messing with her like this? She quickly pulled up the All's Quiet website and searched for Evin Wolfe's name. Within seconds Damien was staring back at her from the screen.

What she needed to do today was get Grant to share his schedule for Damien's work on the Spindrift house. She wouldn't want Grant there when she confronted Damien, so she also needed to know where he would be. It might work better this way. As long as she knew Damien was alone at the job site, and Grant was some distance away, they would have some privacy to come to terms on Damien's presence in Cliff Creek. They were both adults. She wasn't a child anymore. They could make this work. Maybe Angela's new friend could even help make sure Damien stayed away from her and her family. She would have to come up with a reason, but that shouldn't be hard if he kept breaking and entering. She could deny knowing him. She could press charges and get a restraining order. She tucked the thought away when she heard Grant coming down the stairs carrying Anya.

"Good morning!" Jaclyn called out.

"Hi Mommy!" Anya wiggled out of Grant's arms and jumped into Jaclyn's lap.

Jaclyn opened her blanket and welcomed Anya into its warmth. Without spilling her coffee she wrapped them both up and Anya shared her dreams with Jaclyn.

Grant grabbed coffee and sat across from the girls on the matching couch.

"Let's have a family day today. What do you think?" Jaclyn directed her question at Grant, but Anya screamed with delight.

"What do you think, Grant?"

Grant met her eyes and shrugged his shoulders. "What are you thinking? Can we talk without fighting?" He mouthed the word fighting so as not to upset Anya.

"Yes, we can." She tried to smile at Grant, but she knew he didn't trust that she was serious.

One by one, the other girls woke up and climbed on the couch with Grant. Jaclyn put on cartoons and went to fill her mug with coffee.

Grant wiggled his way out from under the girls and joined Jaclyn in the kitchen.

"Any coffee left?"

"Absolutely!" She grabbed the pot and offered to pour. Grant held out his mug.

"So, the girls are being entertained by Spongebob. Can we talk for a bit?"

"Yes."

"Okay, why have you been acting so strange lately? You're scaring me, Jack."

"I don't blame you." Jaclyn took a deep breath and continued. "The story I'm working on involves a local business owner who has a past history of violence. He's being investigated by the police and he has discovered that I'm asking around about him. I'm worried that he will find out where I live."

"Jack, why couldn't you share that with me earlier? I still wouldn't know who it is, but I could have protected you."

"I know. It was foolish. I just didn't want to drag you or the girls into something that could be dangerous."

"I appreciate it, Jack, but can we face this together now? When is your deadline?"

"Not until Wednesday. I promise I will keep you posted on anything suspicious. I'm sorry I've been acting a little crazy."

"Well, maybe just a little more crazy than usual." Grant winked and took a sip of his coffee.

A memory transported Jaclyn back to when they had first met. The brilliance in Grant's eyes had not dimmed over the years, only the lines radiating out from their shores had deepened with age and life and wisdom. He was strong and stable. He road the waves of life's turmoil and uncertainty, not succumbing to the rip current of defeat. At times, she could see the sadness their marriage had wrought, but he stayed faithful and confident. Yet, she couldn't even stand in the shallowness of life's most peaceful waters without being knocked over by the stormy sea within her heart. She was tired of waking every day fighting to breathe again. To feel alive enough to join with the rest of the living in the rhythms of daily life. She was broken inside. Shattered hopes, dreams, and self-esteem hiding behind a curtain of shame, drawn tightly around her real identity. She presented to her world only an outline of the person she had always hoped to be, but her exhaustive efforts to fill in the emptiness proved fruitless no matter how hard she tried.

She glanced away from Grant's empathetic gaze, unable to receive his offer of hope.

"Well, a little crazier is an understatement." Jaclyn laughed. "What do you say we make these girls some breakfast?"

Grant clapped his hands and stood up. "What do you say these girls make us breakfast? Girls! Come here. You are cooking!"

The girls all came running, excited to be in control of breakfast. They were all in agreement that they would make pancakes that looked like their mom and dad. Mandy got out the griddle, while the other girls collected ingredients. Anya pushed a stool over to the counter and climbed up and onto the counter.

"Anya, scoot back so you don't burn yourself on the griddle."

Jaclyn could always trust Mandy. She had been a little mother since Mackenzie was born. She smiled and reluctantly let Grant lead her back to the living room.

"They will do just fine." Grant laughed.

"Like last time?"

"That was three months ago, at least. They are so much bigger now."

Jaclyn couldn't help but laugh with Grant, both remembering how the girls had tried to stir the pancake batter in the blender, but forgot to put the lid on.

"Okay, but you are in charge of helping them clean up."

"Yes, ma'am!"

Jaclyn's head pounded with stress. She sat with Grant on the couch watching Spongebob, allowing him to put his arm around her.

Normally, she would find an excuse to get off the couch and find more personal space, but she needed Grant to share when Damien would work on the Spindrift house. So she stayed.

"So, what does your week look like?"

"Well, it's a short week with Thanksgiving, so I will have to divide and conquer. I have a sub soundproofing the theater in the Spindrift house all day Monday and Tuesday, and Wednesday afternoon. I will join him Monday and Tuesday, but Wednesday I need to be at the shop working with a couple of my PM's on plans for two new homes."

"Sounds busy. Who is doing the soundproofing?"

"A new company called All's Quiet. I met with the owner Thursday and his operation is impressive. But, the guy himself creeps me out."

Jaclyn sucked in her breath. "Really? Why's that?"

"I don't know. I can't really put my finger on it. He seemed almost confrontational. It's the way he looked at me. But, I really need his expertise. He should be able to finish the job before Thanksgiving. I'm probably just reading too much into it. Some guys feel the need to be macho like that."

"Grant, I don't want you getting hurt. Isn't there anyone else who could do the work?"

Grant thought about her question. "Well, not really. To do something like this without a local sub would be super expensive. The fact that he is in town means I don't need them to fly someone here to install the soundproofing."

Jaclyn searched for another argument against Damien doing the work. "But, can't anyone install it? You could use their material, but pay your own guys to put it in."

Grant chuckled. "I wish. But, this stuff is tricky, Jack. I don't have anyone who knows how to do it. I sure don't know how to do it."

Jaclyn was quiet and Grant pulled her closer. "Seriously, Jack, it's okay. He's just a big lug nut. He drives a ridiculously big black truck. At the job site Friday he even peeled out on the dirt driveway. Ridiculous. But, harmless."

Jaclyn's heart was pounding, and she felt nauseous. Why did Damien have to mess with her family? This was between him and her. No one else. Lug nut? If Grant only knew the extent of his gut reaction towards this man.

Grant reached for Jaclyn's hand and she genuinely embraced it with her own. Intellectually she knew Grant was nothing like Damien. He was honest and caring. Ironically, she was more like Damien that she was comfortable admitting to herself. The thought made her shudder.

Grant felt her body shake. "Are you cold, Jack? I can turn the fire on."

Jaclyn was glad for the diversion. "Sure. Thanks."

Wednesday afternoon she would end it. She would validate with Pete that Damien would be the one working at the Spindrift house Wednesday afternoon and ask that he give Damien the message that she would meet him there for the interview.

Three more days. Seventy-two hours. Her heart stopped pounding and an unusual calm settled over her. She was tired of being held captive by this man all these years. It was time to stand up for herself. Bolstered again by her resolve, she laid her head on Grant's shoulder and relaxed.

• CHAPTER 10 •

A loud beeping filled Jaclyn's dream. It was getting louder and louder, and from a distance, she could hear Grant saying her name. She tried to respond, but no sound would come out. She screamed over and over, but no one seemed to be able to hear her. Grant's voice got louder and louder. He was in trouble. She had to run to him, but her feet were stuck. Everything around her was dark. Her heart pounded louder and louder. Then, hands grabbed her shoulders, and she started to scream.

Grant whispered close to her ear. "Jack! Wake up!"

Jaclyn opened her eyes and pushed Grant's hands off her shoulders. "Stop it, Grant! What are you doing?!"

"Jack, Shh! The house alarm is going off on our phones. Quiet."

Jaclyn bolted upright, straining to hear any sound from downstairs, nausea rising in her throat. Once he was confident that Jaclyn was completely awake, Grant walked to their bedroom door and listened. He could clearly hear banging downstairs.

"The girls, Grant. The girls. We need to get to them." Jaclyn had joined him at the bedroom door, her mouth close to his ear.

Grant turned and looked into her eyes. "Do you still have my gun in your office?"

"Yes, in the filing cabinet, but it's locked. The key is with my others in my purse downstairs."

Grant turned away. "Damn it. Stay here, I will see what's going on." He opened the door as quietly as possible.

"Not without me," Jaclyn whispered. She was so close to him they were touching.

"Stay behind me then." Grant had grabbed his Swiss Army knife and held the knife extended in his right hand.

Quietly and cautiously they descended the stairs, stopping every few stairs to listen. A loud repetitive banging was coming from the front door. Jaclyn grabbed the bottom of Grant's shirt and hung on. They moved as one. She whispered a plea to God for protection.

"Watch my back." Grant walked the ten feet to the front door while Jaclyn kept scanning the room for anything out of place. When he reached the front door, he found it locked. He looked through the peephole in the door and busted out laughing.

"What is so funny?" Jaclyn whispered.

"Your wicker chair is levitating and banging against the door. Wow! This wind looks vicious."

"Let me see." Jaclyn pushed Grant to the side and looked out at the storm. She instantly felt relieved that it was just their outdoor furniture that was being torn to pieces and not them. "But, why would the alarm go off if a door wasn't open?"

"Good question. Let me go grab my phone. I never looked to see what area of the house was sending the message." Grant ran back up the stairs and quickly returned holding his phone. His expression looked panicked.

Grant grabbed Jaclyn's hand and pulled her back. "Jack, get behind me."

She quickly got behind him without arguing. "What is going on?"

"It says the garage door is open."

"I will check on the girls. Wait here!" Grant waited at the bottom of the stairs until Jaclyn returned. He searched the great room from where he stood and saw nothing out of place. If this were a burglary, they sure didn't make it far into the house.

Jaclyn returned and grabbed the back of Grant's shirt. "They are all asleep. I shut their doors. Should we call the police?"

"I already requested it. The company is sending someone now. It is part of the service."

Jaclyn tugged at Grant's shirt, pulling him back. "Should we just wait?"

Grant took Jaclyn's hand off his shirt and gripped it. Without looking away from the kitchen he whispered, "I will look first."

Jaclyn pulled her hand from his. "Well, I'm coming, too, then."

"Jack, please stay here close to the girls!"

"No, I'm coming!" Jaclyn tried to push past him, but he shouldered her out of his way.

"So stubborn," Grant mumbled under his breath as he fought to stay a couple of steps ahead of her. He held his knifeless hand out to the side to prevent her from doing anything stupid.

Once they reached the threshold to the kitchen, Grant reached for the kitchen light switch and flipped it on. Bright light flooded every inch of the large room. The door to the garage stood wide open and on the floor laid what looked to be the neighbor's cat. Blood pooled beneath its lifeless body. Jaclyn stifled a scream. They both took a step back and searched the kitchen with their eyes. Nothing else seemed out of place.

Just then, there was a loud knock at the front door. Still moving as one, they returned to see who it was. Looking through the peephole, the officers assured Grant of their legitimacy by holding up their badges. He unbolted the door and, with a strong gust of wind and a barrage of leaves, the officers stepped into the entryway. After Grant shared a brief explanation of what they found, the officers asked Grant and Jaclyn to stay put while they went to investigate, guns drawn.

Grant and Jaclyn stayed, glued to each other, sitting on the stairs, until the officers had searched the entire downstairs. One officer went upstairs to search while the other explained their findings.

"Well, it looks like a sick practical joke. There is no sign of forced entry; it appears like the garage door was unlocked and so was the door into the kitchen."

Jaclyn glared at Grant and he blatantly ignored her gaze.

The officer continued. "It looks like they shot the cat in the heart outside and carried it inside and dropped it on the kitchen floor. There is blood from the driveway all the way into the kitchen. But, no footprints."

Jaclyn stared at the officer. "Is the house secure now?"

"Yes, all looks clear," the officer said coming from upstairs. "Amazingly, your kids are all sleeping peacefully."

Over the next half an hour, Grant and Jaclyn assisted the officers in filling out a report. Jaclyn brushed off any chance of this being the work of the company she was investigating. She told the officers she would talk to her boss about revealing her sources, but she was sure he would deny it.

"Well, here's my card. Call me tomorrow with your boss's response. Meanwhile, we will have our forensics team run the evidence and see what they can come up with."

The officers locked the garage doors and taped off the area in the kitchen where the cat laid. Then they asked Grant and Jaclyn to keep the kids away until the team could come to lift any fingerprints and gather anything that may contain DNA.

"It might be a good morning to take your kids out for breakfast. Crime scene investigators should be here early to mid-morning to bag the cat and take samples of hair and blood from the trail through the garage. They will call first. Sorry for the inconvenience."

By the time the officers left it was nearly four in the morning. Together, Grant and Jaclyn curled up on the couch staring at the front door. The wind outside howled and Jaclyn's stomach turned. Should she tell Grant what was going on with Damien? Was this his demented idea of scaring her or was this whole thing unrelated to Damien? She couldn't chance revealing her past if it wasn't related. The idea of revealing the shame she had carried for two decades paralyzed her efforts at vulnerability. For now she felt stuck with her own pathetic idea that she could settle the matter with Damien all by herself. Fifty-seven more hours and the results would be known.

Grant set his phone alarm for six and they both tried to catch a little sleep on the couch before they needed to get the girls ready for school. Within what seemed like minutes his alarm rang and they both groaned.

"Well, here we go, Jack. Let's get through this day together, okay? No secrets?"

"Sure." Jaclyn knew she was lying, but she also needed Grant to not suspect what she was doing.

They both went to wake the girls and surprise them with going out for breakfast before school. They all stayed upstairs to get ready, then left through the front door. For once, Jaclyn was relieved that the cars weren't in the garage. Grant carried Anya so the violent gusts of wind wouldn't knock her over. They took two cars so Grant could go to work and Jaclyn could meet the forensics team after breakfast.

The stacks of pancakes made into funny faces and smeared with butter, syrup, and whipped cream thrilled the girls. And Grant even joined in the fun by making his eggs, hash browns, and bacon into a face they all agreed looked like grandma Friedman. While they all laughed and played with their food, Jaclyn sipped her coffee and picked at her eggs and bacon, far from hungry. Grant noticed and squeezed Jaclyn's hand and offered a knowing smile. He kissed her on the cheek and whispered in her ear that, even though their night had been awful, they were in this together. Jaclyn winced. If Grant only knew how untrue his statement was. Shortly before eight, Grant announced that he had to head off to work. He kissed Jaclyn and the girls goodbye and left for Spindrift. The thought of Grant working with Damien all day made her queasy.

Soon enough, the girls were all at school and daycare and Jaclyn was back home, waiting for the forensics team. She stood outside the tape in the kitchen and stared at the cat. Was this to be her end, too? What possessed Damien to go to these lengths to terrorize her? That was twice now that Damien had been in her home. At least twice that she knew of for sure. Goosebumps covered her body at the thought. How many more times had he been near her and she hadn't known? The thought made her physically ill. She grabbed a couple of antacids and sat in the living room facing the kitchen. She had read once, while working on a story about a serial killer, that sociopaths kill animals before they eventually kill people. And in her kitchen was a slaughtered cat, a direct message from Damien to her. He definitely wasn't in her neighborhood to make amends. He meant to scare her into bowing down to his desires. The thought of what that could mean now, twenty-three years later, was frightening.

Just before noon, the forensics team arrived. They photographed every angle of the scene of the crime, then bagged evidence, including the cat. When they were done, a cleaning crew cleaned and sterilized the kitchen and garage floors along the path of blood. And, in less than an hour, there was no evidence that a crime had even occurred in her home. After letting the team out, Jaclyn locked all the doors, turned on the alarm, and left for the Courier. She had to get her work done or she would find herself without a job when this whole thing with Damien was over. But, would it ever really end? He had haunted her even when he was supposedly dead. The thought that she would never be free from his terror caused her to shudder. Sitting up straighter behind the wheel, she cursed out loud. She had to believe it would end soon. There was no other choice if she had any hope of retaining what was left of her sanity.

As she neared the Courier, she slowed enough to see what was going on at All's Quiet. They must have officially opened the store because cars filled the parking lot. She searched for a big black truck as Grant described Damien as having, but didn't see it. He must be at the Spindrift house. She found her parking space at the Courier and sat in her car listening to the wind howl. She needed a few minutes to process the last twenty-four hours and these could be the only free minutes of her day. From where she was sitting she could see the comings and goings of the All's Quiet customers. A steady stream flowed in and out, probably all trying to get their order in while the grand opening sale was still in effect. She would call Pete later today and set up her appointment with Damien for Wednesday at one in the afternoon.

A fist pounded on her window and Jaclyn screamed. She dropped her coffee, and it splashed across her dash on its way down to the floorboard. Covering her head and struggling to get down away from the pounding, Jaclyn kept screaming. Her driver's door opened, and she crawled into the passenger seat reaching for the passenger door handle to escape. The wind filled the Jeep, howling as it also sought an exit.

"Jaclyn! Whoa! Whoa! Whoa! It's just me!"

Jaclyn turned to see Mark, her editor chuckling with two coffees in his hands.

"My, my, you are jumpy today, young lady! Get yourself together and let's go inside. You will freeze to death out here."

"Mark! Good Lord! Don't do that! You are nuts. You could have killed me with your joy!"

Mark laughed a deep belly laugh and extended his hand to help her out of the car. "What a way to go though, right? Come on, get out. I'm freezing."

"Well, give me a minute, you maniac. I'm kind of tangled up here." Jaclyn freed herself from the middle console and gathered her purse and now empty coffee cup. "I'm glad you have two cups of coffee because you spilled mine, you crazy old man."

"Watch it, young lady, I will demote you to classifieds if you don't treat the elderly with respect." Mark howled at himself. His white beard and bald, hat-covered head framed the twinkle in his eyes. And his far away West African accent made his words even more playful.

"Mark, you are crazy. But, you are my boss so I will get my act together." Jaclyn smiled and accepted his offer of one cup of coffee.

"I will tell Jane you stole it from me."

"No, you will tell your secretary you scared me nearly to death and spilled my coffee and you will have someone run to get her a new one."

"Yes, Ma'am!"

Once inside, Jaclyn turned to go to her desk, but Mark asked her for a few minutes in his office. She followed him, hoping he would not lecture her about her missed deadlines.

Before he even shut his office door, Jaclyn began her defense. "Mark, I know I'm late on briefs, but they are easy and I've had one hell of a week at home. I will get..."

"Jaclyn, stop. For one minute, stop talking. I didn't call you in here to jump on your case about deadlines. Yes, you're late. But, I'm worried about you. You just don't seem yourself lately. I mean, you being brash and crabby is what I look for every day to make sure you are acting normal. I love you just how you are. You know, had my own daughter survived the car accident ten years ago, she would be the same age as you. I care about you like you're my own daughter. Now, tell me what's up."

"Mark, I'm good. Really."

"Jaclyn, you're sad and afraid. Don't argue with me. What is up?"

Jaclyn's eyes filled with tears. She sat silently and tried to compose herself.

"Listen, I've been there. My first marriage failed when I was a young arrogant man, thinking I didn't need anyone's help. What I discovered was that I could definitely destroy things with no help. My only hope for redemption was wrapped up in our daughter. I vowed to be the father I failed to be when she was younger, but then a drunk driver took away that opportunity and I sunk into a depression deeper than any light could penetrate. That is any light but the light of redemption itself. Jaclyn, I needed to talk. I had to break the silence that held me captive. I needed to be vulnerable. It took a lot of counseling and a lot of coffee with my dear friend Frank. He was a retired pastor, and he was just as mad at God as I was. But, together we began to recognize that God doesn't work on us when we sit in a building. He works on us when we're in the fire. I came to realize that as messed up and marred as my life was, I held value in this world. I was created for much more than anger and self-pity. I needed to acknowledge my value and begin opening myself up to the world. I turned on the light and gave up covering up the abuse I inflicted on my wife and young daughter as an angry young man. I began to tell my story, hoping and praying someone would lay me flat for what I had done. But, the judgment didn't come. Just grace. Lots of it. Soon I was being asked to tell my story and, with every telling, humility grew in my heart. Years after our daughter died, my ex-wife and I even mended our relationship. We are not re-married, but we have become broken, yet redeemed, friends. We share a common grief, but we have also discovered a common purpose and hope for our futures. Jaclyn, this life's too short to live in the darkness. Don't befriend the night when the day is calling you to a greater purpose."

Mark reached out for Jaclyn's hand and guided her to the chair near his desk. He pulled a chair next to her and faced her. He grabbed both of her hands and asked her to look at him.

"Jaclyn, you are worth being loved. I'm not sure what your demons are, but you don't deserve the darkness they are convincing you is all you can expect from life. You don't need to tell me anything. But, think about what I've said. Your work here is nothing compared to the story your heart could tell a hurting world. Consider telling it."

Jaclyn just nodded her head and released a hand to wipe her nose. Mark handed her a couple of tissues from his desk and smiled.

"Now, get to work, you slacker!" His smile warmed her heart. She stood and gave him a big hug. Surprised by her unusual tenderness, Mark held her tightly, not letting her dash away.

"Thank you," she whispered in his ear, then gathered her things and left his office.

At her desk, she regained her composure and worked to finish the briefs. Several hours passed as she focused on her work, but as much as she tried, she couldn't get Damien out of her mind. What were he and Grant doing in Spindrift right now? Was Grant safe? She knew she couldn't bring any more attention to her fears or Grant would have her committed. She knew she had been acting crazy. Once the briefs were done, she pulled up Facebook and again looked for Damien's profile. Nothing. She searched for Evin Wolfe. Nothing but a few other Evin Wolfes, one in Vermont, one in Dallas, and one in Canada. Not one of them looked like Damien. For the next several hours she searched public records and made several calls trying to gain access to more information on this maniac. She found nothing but refused to give up. It was nearly six o'clock when she heard her phone vibrating in her purse. Where had the time gone? She saw it was Grant and winced as she answered.

"Jaclyn! What the hell?! Where are you?"

Jaclyn instantly went on the defensive. "I'm still at work. Calm down!"

"Calm down? I've been trying to reach you for hours. You were supposed to pick up girls from school! The school tried to reach you, too. I had to leave Spindrift to get them, so I needed to reschedule a meeting with potential clients. We ordered pizza and are waiting for you."

She could hear Grant breathing hard into the phone. "We never agreed I would pick up kids. Grant, sorry, but I have a job, too! Just stop yelling. I'm on my way now."

Grant hung up.

Jaclyn looked at her phone and noticed a missed call from the school and seven missed calls from Grant. She deleted all the voicemails without listening to them. She didn't need to hear anyone else but herself beating herself up. As she pulled out of the parking lot, the lights of another vehicle lit up behind her, blinding her in her rearview mirror. She tilted the mirror up slightly to soften the glare and continued to drive home, a routine fifteen-minute drive without traffic. A couple of miles into her commute she noticed that the vehicle was still following her. Jaclyn sat up tall and looked in her rearview mirror. She took several unnecessary turns and attempted to speed up to gain some distance from the vehicle, but the large vehicle stayed right behind her. Adrenalin pierced her heart when the vehicle drove beneath a streetlight and she saw that it was a large black truck. She continued to avoid her normal route and attempted to lose the truck, but it stayed close. Finally, she thought it best to go home and headed in that direction. When she got to the corner to turn onto her cul-de-sac, the truck sped past her, revving its engine. She gunned it up the street to her driveway, looked behind her but saw no truck, parked in the driveway, and quickly entered the house.

"Well, thank you for coming home." Grant's sarcasm grated on her nerves and she completely ignored him. She set the security system and walked into the kitchen. Another day and a half and this all had better end. Grant followed her and leaned against the kitchen wall, passive-aggressively waiting for an explanation. She refused to give him one as she ate a piece of cold pizza and avoided his cool gaze. She knew she had been neglecting her time with the girls so she stood and left the room to go give the girls baths, get them in their jammies, and read them stories. At least it would take her mind off of Damien for a short time. She didn't see Grant for the rest of the night. Finally, when the girls were all tucked in, she grabbed a blanket from the living room and settled on the couch up in her office. It was there that she awoke with a start the next morning.

• CHAPTER 11 •

Adrenalin pierced her heart as she realized her life was still the nightmare it had been when she had fallen asleep the night before. For several minutes, she lay still under the soft blanket and listened to the quiet of the house and the raging storm outside. The forecast called for diminishing winds later today, but those winds were to usher in freezing rain, sleet, then snow by late Wednesday afternoon. She closed her eyes and felt a similar storm in her heart. Mark's words battered against the walls she had built around her heart, threatening to crack the facade she had created as a young girl. How could he tell her she didn't deserve the darkness she was living in? He did not understand what her struggle was against. He didn't know just how dark the darkness had become. She deserved every blinding part of it because she was afraid. She had always been afraid. From the beginning, she should have fought back, but she succumbed. She laid down and let life happen to her. And now, as an adult, a wife, and mother, she was weak and defenseless. She couldn't be herself because she didn't know who she was. She was a fake and a liar. She was doomed to live encapsulated in this cocoon of self-hatred and dead desires and dreams. She was beyond forgiveness and redemption. All she had left was to fight back to protect her family, whom she should have protected from the very beginning. This was all her fault. A deep sob found its way out and Jaclyn realized she was crying.

When would this end? Would it end? She looked at her phone and it was only four o'clock. Her heart was pounding out its daily rhythm of anxiety and stress, therefore, there was no chance of entering the solace of sleep anymore tonight. She walked to the kitchen and put on a pot of coffee, careful to not step where the cat had been. What kind of demented mind does things like that? And why did she deserve it? Mark had said she was worth being loved. As a young child, she had believed she was worthy of love. Before her mom died, she knew nothing but being loved. She sipped her coffee and allowed herself a moment to remember mandatory family dinners in their home. They would all linger around the table long after eating and talk and laugh together. Her mother was her hero. She had worked a full-time job as a seamstress for a local theater group but could somehow still make sure there was a hot meal and plenty of attention for everyone. And she had loved stories. She loved telling them and hearing them from her family. Jaclyn's love for journalism stemmed out of the many true stories told around her childhood table. Even when guests would join them for dinner, her mom would draw out spectacular events in the person's life. Jaclyn had even started writing some stories she heard down in her journal and illustrating them like she imagined them playing out. She still had those journals but hadn't looked at them since her mom died.

Jaclyn's mom's death had hurt her deeply, disintegrating any sense of belonging and safety. So, when Damien offered kind words and compassionate hugs, she soaked them up like a dry, brittle sponge. He offered to pick her up from school and bring her back to the nursery so her dad didn't have to leave work. Often they would stop for a Coke or ice cream and she could share her broken heart with him. He talked about losing his own mother when he was about her age and she felt understood. After a couple of months, she depended on Damien, not only for rides but for validation. She wrote about him in her journal, calling him her knight in shining armor. The thought made her shudder now, as she slowly sat down at the island. She didn't want to remember, but her mind wouldn't stop. She closed her eyes and could vividly see the motel they stopped at one afternoon before going to the nursery. She questioned what they were doing, but he said it was a surprise and that she would love it. He unlocked the door to room 106 and she couldn't see anything but balloons. She laughed and made her way inside. He closed and bolted the door. On the bed were several wrapped gifts. Damien smiled when she looked at him and he said they were all hers. He went on about how proud he was of how strong she had been since her mother's death and she deserved these gifts and so much more. She giggled as she opened every gift, thrilled that all the gifts were things she had shared with him she wanted. She gave him a big hug, but he held on too long. She tried to step away, but he lifted her off the ground and laid her on the bed. She tried to laugh and get away, but he yelled at her to stop. She stared into his eyes and they grew darker than she had ever seen them before. He told her he had one more gift, one that she could tell no one about. As he undressed her, he told her in a low, gravelly voice that he would kill her father and brother if she ever told them or anyone else about this gift. He called it the gift of womanhood. He praised her for her beautiful body and maturity. He said that any boy she dated would be the luckiest man alive. He began to take off his clothes and tears welled up in her eyes.

"Good morning, Jack." Grant had walked all the way to where Jaclyn was sitting without her noticing him.

Jaclyn jumped then tried to get up and spilled her coffee all over the island.

Grant reached for a towel. "Whoa, Jack, it's okay. It's just me."

"Damn it, Grant, don't scare me like that!"

"Jack, I just walked into the kitchen. I don't know how to do it any other way. What is wrong?"

Jaclyn took a few deep breaths and tried to regain control. "Nothing. Just jumpy I guess since yesterday's murder in our kitchen." They both laughed nervously.

Grant reached for Jaclyn's hand. "Yeah, me, too. Listen, I'm sorry about how I acted yesterday. I know you've been overwhelmed at work and I shouldn't have taken my day out on you. I think we were both on edge after yesterday morning."

Jaclyn stiffened at his touch. "No, it's fine. I should have paid more attention to the time. I'm sure I put you in a bind."

"Well, that was yesterday. Let's focus on today." Grant squeezed her hand gently before she pulled it away.

Jaclyn marveled at how Grant could turn things around. Her whole being stewed in past regrets and failures and she could only raise her head to the surface for brief moments of positivity.

Jaclyn switched gears. "Okay, sounds good. Today I need to meet some deadlines and arrange some interviews. Are you still going to be at the Spindrift house?"

"Yep. We got a lot done yesterday, but we are nowhere near finished."

"How was Damien?"

Grant looked up to meet Jaclyn's eyes. "Who?"

Jaclyn panicked and started to laugh. "I mean Evin. Geez. Damien is one of my other sources. I have too much going on in my head."

"Ah, gotcha. Well, Evin was quiet. He said he would normally send his crew out to do the work, but he has a particular interest in the layout of this theater and wanted to do it himself. He was actually pretty cool yesterday. I may have misjudged him."

Jaclyn's stomach did a flip, and she struggled to say anything positive. "Good."

Grant watched Jaclyn's demeanor change right before his eyes. "What's wrong?"

"Nothing. Why?"

"The look in your eyes when I said Evin wasn't such a bad guy. What was that reaction about?"

Jaclyn took a breath before speaking. "I just didn't like the way you said he treated you the first time you met. It is hard for me to get that out of my mind."

Grant smiled. "You are protective, aren't you? Well, thank you. But, he's harmless. How was your day at work?"

Jaclyn was happy for the diversion. "I actually got a lot done. It's amazing when you forget about everything else and just work." She covered her face with both hands. "Sorry."

"Jack, you're forgiven. Let it go." Grant kissed her on the cheek and poured himself a cup of coffee. "Seriously, let's move on. It's a new day."

They could both hear the girls giggling upstairs. They smiled at each other and Jaclyn volunteered to make sure the girls were on task getting ready for school.

"I'll get breakfast going." Grant pulled out the frying pan and grabbed eggs from the fridge.

"Thanks. Once the girls are on task, I will shower and get ready. Want me to take the girls to school?"

"If you could, that would be great." Grant grinned and winked. "Love you, Jack."

"Yep." Jaclyn grinned back, avoiding Grant's eyes. She hated herself for not being comfortable with vulnerability. Grant was so good at it and he didn't have an easy childhood either. Envy pushed her introspection back deep inside. Once the girls were in their rooms dressing, she hopped in the shower and focused on everything she needed to do in the next twenty-four hours.

Jaclyn dropped Anya off at daycare first because she did not have time to watch the other girls on the playground. She let the girls stay in the Jeep, but locked them in with a stern warning to not unlock the doors for anyone. When she got back in the car, the radio was blaring one of the girls' favorite songs. They were all singing along and Jaclyn put the car in gear and joined in on the chorus. The girls all shouted with glee at their mom's willingness to be silly. At the school, the girls all took turns giving Jaclyn a kiss and a hug before jumping out of the car. She smiled at each one without speaking, working hard to keep the tears in her eyes from spilling over. Mandy was the only one who noticed.

"Mama, are you okay?"

"Oh, honey, yes." Jaclyn sniffed and quickly brushed her eyes with the back of her gloved hand. "I'm good. Just so proud of you and your sisters. Have a great day, baby!"

Mandy jumped out of the Jeep and blew another kiss to Jaclyn before running off to her friends on the playground. Jaclyn started bawling as she pulled away from the curb. She was in awe of how quickly Mandy had worked through her anger about the missed sleepover. Her love for all the girls was intensely raw and strong this morning, and with new resolve, she forced down any fear of Damien and began to feel almost militant. She needed to get to work and map out her day tomorrow.

As she pulled into the Courier parking lot, she slowed to a crawl and perused the All's Quiet lot. No black truck. She shuddered remembering the truck that followed her home last night. Where was he now? Probably close to meeting with Grant. The thought of him being near anyone she loved made her sick. Before getting out of her car she pulled up her hood and zipped her coat as high as it would go and pushed the car door against the driving wind. She hugged her backpack to her chest and ran, hunched over to the main door. Once inside she took a deep breath and undid her coat so she could straighten up. Mark stood sipping his coffee and watching her undo herself from the clutches of the elements.

"Good morning, sunshine!"

"Oh, hey Mark. Good morning."

"Got some briefs for me?"

"Yes, sir!"

"Great, I will look when I get to my office. I sure wish you all could just print them out for me like we used to do. This computer Internet stuff drives me nuts."

Jaclyn laughed, patted him on the back, and made her way to her office. She was the senior reporter on staff and had earned an office a couple of years ago. She had always coveted that space before they gave it to her and she vowed never to lose it. Therefore she spent the first part of her day getting ahead on her work for the paper. She was able to schedule three interviews and do one over the phone on the spot. She made edits on the story due to run today, then tried to reach Pete Black.

"All's Quiet, this is Pete."

"Hey, Pete. Jaclyn from the Cliff Creek Courier."

"Yes, Ma'am! Were you able to meet with Evin Saturday?"

"Actually, he didn't show, and I didn't have his cell number."

"Oh boy. Typical. So sorry. Let me see if I can get you in...."

"Pete, is there any way I could meet him on site at the job in Spindrift? I would like to grab some photos of the work he does to go with the story."

"Well, that's one way of catching the prey."

"Excuse me?"

Pete laughed. "Just an expression, Ma'am. Let's just set it up. He will definitely be there. I'm not even going to tell him. That way he can't run away from you. He'll be there from around noon until five or six."

"Thanks, Pete. I appreciate it."

"Do you need the address?"

"I've got it. Thanks! Have a good day."

"You, too, young lady!"

Jaclyn hung up the phone and opened her notes app. She began typing her list of items to bring with her to Spindrift and everything she needed to get done before Thanksgiving dinner. Thank God Angela is bringing the turkey. She felt bad for not paying much attention to Angela in the past week. She quickly typed out a text to her to lessen her guilt. But, before she could send it her phone lit up with a call. It was the girls' school.

"Hello, this is Jaclyn."

"Hello, Mrs. Friedman, this is Stacy at Eagle Crest Elementary School."

"Yes? Is everything okay?"

"Mandy is fine, just a little shaken. Apparently, a man was talking with her through the fence during recess and he scared her. We didn't get his plates, but Mandy described his vehicle as a big black truck. We've alerted the police."

Jaclyn was in the car and backing out of the driveway before the secretary had even finished her sentence. "On my way. I want her to come home." She hung up without saying goodbye.

She cursed and screamed as she sped through town to the school, ignoring every law and begging God for the mercy of not being pulled over. She parked in the fire lane and ran into the school. Mandy was sitting in a chair in the office.

"Baby, are you okay?" Jaclyn embraced Mandy with trembling hands.

"Mom! Yes, I'm fine. I don't want to go home, mom. They told me I could stay inside during the next recess. Please, mom! I want to stay here."

Jaclyn leaned back but held tightly to both of Mandy's shoulders. "Honey, I don't feel comfortable with you here until that creep gets arrested."

Mandy pouted while Jaclyn signed her out.

"Mrs. Friedman, we will keep a close eye on…."

"No!" Jaclyn shouted, then apologized. "I'm sorry, but I want her to come home."

The secretary held both hands up and said, "No problem."

Mandy crossed her arms all the way to the Jeep, refusing to run with Jaclyn through the freezing rain that had just started. They were both soaked by the time they got to the car. Jaclyn watched Mandy in the rearview mirror, praying that someday she would forgive her for her paranoia. Mandy shivered but didn't utter a word. At home, they both changed into dry clothes. Mandy stayed in her room, ignoring Jaclyn's suggestions for renting a movie or making brownies. So she sat on the couch and rented a movie that Mandy had been begging to see. It was PG-13 and Jaclyn had told her they could watch it together, only if the other girls weren't home. She pushed play and sat back and waited. Soon enough she caught Mandy sitting on the bottom stair with her chin in the palms of her hands. Jaclyn patted the couch next to her and Mandy drug her feet on the carpet as she slowly walked to sit down. Jaclyn didn't say a word and pretty soon Mandy was leaning against her, totally engrossed in the movie.

Should she tell Grant what happened? By the time the credits were rolling, and Mandy was begging to make brownies, Jaclyn finally decided that she needed to tell Grant before he heard it from Mandy. After helping Mandy mix up the brownie batter she texted him a brief message about what happened. Forty-five minutes later he still hadn't texted back. "It's a good thing no one is really in trouble. You would never answer our calls for help," Jaclyn whispered under her breath as she went to get their coats.

On the way to pick up the other girls, she kept her eyes open for a black truck but didn't see one. Shouldn't Damien have been with Grant when this happened at school? Maybe the man Mandy saw wasn't Damien. She was sure there was more than one creep in town.

By the time Grant got home the sleet had turned to snow. The wind had died down, but the roads had become treacherous. Grant grabbed a shovel and cleared the area around the front door so no one would get hurt. He propped the shovel by the door, knowing he would shovel more before the night was over, and walked in the house.

"Daddy, daddy, daddy!" Anya ran to meet Grant at the front door.

"Hi, Pumpkin!" He kicked off his boots and swung Anya up into his arms.

Mackenzie and Jenae heard the commotion and came running. They joined in and ended up tackling Grant to the floor. He set his backpack to the side and began to tickle the girls until they were in danger of wetting their pants. He glanced up at the couch during the attack and saw Mandy sitting on the couch watching. After a few minutes, he settled the girls down and sent them off to hide and began counting.

As he continued to count, he sat next to Mandy. "Hey, kiddo! How was school?"

"Fine. I didn't get to stay though."

"Why not?"

"Mommy picked me up because some weird guy was talking to me and I got scared and told a teacher. I did the right thing. Why couldn't I stay?"

Jaclyn had caught his eye from the kitchen and pleaded with him to take the threat seriously.

He looked back at Mandy's frown. "Well, sweetie, your mom did the right thing. We never want to take a chance on you, or any one of your sisters, getting hurt. Even if it means taking you out of school. By tomorrow that guy will be gone and you can enjoy recess. And, there should be plenty of snow to play in." Grant started to tickle her, then heard the other girls yelling to come to find them. "Come help me find those crazy girls!" He grabbed Mandy's hand, and they crept towards the stairs and climbed them like ninjas.

Before dinner, Grant found Jaclyn in the kitchen pouring a glass of red wine.

"May I join you?"

"Sure." Jaclyn reached for a glass, filled it halfway and handed to Grant.

"Are you okay?"

"Yep. I don't think this is related to my story at all. The secretary said they report incidents like this several times a year. He was just a creep and they've probably picked him up by now."

Grant could tell that Jaclyn didn't believe her own words. "I think you did the right thing, Jack."

Surprised at his agreement, Jaclyn looked up from her wine. "Really? Are you being sincere?"

"Of course I am. Moms have a radar for things like this. I trust your intuition."

"How come you couldn't trust me about canceling Mandy's sleepover?"

Grant took a sip of wine and tried to think of a reply. He had just wanted to encourage Jaclyn, not get into an argument. He took one for the team. "I was wrong about that. Forgive me." He grinned and winked at her.

Jaclyn could clearly see Grant's attempt at sincerity, even though she knew he thought she was being overprotective. She, too, conceded. "Thanks. I forgive you." She gave her best shot at a smile back at him.

Just then, Jaclyn's phone rang.

"It's Angela. Do you mind if I take it? I've been ignoring her for the last week."

"No problem. I'll set the table."

Jaclyn retreated to the corner of the kitchen so she could hear better. "Hey, Angela. How are you?"

"I'm doing well. Listen, I just wanted you to convince Jason that it would be okay for him to join us for Thanksgiving dinner. Can you talk to him for a few minutes? We are out to eat and just waiting for our food."

Jaclyn sighed, not having any patience for something so trivial. "Sure. Put him on."

"Hello? Jaclyn?"

Jaclyn dropped her phone and stepped back from it. Grant turned his head at the sound. "Jack, what's up?"

Quickly trying to regain her composure she bent over and retrieved her phone. "It just slipped out of my hand." She walked out of the kitchen and held the phone to her ear. "Hello?" Silence met her shaky voice. He had hung up. She sat on the couch and rubbed her temples. She was losing it.

•   C H A P T E R   1 2   •

It was morning, and the sun was lighting up her whole room and a gentle breeze was playing with the curtains on the open window. Birds sang in the trees and Jaclyn could hear her mother singing in the kitchen downstairs. She jumped out of bed, eager to see her mother, and leaped down the stairs hoping she was baking so she could join her. The kitchen transformed into her childhood kitchen and she could see her mother's back as she stood at the sink doing dishes. Jaclyn gleeful called to her mom as she ran into the room, but she didn't turn around. Then, from behind her, she could hear her dad yelling for her mom's help with his tie. Her mom turned and dried her hands on a towel, chuckling to herself about her husband being so needy. She walked right by Jaclyn without saying a word, even though Jaclyn had yelled her name. She followed her mom into her parents' bedroom where her dad stood before the mirror struggling with his tie. Her mom kissed her dad on the cheek then stood behind him and tied his tie, both smiling and looking into the mirror. Then Jaclyn saw him. Damien. He laid on her parents' bed, propped up against the headboard with several pillows. Jaclyn screamed, but neither her mom nor dad moved. They kept smiling and working together to get his tie just right as Damien patted the bed next to his body. Jaclyn tried to run, but her feet wouldn't move. She looked down and someone had nailed her feet to the floor, but she couldn't feel anything. She screamed louder, but no one, but Damien could hear her. He began to laugh as he scooted himself off the bed. Her mom and dad finished with the tie and walked out of the room holding hands. Jaclyn cried and screamed, but no one would help her. Damien grabbed her shoulders and lifted her off the ground, ripping her feet from the nails. She blacked out.

Pain in her feet woke Jaclyn and she bent to grab them. They were whole, not ripped apart. Her heart pounded and her breathing was labored. Sweat soaked the sheets. She tried to slow her breathing by taking deep breaths. Eventually, her heart returned to a normal rate and she felt more in control. She rolled onto her back and laid one arm across her eyes. Why was she so alone in her pain, both when she was awake and asleep? Her mom couldn't have known about Damien before she died. He wasn't a problem then. But, her dad was around. She knew he suspected something was going on that wasn't right, but he was never there when she needed him the most. Just like in her dream, no one could hear her inner screams for help, except Damien. He knew. And he thrived on it. Jaclyn's stomach hurt and nausea pressed its way up the back of her throat. She willed the nausea to stand down and eventually felt strong enough to get out of bed.

Grant had left before Jaclyn even woke up. He had agreed to meet with some customers at the shop before they needed to be at work. She stretched one last time under the warm covers, deciding that she could let the girls sleep in a few extra minutes. Making her way downstairs and into the kitchen, she poured some coffee and sat on the living room couch. She tested the silence. A supernatural calm invaded the space around her and then within her. She felt different. Something inside was shifting, and it didn't feel good, but it didn't feel wrong either. It was a longing, a deeply ingrained, almost innate need. She wanted, no, she needed to belong. But, belong to what? She was a part of a family; she had co-workers, and they counted themselves part of the congregation of a small church, even though they rarely attended. She belonged. But, was she accepted? Did anyone really care that she was even alive? Why Grant stayed with her would always be a mystery to her. She would not stay married to herself. The girls were stuck with her. And, she belonged at work because she was a damn good journalist. But, she gave little credence to being a part of the church, because she really didn't think anyone there even knew they existed. Angela was the one person in her life who tried to draw her out. She annoyingly never stopped encouraging her and questioning her. But, Jaclyn never felt like she could reciprocate. What did she have to offer others? She felt like a shell of a human, just going through the motions of life. What more was there? Love was so ambiguous. Had she ever really felt loved?

When she was a little girl, she remembered the joy and peace of knowing she was safe and cared for and enjoyed. Her mother had filled each day with joy. She used to watch her mom stand at the kitchen sink long after she washed the dishes with her head bowed. Just once during this time had she tugged on her mom's shirt and begged for attention. Her mom had simply put her finger up and whispered, "When I'm done talking to my father." For months she had thought her mother's father, her grandfather, was invisible. She knew her grandparents had died before she was born, so this mystery filled her with questions she was afraid to ask: Why don't you ever talk to your mother? Does grandpa not like me, because he doesn't talk to me? What does he say to you? Then one night while her mother was saying prayers with her, Jaclyn prayed that grandpa would talk to her just like he talked to her mom. Her mom had laughed and asked what Jaclyn meant. Jaclyn explained that she wanted to talk with grandpa just like her mom did after washing dishes. Her mom had hugged her and then explained that her father was also Jaclyn's father. Their heavenly Father. They had talked for a long time that night, her mom explaining God's love to her and his sacrifice of his son Jesus who was their savior. Jaclyn loved the stories her mom told about God's miracles and how she didn't have to fear death, because God made a way to live for eternity. They never had talks like this with dad, just when her mom was tucking her in at night. Much later, she would learn that her mother had also been sharing the same stories with her brother. But, before a year had passed since learning that her mother's Father was also her own, her mother died. The aneurysm had taken her in an instant. And it took her at the kitchen sink. Why had she never put that together until now? Her mother had probably been praying when she died. Maybe that's why her dad never took her or her brother to church again. He said nothing about God to them. He just didn't talk about him. If God was love then where was he? She could really use him but she felt nothing. She didn't feel protected or safe or loved. All she felt was this deep, gnawing, gut-wrenching longing for more. Keeping this desire silent was becoming more and more difficult. Lately, she just wanted to scream it out loud. But, she knew those closest to her were already questioning her sanity.

She started when she felt Anya's warm chubby hand on her arm.

"Mommy!"

"Good morning, baby girl!" Jaclyn picked her up and tucked her beneath her blanket. "Do you know how much I love you?"

"Yes. So much!" Anya held her arms so wide that she held her breath. "Miss. Meaghan says God loves us more than people do!"

All the girls had attended the preschool at the neighborhood church, only because it had been the cheapest option. Jaclyn felt a stab of guilt at the thought.

"Well, that must be a lot, because I love you more than my arms can stretch!" Jaclyn mimicked Anya's wingspan.

"Mommy! You're silly. God's arms can go all the way around the world!"

Jaclyn hugged Anya close trying with all her might to absorb a fraction of what Anya knew about being loved. If she were to die would her girls know that she loved them? She had never felt so inadequate. She offered a hesitant prayer that she would survive her encounter with Damien, so she would have more time to learn to love them better. Her prayer echoed in her mind. It felt empty, just like her longing.

Soon enough, all the girls were awake and routine kicked in. By eight-thirty, all the girls were at school and Jaclyn made a split second decision to stop at the grocery store before going home to pack for her meeting with Damien. She had had no problem navigating the route to the daycare and school because the main roads had been plowed and they had spread the salt and sand mixture near the intersections. But, her decision to take back roads to the grocery store proved to be a bad choice. Sometimes she regretted being overly confident of her Jeep's abilities. The snow was no problem, but the layer of ice beneath it from the day of freezing rain made her Jeep as useless as a rear-wheel drive sedan. She drifted into the curb twice, but there was no one in front of her to hit. She slowed down and drove much slower than her racing pulse, and eventually arrived at the store.

Once inside, she was drawn to pre-made dishes: mashed potatoes and cheese; green bean casserole; fresh rolls; cranberry stuffing; and roasted sweet potatoes with beets and parsnips. They were all wrapped with easy directions to heat and serve. Why did she feel so fatalistic? Surely she would spend this Thanksgiving with her family. But, her gut was telling her to make it easy enough for anyone to cook. She settled it in her mind that this way was best because of the stress she had been under during the last week. That made sense. She grabbed a couple of bottles of sparkling apple juice for the girls so they felt part of the toasts the adults would make with their wine. Toasts of thankfulness. This had been Grant's family tradition since he was a kid and she had always enjoyed the moments of reflecting on what was good in her life. What would her toast be tomorrow? Hopefully, it would be that she was alive. She navigated her cart to the baked goods looking for a couple of pies. They were definitely picked over. She had never seen such a crowd in the store before. At least she felt in good company. All procrastinators. Or, too busy to shop because of being pursued by a maniac. There was only one apple pie left, but before she could grab it, another lady put it in her cart. Tears overflowed the swollen rims of her eyes and she let them fall. She grabbed one of the last pumpkin pies and a pecan pie, which no one liked, but it would have to do. Apple pie had been her mother's favorite. They had made many of them together, both of them laughing as they had smudged each other's cheeks with flour. The line at the register was long enough that Jaclyn had time to compose herself before interacting with the cashier.

Finally, back home and groceries put away, she still had a couple of hours before she needed to leave for Spindrift. She sat on the floor of her office with her backpack opened in front of her. She unlocked the cabinet, lifted the gun out, checked that the magazine was in place, and the trigger guard was engaged. For several minutes she held the gun, feeling its weight and sensing its capacity for destruction. She stood up, locked the door, and walked back and forth across her office imagining potential scenarios that could take place in Spindrift. Twisting, she raised the gun with both hands and steadied herself, acting out being surprised by Damien behind her. After roleplaying for several minutes she lowered the gun and again checked the trigger guard. She wrapped it in the towel and lowered it into her backpack. Next, she made sure that her phone was fully charged hoping there would be enough service at Spindrift to call for help if needed. She threw the backpack on her back and headed downstairs.

Jaclyn put the backpack by the front door and sat by the fire. She still had a good hour before she needed to head out. From where she sat on the couch, she could see the snow falling heavy on the front yard. Gusts of wind were aggressively flipping and slamming the snow up into the sky and back down to the ground, only to lift again with the next gust. The beauty and the power of the wind mesmerized her. It couldn't be seen, but its effects were damaging. Just like her life. No one could see her hurt, but her emotions were constantly being slammed back and forth between her past and present, causing drifts of insecurities that were at times impossible to get past.

Jaclyn lifted her phone and called Grant. She wanted to make sure that he was in Pineridge, and not Spindrift. She needed to have this conversation with Damien alone. What would she say to him? She had role played the conversation in her head hundreds of times in the past few days, but she was no closer to what she would say.

"Hello?! Jack?!"

"Oh, hey, Grant."

"Did you call me? Or did I butt dial you? You didn't respond when it connected."

"Sorry. My mind is spinning. I have a busy day ahead of me. But, I wanted to say good morning and see what your day looks like."

"I am so swamped at the shop that I'm not going anywhere but my desk today. How about you?"

"I will be at the office, too."

"Drive no more than you have to, okay? The roads are getting worse by the hour."

"Yeah, I know. I will get kids and see you tonight."

"Love you, Jack."

"You, too." Jaclyn hung up and whispered, "But, you wouldn't love me if you really knew me." She allowed a few tears to breach her sleep-deprived eyelids, then slowly pulled herself together.

As it neared noon, her stomach burned with anxiety. She needed to gain control over her emotions or she wouldn't have any chance of taking the upper hand with Damien. But, the more she envisioned being near him, the more she believed he would crush her. Old buried fears and beliefs constricted her throat. Hot tears burned the backs of her eyes. The only way to protect her family would be by sacrificing herself. But, what would that look like? What did Damien want? Why couldn't he leave her family alone? She decided that she would need the gun out when they met. She needed that courage. She needed to send him a message stronger than her weak words and failing emotions. She took a moment to look at the girls' school pictures on the wall. She knew every cowlick of hair, dimple, and unique shape of their warm brown eyes. Her resolve grew as she drank in their smiles with her eyes and burned their faces into her memory. She would do it for them. She would conquer her fears or die doing so, but she would do everything she could to make sure that they would not lose their innocence as a child like she did.

Jaclyn put on her boots, coat, hat, and gloves then grabbed her backpack. She took a long look at herself in the mirror by the front door and said to her reflection, "Let's do this!" She started the Jeep and sat in the driveway while it warmed up. The wipers swept away most of the wet snow from the windshield, but a layer of ice lay beneath, obscuring her view. She stared straight ahead, their home looking like a Monet painting of swirling blue strokes. She could just get the ice scraper out, but she had the time and could let the defroster do the work. Damien didn't know she was even coming. Would all this terror end today? It had to. She couldn't go on. She felt sick. Lack of sleep and no appetite showed on her face. She felt old and looked tired.

Before she knew it, she had been sitting there for twenty minutes. The windows were mostly clear, so she entered the address into the dash screen, backed out of the driveway, and made her way to the highway leading south out of Cliff Creek. Spindrift was a good fifteen miles from their home and the weather was only getting worse. As she navigated the city streets, she decided that asking Angela to get the girls from school might be a good idea.

"Hello, friend! I thought maybe you had moved." Angela chuckled at her own teasing.

Jaclyn mustered up a laugh. "No, so sorry, still here. Listen, do you have any showings today?"

"Nope. I had one, but they canceled because of the weather. It is nasty out there. I'm not ready for winter."

"I know what you mean. Say, I have an interview this afternoon near Spindrift and I'm not really sure how long it will go. Would there be any way you'd be willing to pick up the girls and bring them to our house?"

"Jaclyn, you know I would do anything for those girls. Including driving in this mess. Don't worry, I will get them."

Jaclyn breathed a sigh of relief. "You are an angel, friend. Also, just in case I forget, I bought everything else for Thanksgiving dinner and it's all in the fridge. Everything is pre-made, just heat and serve. It will be an easy meal to make. Thank you for getting the kids! I will get home as soon as I can. Talk to you la…."

"Whoa, whoa, whoa. Don't hang up on me. I think you owe me an explanation for a few things."

"Angela, I wish I could talk, I really do, but I'm on the clock."

"Jaclyn, please, you can take a few minutes. What is up with you lately? You are avoiding me, that is very clear. And, why are you buying prepared dishes? We always have fun spending the day cooking together and drinking wine. Fess up, friend!"

"Please, this is no time to analyze my life, Angela. I need to go."

"You ignore most of my calls and texts, you forget our coffee dates, and you are just plain and simply acting strange."

"Sorry I don't meet your standards for a friend. I suck. End of story. Got to go."

"Stop it, Jaclyn! You are hiding something. What is it?"

Jaclyn gripped the steering wheel tightly and cringed. She took several deep breaths, struggling with not hanging up. She could tell Angela everything right now. She could ask her for help. What would Angela say? It appalled her that she had kept this secret for over twenty years. A secret that had taken its toll on her emotions, was killing her marriage a little more every day and proved to be detrimental when trying to parent and raise healthy kids. She was pathetic. But, she decided that coming clean now was not an option. She was in this alone.

"Jaclyn, are you there? Are you okay?"

Jaclyn failed to keep a deep sob from escaping into the mouthpiece.

Angela softened her approach. "Listen, let's talk, friend. There is nothing you could say that would change my love for you. You are a dear friend. You are family to me."

All she had to do was end the call. Why was she hanging on? But, she couldn't talk. She didn't even know what to say. Although drawn to Angela's invitation of acceptance, it repulsed her to need it.

"Jaclyn, you need help. Let Grant and I help you. We can find someone for you to talk to. You are not thinking right. And the fact that you bought pre-made food for Thanksgiving scares me to death. Where will you be tomorrow, Jaclyn? Because if you will be there, I know you would want to be cooking. Where are you right now? Let me come to you. We will go get the girls together."

Anger replaced Jaclyn's despair, but she still could not talk.

Angela listened to Jaclyn's heavy breathing and prayed for her. "I love you, friend. What's wrong? Tell me and I can help."

Jaclyn was nearing Spindrift and needed to get off the phone. "I need to go, Angela. Thanks for getting the girls."

"Jaclyn quit being stubborn!"

Jaclyn raised her voice. "No! I'm not being stubborn and I'm not crazy. I don't need your help. Go hang out with your boyfriend and mind your own business. Now, leave me alone!"

Before Angela could reply, Jaclyn hung up and threw her phone onto the passenger side floorboard, regret instantly hitting her hard. Surely Angela would still go get the girls. Wouldn't she? She would apologize to her later. Angela was right, she was a mess. But, not in the way she was assuming. Anyone with a maniac terrorizing them would act the same way. She wasn't crazy. She just wasn't.

Jaclyn slowed down as the visibility decreased. She knew she was almost to Spindrift, but couldn't see a thing. The ice had melted and a thick slush was building up everywhere the wipers couldn't reach. The turn onto the driveway was coming up. There was no one behind her that she could see so she inched forward looking at addresses on mailboxes. She finally saw 505 and turned onto the driveway. She remembered that when Grant was describing this new home to her, he had mentioned how long the driveway was. Nearly a quarter of a mile. As she turned up the slight incline, the tires seemed to get hung up on the deepening snow. She pressed harder on the accelerator to get some momentum and the engine cut out. She put on the brakes and tried again to get some traction. The Jeep still lacked power, but the tires took hold and she crawled up to the crest of the small hill. From there, the driveway sloped downward and disappeared into the blowing snow. The Jeep rolled forward until she pressed the accelerator again. This time, the engine jerked and then stalled. What was going on? She tried to turn the engine over, but all she heard was a cranking sound.

"Damn it!"

She was out of gas.

• CHAPTER 13 •

Jaclyn's anger swelled to her breaking point. She put the Jeep in park and repeatedly slammed her hand on the steering wheel, screaming a long litany of profanity. How could she have forgotten to fill the car with gas? Her yelling quickly turned to tears, and she sobbed uncontrollably. She allowed herself the release of emotion but quickly knew she had to get herself together. Wiping her tears, she took a few deep breaths and regained control over her emotions. She wasn't about to give up without a fight, and she needed to be present and thinking clearly to fight smart. Finally, gripping the steering wheel with every ounce of determination she could muster, she stopped reacting and began to form a new plan. This nightmare with Damien had to end. She just couldn't make it another day living the way she had been living for the last week. She couldn't even continue living the way she had been living for the past twenty-three years.

Jaclyn grabbed the backpack from the passenger seat and laid it across her lap. She took a deep breath riddled with tremors of profound despair and desperation. But, her next breath was stronger. She waited until she felt totally in control, then she unzipped the backpack, marking time as if these may be the final movements of her life. With great caution, she lifted the gun up and out into the cold gray light of day and tried it in her right hand; her palm sweaty with fear. Her wrist shook until she cupped her left hand under her right, curling her fingers lightly to steady herself with the strong grip. With outstretched arms she raised the gun to eye level, imagining Damien within its sight. She stopped breathing. The thought of her being in control of him fueled her mission. She could do this. She had to do this. Then, making sure that she didn't touch the trigger, she laid the gun on the dash and put on her gloves and hat.

Since leaving home, the temperature had dropped at least five to ten degrees. The snow was coming down heavier every hour, and the wind seemed bent on setting a record. She stepped out of the vehicle into the deepening snow, shut the Jeep door, and scanned the landscape. Nothing, but white. She tried a few steps. Her feet sunk in the snow several inches. The crunch of her boots echoed across the land then faded into nothingness. She looked up and scanned the surrounding area. The driveway was difficult to see, the surrounding land covered by the new blanket of snow. Finally, with a deep breath, Jaclyn grabbed the gun off the dash, shut the door, and set off in what she believed was the direction of the house.

The gun swung in rhythm with Jaclyn's cadence as she labored up the slight incline. Her thighs and calves burned as she pushed hard against the slope and cold. As she focused on forcing one foot in front of the other, she was reminded of a similar ache she had felt as she walked from the family car to the cold hole in the ground. A half circle of people had gathered to grieve and to encourage. Her father and brother, steeped in their own pain, stood beside her. The three of them standing without touching, three pillars of shock and disbelief. As Jaclyn continued the slow walk up the snowy driveway, she could feel the same sharp piercing of her heart she had felt when her mother's cold body, entombed in the heavy wooden box, was lowered deep into the ground. That day, her feet had felt heavy, almost impossible to lift, as she walked where she did not want to go. Her mind had been numb to any emotion, and she shed no tears. She seemed to watch herself from a distance, an innocent bystander to a great tragedy.

Today felt the same. But, today it was her that was the walking dead. She felt nothing now as she trudged up the long driveway. The cold seemed to be coming from within. This shouldn't be happening. Her mother shouldn't have died. Damien shouldn't have stolen her innocence. And she shouldn't, as a wife and mother, be facing her own mortality with a gun in hand and unbridled anger fueling her steps. She had grown older, gained more responsibility, and built a life of her own, but her ten-year-old self remained stunted, needy, scared. Even after Damien presumably died, she suffered. Like the woman in the Bible who looked back at the destruction of Sodom and turned into a pillar of salt, she couldn't stop looking back at the horror Damien had inflicted upon her life. She, too, was frozen in time. She continued to go through the motions she had learned were normal by watching others around her, but her heart was imprisoned and her spirit smothered.

Eventually, she rounded a corner of the driveway, hoping to see the home, but it was a total whiteout. Nothing, but swirling flakes and the illusion of flat terrain. More than once she had stepped on a rock beneath the snow and had fallen. Each time she slipped she held the gun high, taking the brunt of the fall with her hips, knees, and back. She breathed heavily and her head throbbed. Sleep had evaded her for days now, her only times of rest invaded by nightmares. And now, although she was awake, the nightmare was gaining ground in her conscious state.

Finally, a faint outline of the house could be seen through the blanket of low clouds. And, with each step, its unique architecture came more into focus. There appeared to be no vehicles in the driveway. Maybe Damien had gone to get lunch. Although she could now see the house, it was nearly one-thirty by the time she reached the front porch. The crunch of her boots on the stairs split the sinister silence. Once on the porch, she gathered herself together, pulling her resolve back from the depths of any lingering fear. She took several deep breaths and listened for sounds of a truck on the driveway. It was quiet, except for the gusts of wind in the nearby trees. Convinced she was alone, she turned to face the house. Her eyes took in the home's breadth. It was huge. She reached out with her left hand, held her breath, and tried the front door. It was unlocked. Grant would not be happy with Damien for leaving it that way, but she was thankful. She opened and shut the door. Then, standing still in the majestic entryway, she listened. The house gave away no sounds of life; her breathing all she could hear. She stood for several minutes taking in every corner of the spacious layout. The entry, living room, kitchen, and dining room were all one, covered by a cathedral ceiling and encircled by mostly glass. All beauty lost on the evil at hand.

Jaclyn set her backpack by the front door and took off her coat, hat, and gloves. She wanted nothing to hinder her when she encountered Damien. She locked the door to avoid any surprises. She wanted to know when Damien arrived. Before heading to the basement, she searched all the rooms on the main level, her attention aimed mostly at listening for the attempted turn of the locked front door handle. Each room stood empty, a promise of a future life, but now only an empty womb. She, too, felt hollow, empty of life, just a shell holding out for the fulfillment of a promise and desolate hope.

Slowly, one step at a time, she descended the stairs into the basement. Gray light flooded the large great room at the bottom of the stairs. A fireplace graced one long wall and large windows spanned the opposite. An alcove housed a hot tub sitting on a newly tiled floor, but not yet enclosed with sheetrock. She stood on the cold cement with the gun raised with both hands as she scanned every inch of the roomy space. Stacks of supplies littered the room and her eyes crawled over every object. The house was cold. The basement was even colder.

Off to her left, she noticed double doors. She pushed open the left door and searched for the light switch with her left hand. The room was dark, the only light coming from the dense daylight behind her. Her right hand held the gun out in front of her. She heard a noise in the dark. Her heart spiked with adrenalin and she stood completely still. After a few moments of silence, she again searched for the light switch. The arm holding up the gun began to ache. Finally, her fingers hit the switches. She flipped them all on. Nothing.

Her heart beat faster. She felt nauseous. She reached for her phone for its light. But, it wasn't on her. Damn! She had left it in the car. Thrown it on the floorboard in anger. How could she be so stupid? Following the wall with her left arm outstretched and her back against it, she ambled around the perimeter of the large room. Within only a few feet, her foot hit a metal stand. A work light. She felt her way up the stand to the light and felt for the switch. Another sound made her freeze. She willed herself to breathe shallow, to not make a sound. For several minutes she listened. Nothing. It could be the house creaking from the wind and cold. It could be mice. She steadied herself and, finally, with the gun still outstretched in front of her, she depressed the switch. Bright light flooded the substantial in-home theater.

Jaclyn cupped her left hand under her right, finding some much-needed relief for her right arm. She stood still and scanned the room. The floor was terraced concrete, several large bolts protruding out of each level for rows of chairs that would grace that space soon. The elevated wide wall in front was marked up with chalked reminders to the crew. Wiring hung from the ceiling where can lights would be installed. Off to the right, an expansive wet bar filled in the back of the theater. Slowly she moved towards the bar to check behind it. Nothing. Only a half door opening without the door. She leaned on the counter wondering if Damien was going to stand her up again. It was nearing two o'clock. Where was he?

Jaclyn set the gun on the bar and rubbed her hands together. The revolver was heavier than it looked. Her right hand spasmed until she kneaded the knots a bit. On a whim, she turned and bent down near the half door and peeked in. The shaft of light coming from the work light cast a long beam into the dark alcove. She scanned the storage space and turned to stand up. Before she got to her feet a hot white light coursed through her brain and she fell.

Moments later she came to with no recollection of what had happened. She tried to take a breath, but something covered her mouth. Opening her eyes the light from the small door reflected in Damien's eyes as he looked into hers. His mouth turned up in a slight smirk of victory. As far as she could tell, they were both in the crawl space on the cement floor. She tried to say something, but Damien pushed harder against her mouth, pressing the back of her head against the cold cement.

"Thank you for stopping by," Damien spoke with a raspy low voice close to Jaclyn's ear. "And, thank you for the gun. What a nice surprise."

Jaclyn began to writhe against his strength, guttural noises coming from deep within her. Damien pulled himself to a kneeling position and slapped Jaclyn's face hard with his free hand. Tears stung her eyes, and she laid still. Their eyes met and Jaclyn shivered. His look was the look of the devil himself. She quickly closed her eyes and prayed for mercy. Consumed by fear, and light-headed from breathing shallow and fast, she took several deep breaths. When she opened her eyes, Damien was looking straight at her. She again saw pure evil and felt intense hopelessness. She was all alone. She had set herself up for destruction her whole adult life by not letting anyone in. Damien was the embodiment of her fear, but the silence was the murderer of her life. Silence had killed her joy and hope as a young girl, and she had walked like a zombie into her adult life. Damien should have been thrown in jail decades ago. But, she had let silence take over in her life. He had gone free, but she started to die. The silence had grown and controlled her more and more every year. It killed a little more of her every day. As she lay on the cold cement breathing hard against Damien's hand, she searched for any life within herself. And deep in her heart, she felt it. She squeezed her eyes closed, blocking out the evil and she pictured her family. She saw her girls and Grant. She pictured Angela and her sharing coffee. She needed all of them. And she needed them to know everything about her. It was a risk she should have taken before she ended up in this predicament. Now, she may never see them again. But, that can't happen. She had to get herself out of this and live. It was time. She needed to break the silence.

Her breathing slowed down with her new resolve. And when Damien sensed her relaxing, he grabbed the roll of duct tape next to him and placed a gag in her mouth and taped over it. Then, rolling her over, he taped her wrists together, circling the duct tape several times more than necessary. Next, he taped her feet together, then sat looking at her. He let out a laugh filled with contempt.

"Well, Jaclyn, it's been a long time. How have you been?"

She glared at him, desperately holding on to the hope she had felt moments before.

"Don't want to talk, huh? That's okay. I've got a lot to say. First, let's clear the air. I'm sorry I made you believe I was dead. It was wrong of me to not punish you immediately for making your dad worried about our relationship. I tried to warn you nicely. Do you remember, pretty lady? It would have been so easy to kill your dad. He was never very strong. And your brother? What a joke. I can't believe I worked for them as long as I did."

Damien sat back against the wall and chuckled at the memories. He took in the sight of Jaclyn, looking at her from head to toe. "You are a beautiful woman, Jaclyn. I knew you had potential when you were a child. You were such putty in my hands back then. Too bad we didn't get more of your formative years together. I could have helped you learn to conquer every man you came in contact with. And we could have made good money at it. We could have been a good team, but you blew it."

Suddenly, Damien's demeanor changed from reminiscent to angry. "So, you are the reason we sit under this house today in this God forsaken land. Don't even think of blaming me for your stupidity. But, it's okay. I'm patient, and actually, I like it better this way. Your husband has a thriving business and you can get me some of his money to pay your debt for screwing up my life."

Adrenalin pulsed in Jaclyn's heart as Damien spewed his hatred all over her. She wanted to kill him. She wanted silence to smother him as` it had done to her. She searched for a way out of her restraints, but the duct tape was thick and strong around her wrists and ankles. Damien made a move towards her and she rolled onto her back and began to kick in his direction. Before he could grab her, she kicked his face hard and blood began to flow from his bottom lip.

Damien lunged his whole body towards Jaclyn forcing her legs down with his weight. Her head hit the cement and she let out a muffled wail. Once she stopped resisting, Damien breathed heavily on her face, his hot, acrid breath causing bile to rise in Jaclyn's throat.

"Kind of like old times, huh, pretty lady?" Damien stroked her hair away from her face. "But, you are definitely not as compliant as you were when you were young. It's a shame, really. I feel bad that you came here believing that you had a chance at resisting me. I thought I had taught you better. I really hate that our time together had ended so abruptly. You could have learned more, like the others."

Jaclyn's eyes grew wide. Others?

Damien laughed as he saw her surprise in the dim light from the door. "Surprised? Pretty arrogant to think you were the only one. You're not that special, Jaclyn." He continued to laugh, spit hitting her face.

Jaclyn grimaced as his weight pushed her body into the cement. And she willed herself to not think of his foul breath and spit on her face. If she vomited now, with the gag in her mouth, she would surely die.

"You like this, huh?" He moved his body on top of hers, mocking her predicament. "Just lay back and enjoy."

With every ounce of energy she had, she raised both legs up hard, forcing his legs apart.

Damien spewed a string of profanity and rolled off of her, half moaning and half laughing as he waited for the pain to subside. "So, that's how you want this to go, huh?"

Once he was able to get to his knees, he grabbed Jaclyn by her feet and pulled her into the farthest corner, a good six feet from the door. She didn't fight, for it was painful enough to be scraped over the rough concrete. Her back was rubbed raw, but she held her head up to keep it from bouncing across the floor. Once she was where he wanted her, Damien sat back and kicked her onto her stomach. She laid her right cheek on the cold concrete slab and winced in pain.

Damien enjoyed her discomfort. This time he laid next to her, avoiding her legs, and again pushed her hair out of her eyes. "What do you want to say to me, Jaclyn? You are not enjoying this? Too bad. You are the one who decided this is what needed to happen. Women always have to do things the hard way." He rolled onto his back next to her and smiled. "Oh, Jaclyn, you have always made my life interesting."

Jaclyn turned her head to keep him in her sights.

"I have loved following you all these years. You entertained me even from afar. It's so nice that you have always had such a public trail of accomplishments with your writing. And, I have thoroughly enjoyed watching your family grow. Thanks for all the nice photos you put on Facebook. That Mandy looks just like you when you were her age. I can't wait to really get to know her if you know what I mean." Again, he couldn't hold back his demented joy at the thought.

Jaclyn began to cry, tears rolling down her face onto the cement.

Damien rolled back to face her. "Oh, so sorry. Did I say something wrong? I seem to keep doing that. Well, don't worry, sweetheart. I need you alive. At least for now." And with that, he crawled to the opening and stood up behind the bar.

Jaclyn could only see the lower part of his legs, so she couldn't tell what he was doing. But, it sounded like he was fidgeting with something at the bar. Then she heard him release the magazine clip on the gun. She had been so stupid to set the gun down.

"Nice gun, Jaclyn. This yours or the hubby's?" Damien pulled the slide back and reinserted the magazine. Then he bent down and looked at Jaclyn through the small opening.

Jaclyn could only see his silhouette.

"Fifteen rounds should be enough for me to get my way today." He fired the gun into the corner of the crawl space.

Jaclyn curled up in the fetal position at the deafening sound, her heart pounding against her rib cage. She mentally checked her body for injuries. When the ringing in her ears stopped Damien's laughter replaced it.

"Well, now I only have fourteen left. But, that should still be enough."

Jaclyn started shivering. If she died today, would her kids be okay? Would Damien stop after killing her? Even if he got the money he was asking for, she knew deep down in her gut, he wouldn't be satisfied. He would continue abusing her and her girls. The only way out of this would be for Damien to die or have the police lock him up forever. But, she lost her edge on him. She had been so stupid. She needed a miracle. Closing her eyes, she willed herself to ignore her surroundings long enough to plead with God for mercy. She begged for a miracle, protection, and victory. Left to herself, she was a goner. She needed supernatural help. Opening her eyes, she focused on Damien's movements in the adjoining room, but her mind searched her memory for things her mom had taught her about God.

Just then, Damien's phone rang.

"Hello, Evin Wolfe with All's Quiet."

Jaclyn strained to hear who was on the other line.

"Oh, hey Grant, how's it going?" Damien bent down to look at Jaclyn.

She tried to scream, but she could project only a low muffled moan past the gag and the duct tape. She laid her head on the cold cement floor and tried to think of a plan, but all she could focus on was that she would not make it out of this alive.

• CHAPTER 14 •

Grant laid on his side looking at Jaclyn. He propped his head up with his hand, his elbow digging into the down pillow, so he could get a better look at her. She had tossed and turned all night, but for at least this moment she was calm. She was beautiful. He studied her face for several minutes. He knew the curve of her lips and the angle of her jaw. He longed to kiss her, but he didn't dare interrupt her peaceful sleep. She was such a mystery to him. Even after all these years. He longed to know everything about her, but she kept so much of herself hidden. No matter how hard he tried to draw her out, she resisted. But, he knew he loved her. He would die for her. There was no question in his mind about it, he had to keep fighting to get to know her. He rolled onto his back and stretched. One more day, then he could take a break over Thanksgiving.

As a young boy, Thanksgiving had been one of his favorite holidays because his mom had always hosted both sides of the family. Both sets of grandparents would come and all his aunts and uncles, which meant a boatload of cousins. And enough food to feed a boat loaded with people, everyone bringing their favorite dish. But, early in his senior year of high school, his dad had an affair, and that Thanksgiving ended up being awful. His parents had separated. And from the day his dad left the house, his mom tried to make everything seem the same. He hated her for it. He acted out and shook his head at her whenever she tried to make light of the situation. When Thanksgiving rolled around, she made the same dishes and she worked really hard to pretend she was happy and thankful, but there was a foreboding feeling of death. No one was actually dead, but there were so many people missing Grant felt like a fool pretending that everything was normal. All the cousins his age had been on his dad's side. He tried to play with his younger cousins, but quickly resented being deemed the babysitter. When it was time to go around the table and share something they were each thankful for, Grant had exploded on his mom. He started crying and yelling at his mom for pretending. He pounded his fist on the table, spilled his drink, then ran out of the house. He refused to talk to his mom for the next week.

He made an inner vow that day that, when he had a family, things would be different. His family wasn't going to ever pretend. They would talk about everything and love each other fully. There would be no secrets. But, here he was, lying next to a woman with whom he shared a home and four children, but he didn't really know her. Every day they were pretending to be something they were not. For the first time in his life, he felt compassion for his mom. Had his mom known anything about the secrets his father kept from the whole family? Did she lay in bed at night and wonder whom she had married? Tears began to run down the sides of his face. He needed to apologize to his mom. Tomorrow he would call her. She had never stopped loving him and supporting him, even though that day stood between them like a brick wall. It needed to come down. He would make sure of it. Now, if he could figure out how to tear down the wall between himself and Jaclyn. And, when it came to that, he was at a loss.

Grant slid out from beneath the covers without disturbing Jaclyn and hopped in the shower. He let the hot water calm his nerves, but he couldn't stay there for long. He needed to leave the house by six-thirty so he could meet with some potential homebuilders before they had to be at work. At least they were meeting at a restaurant so he could grab breakfast and coffee there. He turned off the shower, toweled dry, then dressed quietly and headed downstairs. At this time of day, their home was quiet. And he enjoyed it. He stood at the front door for a long minute and took several deep breaths. He could do this. He could do today. That's all he needed to focus on for now. He had always pulled himself together and pushed forward toward success. He had never been one to give up without a fight. But, his marriage was proving to be the most difficult challenge he had ever come up against. He closed his eyes and saw her sleeping face again. He was in love with her. He would fight, no matter what. Just one day at a time. With that thought lingering, he stepped out into the wind and snow and managed his way to his truck.

Traffic was light all the way to the restaurant. Thankfully, the couple had braved the weather and showed up. He needed the work. After he had picked up the bill for all of them, and said goodbye to his future customers, he drove toward Pine Ridge. During the drive and his walk across the parking lot, he tried to focus on taking deep breaths. He had a full day ahead of him, starting with putting out some job site fires. The project managers better be waiting for him right now. Sure enough, they were seated in his office waiting. He needed to tuck his personal life away for a few hours so he could focus. Grant sat down at his desk without saying a word then combed his fingers through his hair in frustration. The two red-faced project managers stood and faced him as he sat at his desk, his heart pounding aggressively against his rib cage. His early morning meeting with the potential home builders had gone well. They were trusting him to build the home of their dreams. But, how would he ever meet their expectations if his PMs couldn't get their act together? To Grant, the solutions to the problems the PMs faced were clear, but he had to get elementary in his explanations in order for them to understand. He felt his blood pressure rise, and a headache began to form behind his eyes. He willed himself to measure his words before saying them. He was clearly agitated but remained respectful in his troubleshooting. After a good forty-five minutes, they were all satisfied, and the PMs left to do the work. But, as soon as they left his office, another problem walked through his door.

Before tackling the next crisis, Grant leaned back in his chair and covered his eyes with his crossed arms. For a moment, he needed to remind himself of the reason he loved his work. He mentally reached for the positive energy he felt when training his PMs to excel at what they do. Normally, a day of troubleshooting fueled his passion, energized him because he was improving the business. But, today he couldn't restrain his emotions, blasting his PMs with a raised voice and negative tone. He hated himself for it. He couldn't imagine what his PMs were thinking. He didn't blame them for whatever they thought. Finally, he invited those who stood in his doorway to come to take a seat.

His phone vibrated and Grant silenced it without looking. Over the next ten minutes, it vibrated several more times. The next time it vibrated, he sat forward and glanced at it. It was from Davis. He let it go to voicemail. Now definitely wasn't a good time to talk. With a shred of renewed ambition, he stood and went to the whiteboard in his office where he aggressively began to sketch out what he had been explaining for the past half an hour. The PMs moved with him to the other side of his office and stood silent, not used to this behavior from Grant. Most days, he took everything in stride, firm, but kind. There never seemed to be a problem he couldn't address and steer them in the right direction. But, now, this minute, he looked like he may have a stroke. When Grant turned to see if the PMs were getting what he was saying, he caught a couple of them whispering to each other. Grant threw the whiteboard marker across the office. "Obviously, you've got this. Leave! And don't let me hear about this problem again. Fix it!"

His office cleared and Grant slammed his door and made his way back to his desk. He sat in his chair and laid his head in his shaking hands. His phone buzzed. It was Davis again. And again he let it go to voicemail. He couldn't talk to Davis right now. He was too upset. But, after a few minutes, he remembered his inquiry about Evin Wolfe and how Davis was going to see if he could find any dirt on the guy. He reached for his phone and saw that he had missed a lot more than just two calls from Davis. He had called six times. And left a text: Call me ASAP!

Grant felt a jolt of adrenaline shooting through his body as he hit Davis' number and stood to wait for him to answer.

Davis answered after only one ring. "Grant! I've dug up some information on this guy, Evin Wolfe, that will be difficult to hear."

Grant started pacing the length of his office. "Shit. I knew it. Let me have it."

Davis cleared his throat. "Well, it took a while, but it appears this guy you are dealing with ghosted a man in Winnipeg, Manitoba, over twenty years ago."

"What? I don't get it. What is ghosted?" Grant took a seat at his desk.

"It is an identity theft where someone takes on the identity of a recluse person after they die. Unfortunately, it is actually easier to do than you may think."

Grant didn't need this news on top of everything else he was dealing with this morning. "What?! So Evin Wolfe is dead? Then who is this guy who has been creeping me out?"

"Well, everything he has been doing with his business is legit, as Evin Wolfe, of course. This dead man had a clean record until his death at thirty-five, and this name-snatcher has kept that record pretty clear. After the real Evin's death, it shows that the imposter married twice in Calgary. His first marriage lasted a year, the second for only eight months."

Grant leaned back and ran his hand through his hair. "Maybe that's why he seemed so interested in Jaclyn. Sick bastard."

Davis cut to the chase. "Grant, call Jaclyn and warn her about this guy. He's done enough by just stealing this man's identity that I wouldn't trust him anywhere near your family."

"Good idea, Davis. Jaclyn is already paranoid because of a story she's working on for the paper. She had me install a security system in the house and she's really cautious about where the girls may go." Grant had paced the length of his office without realizing it.

"Good for her. That's what I would have suggested."

Grant could tell Davis was holding back more details. "Davis, what else do you know?"

Davis let there be a long silence before offering Grant any more details. "I have put in a request for investigating who stole Evin Wolfe's identity. But, that will take months, maybe years. If he's gotten away with this for as long as he has, his secret is buried deep."

Grant wasn't satisfied. "What do I do right now about the work he's doing on my job site?" He sat back down and leaned his elbows on his desk.

Davis continued. "Well, his business is legit. It's up to you. Not so sure you want to piss him off by firing him from the job he's doing. You just may not want to work with his company again. It really sucks that he's chosen your community to live in. But, in my business, it is difficult to find any community that isn't filled with all sorts of underground corruption and hidden identities."

"Thanks for the encouragement, Davis." Grant forced a laugh to lighten the mood.

Davis nervously laughed, then became serious again. "Well, he could also be an innocent guy who had a bad string of luck and needed a fresh start. But, from what you've told me about his behavior, I'm guessing this guy has a lot he's hiding."

Grant stood and let out a big sigh. "Yeah, I don't think this guy is innocent. He's definitely up to something. I just don't know what."

"Grant, first and foremost, keep your family safe. I'm here for you if you need anything. I just wish it wasn't going to take so long to get you more answers."

"Me, too, friend. Me, too. But, thanks, man. I will let you know how the rest of his time on the job goes. Say hi to Amy."

"Will do. Give Jaclyn a hug from us. And, bro, hang in there. Don't forget that your marriage is worth the pain and the work. Protect Jaclyn and the girls, they are the most important part of your life."

"Yeah, and often the biggest headache." Grant sighed again. "But, I hear what you're saying. You're right. Thanks. Love you, bro."

"You, too. Talk soon."

Grant sat quietly for a few minutes letting Davis' news sink in. With everything he already had going on, why did he also have to be dealing with a criminal at work? He needed a break. But, first, he needed to warn Jaclyn about Evin. But, how? She was so worked up about this story she was covering for the paper that he didn't want to add fuel to her anxiety. But, he also didn't want to have something happen that could have been prevented by warning her. He reached for his phone again and called her. After several rings, it went to voicemail. He waited for several minutes and tried again. Nothing.

Thinking maybe Angela knew where Jaclyn was he tried her number.

"Hello, this is Angela with Hometown Realty, how can I help you with your home today?"

"Angela, this is Grant. Do you know where Jaclyn is?"

Angela bristled. "Well, I'm doing well, thanks for asking, Grant."

"Sorry, Angela. I've just had a rough day today. How are you doing?"

"Sorry to hear that. Sounds like you and Jaclyn are both doing a nosedive in life right now."

"Why? Did you talk to her today?" Grant asked impatiently.

Angela hesitated for a few seconds.

"Well? Did you?" Grant punched his fist in the air while trying to keep his voice even.

Angela's voice was just above a whisper. "Yeah, but I wouldn't call it talking." She paused again.

Grant squeezed his eyes shut against Angela's silence.

"She called me and attacked me for caring about her."

Grant ran his free hand through his hair. Why did women have to draw the story out? He just needed the facts. "Why did she call? Just to let you have it?" He knew his voice had an edge to it, but he couldn't hold back anymore.

Angela took a deep breath and continued. "No, at first she was nice. She called to see if I could pick up the girls from school because she had an interview in Spindrift and didn't know if she would be back in time. In fact, I need to leave here pretty soon to go get them. It's getting close to three."

Grant looked at his watch. Where did the day go? Had he really been in his office this long? And, Spindrift? It had to just be a coincidence that Evin Wolfe was in Spindrift today, too. But, his stomach started to hurt, anyway. He needed to get a hold of Jaclyn as soon as possible. He tried to regain his composure so he could be patient with Angela. "Why would she get so upset if she were the one asking for the favor? I don't get it."

"Well, after asking me if I would get the girls, she told me that she went shopping this morning for Thanksgiving dinner tomorrow."

Grant interrupted. "That really doesn't concern me, Angela. I need to go. Th...."

Angela cut in and raised her voice. "Her shopping wasn't a big deal. But, she said that everything she bought was pre-made and pre-cooked so it would be easy to make. She was talking like she wasn't going to be there tomorrow, Grant. It freaked me out, and I called her on it. She got furious."

Grant froze. "Wait! She never buys pre-made food. I constantly try to talk her into it to save herself some time, but she says it's unhealthy."

Angela let out a frustrated sigh. "Oh, I know, Grant. I know. But, that's not all. She's been acting really strange all week. She's missed our coffee date and avoided most of my calls and texts. It just isn't like her. What is going on, Grant?"

"Angela, I need to go. Thanks!"

"Grant! What is going...."

Grant hung up.

He scrolled through his recent calls until he found Evin's number and tapped it hard. He had to at least know where Evin was.

Damien smiled when he saw that it was Grant. "Hello, Evin Wolfe with All's Quiet."

Grant's heart began to race. "Evin, Grant. Are you at the house in Spindrift?"

"Oh, hey Grant, how's it going?" Damien bent down on one knee and peered through the door. The shaft of light caught the moisture in Jaclyn's eyes and he met them with his own. "Yeah, yeah, I'm at the Spindrift house. Everything is going as planned."

Jaclyn tried to scream around the gag, but it left her feeling lightheaded. She noticed she had been holding her breath. Somehow, she had to let Grant know she was here. But, how?

"I will have some supplies left over. I can take that off your bill." Damien held in a laugh as he watched Jaclyn struggle. It thrilled him the gag was working so well. Then he stood up and leaned on the bar, his back to Jaclyn. "Yep, the job should be done today. I'll make sure of it."

A small chunk of concrete dug into Jaclyn's cheek as she laid face down in the dark corner. Without taking her eyes off Damien, she began to rub the edges of the duct tape against it hoping to rip the tape from her mouth.

"No, you don't need to stop by today. I can handle the rest of this alone. I prefer it that way. But, I can meet with you Friday if you're available, and we can settle up."

Damien covered the mouthpiece, turned, bent down, and whispered to Jaclyn across the dark cement cave, "Settle up with a hundred thousand dollars that is."

Goosebumps spread from Jaclyn's legs to her head. He was a psychopath. And she was bound, gagged, and trapped in this basement dungeon with him. She started hyperventilating.

Damien chuckled then returned to his call with Grant. "No, I would rather not email the bill. I like to work with hard copies only. It must be a Canadian thing. Everyone here wants an electronic copy, but I like to just keep it simple."

Jaclyn willed herself to calm down before she passed out. She could feel a warm trickle of blood as it dripped from her chin. But, unfortunately, the tape held. She stopped working at the tape and laid still, her forehead against the concrete. She focused on her breathing again. She couldn't just give up. The faces of her girls brightened in her mind's eye. And, for a moment, she again stood in her living room scanning their images on the wall. She smiled, the duct tape resisting her joy. Her girls needed her. And she needed them. She had to keep fighting.

"Happy Thanksgiving. See you on Friday."

Grant ended the call and spun around in his chair to face the weather out his window. The snow was relentless, and the wind was molding the flaky moisture into tall cliffs and deep canyons. He knew he should keep putting out fires and appeasing customers tired of delays, but his mind was reeling with the news about Evin Wolfe and Jaclyn's recent weird behavior. His coffee had been sitting for over an hour untouched, but he grabbed the mug anyway and threw back a healthy swig. It was cold. Disgusted by the coffee, he banged the mug on his desk and tried calling Jaclyn again. Nothing. Where was she? He angered at the thought that she may be ignoring him. He just needed to know she was safe. Tomorrow. Tomorrow he would give her an ultimatum. He slammed his fist on the desk and stood up. People who love each other don't give each other ultimatums. Do they? He closed his eyes and shook his head as he held it in his hands. He didn't know. He didn't seem to know anything. Except that he loved her. He tried calling her again. No answer. Where was she? And was she safe?

Then he remembered that he could see her location as long as her phone was powered on. He opened her last text to him and tapped information, then waited. While the electronic ellipses flashed on and off, searching for Jaclyn, Grant stared at her photo on his screen. The photo was one of his favorites. It was candid, and she was laughing. He loved her and was determined to keep her safe. And, once this home in Spindrift met his specs, he would finally be valued in the construction world and his income would reflect it. He knew their financial situation upset Jaclyn, and he had to keep working towards easing that stress. Finally, her location popped up on the map. She was on the driveway leading to the Spindrift house.

"Shit!" Grant jumped up from his desk, grabbed his keys and ran out the door.

• CHAPTER 15 •

Damien again bent down in the crawl space doorway and just stared at Jaclyn. His smile was more of a sneer. Jaclyn knew he was messing with her mind. He wanted her to become so afraid that she would do anything he asked her to do. Just like when she was ten years old. And he didn't have to mess with her very much. The fear was definitely still there. It had never gone away. After they had told her that Damien was dead, she had relegated the fear to a back chamber of her mind, her subconscious its gatekeeper. She believed that she wasn't afraid anymore. But, her subconscious often paralyzed her thinking and emotions for no apparent reason, except it felt like someone, other than herself, was calling the shots. It didn't even have to be anything major when she felt like this. For example, if Grant attempted to decide for both of them, even what type of pizza they were ordering, she would instantly get defensive. It offended her that there was no discussion about it. But, she had no problem making decisions that affected the whole family and fought back if Grant tried to discuss it. She didn't know why she did what she did. All she knew was that she needed to stay in control. Of everything. Any other alternative was unacceptable to her. Releasing control could be deadly. At least that's how she felt.

She felt like she was constantly battling her fight-or-flight part of her brain. She felt bad, but couldn't bring herself to stop.

The cold, dank basement cement seemed to be seeping into Jaclyn's bones. She felt sluggish like someone had drugged her. She felt out of control, her greatest fear, but her mind was still her own. He couldn't restrain her thoughts. Or her eyes, the windows to her soul. If she had any chance of overcoming this beast, she needed to not let him drain her feeble soul from her beaten flesh. Jaclyn kept her eyes downcast, only being able to see Damien in her peripheral vision. He tried to get her to look up, but she refused. Her heart beat so hard that her body moved up and down against the cement. Finally, frustrated, he crawled over next to her and laid down, his body touching hers. Against her will, tears stung her eyes and her nose began to run. Every muscle in her body was taut. Then he began to whisper in her ear.

"Did you miss me all these years?" His hot, acrid breath landed on her cold cheek and turned to moisture.

Jaclyn took quiet, shallow breaths with no movement that resembled an answer. Unable to escape his wicked breath, she felt nausea roll up the back of her throat, but she willed herself to keep it at bay.

Damien licked his cracked lips and cleared his throat. Then he let out a short laugh. "Don't be mad at me, little girl. You are the one who crossed the line and seduced me. I just wanted to mentor you and help you figure out life. Your dad was so busy. You should thank me right now." He raised his rough hand to her wet face and brushed her cheek with no compassion.

Finally, a sob betrayed Jaclyn's resolve and involuntarily came out with a shudder that shook her whole body. She contracted all her muscles trying to pull herself away from his touch.

Damien rolled onto his back and spread his arms wide, exaggerating his shock at her moving away from him. "Whoa, girl! You know that you owe me my life back, don't you?" He smirked as he enjoyed watching her squint her eyes against him. "Maybe we could even be friends. Your husband and I work pretty well together. But, first I need some of his hard earned money. And you will get it for me." He rolled onto his back and laughed even harder. "Finally, my time has come. It's been a rough twenty-some years trying to rebuild my life, but your gift to me will make it all worth it."

Jaclyn kept her eyes squeezed shut and worked hard to picture her girls again, but nothing came. Only darkness. She felt like she was falling, unable to control her body or her mind. All she could think of was giving in to Damien. If she gave him what he wanted, he would leave her family alone. Would he? But, where would she get the money? She would need to do it without Grant knowing. That just wasn't possible. Tears stung her eyes and her stomach reeled. She felt faint but willed herself to stay conscious. She couldn't give in. She just couldn't. She needed to keep fighting. In her mind's eye, she pictured her girls again. Focus on them, she chanted over and over in her mind. Focus on the girls. She needed to live to raise them in a world where they believed they didn't have to live in fear.

She realized that Damien had been talking to her, but he was in his own little world as he explained his plan of retrieving what he said she owed him. He didn't even look like he cared if she was listening or not. She tried, but couldn't concentrate on anything that he was saying. Not a word. Her heart pounded in her ears and her breathing stung her lungs. Suddenly, with no warning, Damien slapped the back of her head hard. The hit jammed her cheekbone into the cement and a sharp pain throbbed behind her eyes. She laid still. Looking down, she could see out of the corner of her eye that he had sat up and was leaning on one arm. She had been wrong. He had been watching her every movement.

Damien's eyes looked like they were on fire. "I would think twice about ignoring me, young lady." His voice was eerily demonic.

Just then, Damien's phone rang. He looked at who it was and smiled, took a deep breath, and answered. "Well, hello pretty lady! What a wonderful surprise."

Jaclyn cringed at the thought of another woman being subjected to his narcissistic abuse. If there were only a way that she could get some noise past this gag so whoever it was could hear her. She used her tongue, trying to push the gag against the tape, but the gag was too big.

Damien raised his voice and emphasized his next words for Jaclyn's sake. "Of course, Angela. No problem. I totally understand."

Jaclyn laid still and looked directly at Damien. Angela? It couldn't be, but at the mention of Angela's name, Jaclyn's mind surged with regret. She had been a terrible friend. Their last conversation had been awful, and it was all her fault. She should have been honest with Angela. She was a woman. Surely she would understand and help her tell Grant about her past. She felt like a fool. She thought she could handle all of this herself, but look at her now. Pathetic. And, now, would Angela even help her after how she had treated her on the phone? She succumbed to the cold concrete with deep regret, listening to Damien's call.

"Sounds good. Is there anything I could do to help your friend Jaclyn?" Damien raised his voice slightly when he said Jaclyn's name.

Jaclyn snapped her head in his direction and she could tell instantly that he got what he wanted. The horrified look in Jaclyn's eyes made his eyes widen with delight. For more emphasis, he turned his phone over and hit the speaker.

"...and stressed constantly. I pray for her and her husband Grant every day, but otherwise, I feel so helpless. At least I can occasionally help with their girls."

Jaclyn froze. It was Angela's voice. Her Angela. Her friend. What the hell was going on? Angela and Damien knew each other?

"I really am sorry, Jason. I was looking forward to seeing you tonight. But, until I know if Jaclyn's okay and if I need to help with their kids, I should stay available for them."

Damien doubled over in silent laughter. "No worries, sweet lady. And please call if there is anything I can do. Are we still on for Thanksgiving dinner at Jaclyn's house?"

"I'm praying that everything is okay and Thanksgiving dinner will still be on. Let's just plan to meet there around eleven."

"Well, keep me posted. Bye, Angela!"

"I definitely will. Bye, Jason!"

Jason?! Who was this madman? Angela and Damien were friends? They were dating?! And he goes by Jason? Jaclyn's anger filled her chest, and she groaned beneath the duct tape. Then she recalled his voice. Damien's voice. It had been his voice that she had heard when Angela handed her new boyfriend the phone. Now, she felt like she was going to throw up again. And as if that wasn't bad enough, Grant knew Damien as Evin Wolfe. Sick. Just sick. This whole thing had to be some demented joke. Damien had three identities and had everyone fooled, except her. And that is how he had planned it. Damn him! She was living a nightmare and was having a hard time seeing any way of getting out of it. And, if she let anyone know what this maniac was doing, he would definitely kill her family. She was sure of it. The only way to stop him now would be to kill him. But, he had her gun, not to mention that she was bound and gagged. She didn't have a chance. Her tears pooled on the cement below her face.

Damien set his phone down, laid next to Jaclyn again, and chuckled. "Ah, don't be jealous, Jaclyn. There is definitely plenty of me to go around. Now, let me go over my plan with you again, so you know exactly what to do. This time listen. If you know what's good for you."

His plan was working. He wanted to mess with Jaclyn enough to make sure she was afraid to cross him. It definitely had worked on her when she was a child. He decided that he should let her leave Spindrift in time for her to get part of the money before the banks closed for the holiday. And, he was confident that he could convince her to make payments to him every month until she had paid him all the money. Maybe she could just keep paying him for life. She owed him. And, he had a knack for threatening to kill her family. As he stared at grown-up Jaclyn, weak and afraid, he felt proud. He couldn't believe that after twenty-three years no one had figured out what he had done. They were all so stupid. He had been there right under everyone's noses as he had traveled north to Canada after the alleged boat accident. He hadn't even disguised himself. The authorities in Colorado had given up so easily and declared him dead. And that he found it rather offensive. But, he was also glad, for it had served his purpose best that way. And the two-week stand he had with the Canadian investigator had paid off, too. He wondered if such sexual favors could have won him a new identity in the U.S. He laughed again.

Jaclyn concentrated on her breathing as Damien stroked her cheek. She wanted to die. She had to escape this horror. Desperate to get away from his touch, she quickly lifted her head and turned it the other direction.

Offended, Damien grabbed her hair and lifted her head off the ground and his demeanor did a . "Really? I'm the one in charge here, Jaclyn. Don't you dare move unless I tell you to move." He slammed her head hard against the cement.

Jaclyn whimpered in terrible pain.

Damien grabbed his phone and turned on the flashlight so he could see Jaclyn's face better. He grabbed her hair and lifted her head so he could see the damage. Cuts and blood covered her face. Her nose looked broken and the gash in her forehead definitely could use some stitches. "Shit! How am I going to send you out to get the money looking like this? You always have to ruin everything, don't you?"

Jaclyn reeled from the pain but felt some relief as Damien let go of her hair and retreated. He crawled to the small opening and stood up. He started to pace across the theater, brainstorming out loud new ways to get Grant's money.

While keeping an eye on Damien through the opening into the theater, Jaclyn continued scraping the tape against the ragged concrete trying to free it from her mouth. There was a shift happening in her heart. She could physically feel it. Logic screamed inside her brain that she needed to be quiet and submissive to Damien. But, in her heart, she knew she needed to speak up. It was time. She needed to use her voice. Most of her life she had chosen not to speak out, but she no longer felt afraid. Whether she lived or died, the world needed to know what this creep had done to her. Grant needed to know. Finally, she felt the tape lift a bit. She tore at that corner more and more, her face numb to the cold and pain. But, the blood made her face slippery, and the tape resisted her continued attempts. She kept going, refusing to stop trying. She felt no fear anymore. She could feel her strength returning. Even though her predicament would say otherwise, she felt hope for the first time in a long time.

Grant slid through the stop sign, thankful there weren't any other cars around. He had to get to Spindrift fast, but he knew he better be careful or he wouldn't get there at all. The second he had seen her location on the phone, his gut told him that she was in trouble. He had an overwhelming feeling that he should call the police to meet him there. From what little information he knew at this moment, he felt like a fool calling for help. But, he couldn't shake the sense of impending doom. Usually, he was optimistic, but right now he was feeling extremely fatalistic. The call to the police didn't have to be a big fanfare, he just wanted their support in case Jaclyn was really in any danger. Maybe he could get Angela to call for him so he could concentrate on the road. He glanced at his phone and hit redial from their last conversation.

Angela picked up mid-ring sounding breathless. "Hey, Grant. Any word from Jaclyn?"

Grant sighed. "Not yet. Her phone goes directly to voicemail. But, listen, I tracked her phone to see where she was, and it located her in Spindrift, just where you said she would be. But, I'm not happy about who I think she is there to interview. Could you do me a big favor and call the non-emergency line at the police station and have an officer meet me at this home in Spindrift? I just want some support if needed. I'm praying that I'm just overreacting."

Angela gasped and tears sprang to her eyes. "Oh, Grant! Do you really think she could be in trouble?"

Grant was careful to not say too much. But, who was he fooling? He didn't know much. "Maybe. She's working on a story with a source who could give her some trouble. She's been really nervous about everything lately."

Angela did her best to sound calm. "I can call the police. What's the address?"

Grant told Angela the address and hung up. He felt a little more confident knowing that an officer would come soon. But, he was definitely nervous about what could be waiting for him at the house. Hopefully, nothing. He knew he would feel like a fool once the officer arrived, but that would be better than running into trouble without backup. If it ended up being nothing, maybe he could meet the officer outside and reassure him it was a false alarm. Up ahead he saw red lights and began pumping his brakes, his heart feeling the adrenaline slice right through it. He had seen the lights too late, his mind wondering about the possible danger ahead, but he stopped without hitting the car in front of him. Even if it was only by an inch. It appeared like the problem was up ahead. "Damn it! Not now." He could see flashing lights and assumed someone had gone off the road. While he waited for the traffic to clear, he tried Jaclyn's phone again. This time it went directly to voicemail. Either the battery died or she had turned it off. Both scenarios would be weird, especially since she always used her phone to record her interviews. His stomach lurched at the thought and he threw caution to the wind and put his truck into gear. It took a couple of times inching forward and backward to get freed from the line of cars. But, once free, he slowly began to skirt the line on the shoulder avoiding the looks, hand gestures, and occasional horns blaring someone's disapproval. He was only six miles from Spindrift and he couldn't afford to just sit still. Ignoring everyone, he crept forward until he came upon the flashing lights. It was a tow truck. There were no police cars in sight so Grant locked in the four-wheel drive and aggressively hit the ditch. He plowed through the deep snow with ease and popped up on the other side of the stalled car, hoping no one saw Integrity Homes through the sludge plastered on the sides of his truck. He knew it was a jerk move, but he had to do it. He had to make it to Jaclyn. He needed her to be okay.

Damien's phone rang again. Before answering, he bent down and peered through the small opening again.

"Oh, it's Angela. She really loves me." Damien laughed. "Hello, this is Jason." He hit speaker phone right away so that Jaclyn could hear.

Angela was breathing hard and talking fast. "Hi, Jason. Sorry to bother you again, but I could really use your help."

"Absolutely! What can I do?"

"Jaclyn's husband just called, and he's really worried about her. She won't answer her phone, so he's on his way to a house in Spindrift where he thinks she has an interview. He wanted me to call the non-emergency line at the police station to see if they could send an officer to check up on them at the residence. Just in case, you know? I started to call the station but remembered how kind you were to offer to look in on my friends to make sure they were safe. If you are free would you mind driving by the house to check on them? No worries if you can't, I just thought I would ask before I called the station."

Damien repressed the laugh he desperately wanted to let fly. "Anything for you, Angela. I'm not busy at the moment. I can definitely have a look. What is the address?"

Angela had calmed down quite a bit and gave him the address. "It could be nothing, but he doesn't want to take a chance. I guess Jaclyn's been working on a story that could be potentially dangerous."

Jaclyn banged her head lightly on the cement, cursing her own choices that had led her to her current predicament. She could have asked for help earlier. But, now all her preparation was for naught. Her car was out of gas, her phone a quarter mile down the road, and the gun that was to be her courage was now in the hands of her nemesis.

"It's always better to be safe than sorry. I'm glad you thought to call me. I will let you know what's up as soon as I get there."

"Thank you for being so kind, Jason. I appreciate it. Talk soon."

"Bye, Angela."

Damien ended the call without taking his eyes off of Jaclyn.

"Oh my, this is fun, Jaclyn. I've waited a long time to reconnect with you. I've really missed our times together. But, it saddens me how serious you've become. You need to lighten up, sweetheart. This whole scenario unfolding today is definitely more than I bargained for. But, boy is it entertaining."

Jaclyn looked away.

Damien left the opening to the crawl space and she could hear him rummaging around with something in the theater. When he finally came back, he had the half door for the crawl space.

"It looks like we will have some company. That husband of yours tends to get in the way, but I will get rid of him soon enough so you and I can settle our negotiations. Then I can send you on your way. Let the family know you were in an accident or something. Your face looks terrible. You need to be more careful."

Damien laughed for several minutes, then, with the help of a small mallet, he nestled the door hardware into the hinges and pounded in the pins to hold it in place.

"Now, please be quiet while I assure your husband everything is okay and get him out of here quickly. If I hear you make a sound, you will soon find yourself to be a widow. You don't want that now, do you? I am not in any mood to mess around."

Jaclyn stared him down, her resolve rising. He stared back, smiling, then chuckled as he shut the door. Jaclyn immediately went to work rubbing the duct tape against the rough cement again, hoping to regain her voice. She had to somehow warn Grant when he got here. She needed to speak up about everything. She needed to get this gag out of her mouth and unleash everything in her heart. And it needed to happen today.

• CHAPTER 16 •

Grant drove for a good mile after passing the tow truck and stuck vehicle before he dared look in his rearview mirror. There was no one behind him. Thank God. He felt like such a jerk. He let out a deep breath he had been holding for way too long. He was light-headed and nauseous. No wonder there was no one behind him. No one else was foolish enough to do what he had just done. But, he knew he had to get to Jaclyn. He had to make sure she was okay. Under normal circumstances, he would have been patient with bad roads and people in trouble. He would have definitely stopped and offered his help. But, today was different. Today, he only had Jaclyn's safety on his mind. Why had he been so hard on her lately? If only he could have listened to her without judging or trying to tell her what to do, maybe she would have opened up to him more. She was so secretive because he was so impatient with her. Plain and simple. Now, she could be in serious trouble and it was because he had been such a fool. A jerk. A know-it-all. He would do better. He had to do better. Starting right now.

Grant gripped the steering wheel tightly, trying to do his best to stay on the road. The driveway to the home was easy to miss, even on a good day. But, today, it was going to be next to impossible to find. His eyes searched the side of the road ahead of him, scanning the white landscape for mailboxes. The wind was blowing so hard that he couldn't see anything ahead of him either. It was a total whiteout. He wasn't even sure if he was still on the road. But, sure enough, he finally recognized a small shed-like structure off to the left that was definitely after the driveway he was looking for. Grant came to a stop then glanced in his rearview mirror. He didn't see anyone coming behind him, so he put the truck in reverse and slowly backed until he finally saw the mailbox. It was a single mailbox, caked in snow, the address unreadable. He was finally here. He turned onto the driveway and whispered to no one, "God please help me. Help us all." He shifted into drive and gunned it up the slight incline of the snow-covered dirt drive. The bed of his truck fishtailed out of control, but the tires took hold enough to continue the climb. But, suddenly, as he crested the hill, Jaclyn's Jeep came into view and he slammed on his brakes. His truck spun to the right, just missing the Jeep, then slid back into a plot of snow-covered mountain sagebrush. The truck stalled as Grant jumped out and ran through the deep snow to the Jeep. He slipped twice on the way, tripping over small shrubs beneath the snow. When he finally reached the Jeep, he threw open the driver's door while yelling Jaclyn's name. It was empty. But, her keys were still in the ignition. Grant began to panic. His heart pounded as his eye caught sight of her phone on the passenger side floorboard. She was in trouble. She would have never fled from her car without her phone or keys unless she was in big trouble. Where were the police? He sat in Jaclyn's driver's seat, grabbed his phone off his belt and called Angela.

"Hi, Grant is Jaclyn oka...."

"Where are the police?" Grant yelled. "What did they say?"

Angela began to panic and tripped over her words. "Um, I don't know, Grant. Um, I actually called a guy I've been seeing. He's a police officer and...."

"Angela! She's in trouble! I need the police! Now!"

Angela yelled back. "He said he was on his way!"

"Well, where is he then? Call 911, now!"

"Okay, okay, I will. Do you really think she's in big trouble? Do you think she's....?"

Grant took a deep breath and composed himself enough to get Angela to help him. In a slow, measured tone, Grant shared what he knew with her. "I don't see anyone else here, Angela. Jaclyn's Jeep is in the driveway with her keys and phone inside. She's definitely in trouble. She would not have just run off into the storm." Then he raised his voice again. "Please, Angela! For God's sake, call 911! Get someone here immediately! This is no longer a non-emergency."

"Yes! Yes! I will do it right now!" Angela was now crying. She hung up without saying goodbye.

Grant made his way back to his truck, trying to maneuver himself quickly through the unstable landscape. Back at his truck, he jumped in his driver's seat, turned the engine over, and attempted to get back onto the driveway. His back wheels spun out of control, throwing snow and sticks, unable to gain any traction. His truck was hung up on some sagebrush. He slammed the truck into reverse, hoping to get untangled from the vegetation, but he only made his situation worse. The truck stalled again and his fists beat his steering wheel with years of pent-up frustration and disappointment in himself. Finally, he grabbed the sides of his head and screamed at himself to stop it. He began to calm himself down and formulate some sort of plan. Like it or not, he knew he would have to walk the rest of the way to the house. "Damn it!"

Grant cursed, then whispered with a burst of renewed ambition, "Jack, hang in there. I'm on my way."

He jumped out of his truck, then fished behind his seat looking for some sort of weapon. All the guns were now at his shop in Pineridge. Finally, he came across a small ax. Gripping the ax tightly, he slammed the door of his truck and started to jog the best he could toward the house. The snow was already deep and his legs burned with the effort. But, he couldn't slow down. He had to get to Jaclyn. Every step he took was taking too long. He tried to hurry but felt like he was running in quicksand. Twice he slipped and fell, the second time hitting his knee hard on a large rock under the snow. Cursing, he bounced up and pushed forward, ignoring the sharp pain shooting up his leg. Time seemed to stand still. He ran, but couldn't mark his progress, everything was white. His footsteps filled with snow almost immediately after making them. He didn't see Jaclyn's trail, nor did he leave one anyone else could follow. It was nearly impossible to look ahead with the blowing snow. The wind gusted, and he accidentally started veering to the left side of the driveway. Suddenly, he lost his footing and slipped down the embankment. His right hip hit the ground hard and a shrub branch stuck him in the neck. Grant cursed as he untangled himself and climbed up the embankment on his hands and knees. He regained his balance once he was on level ground. He sat back on his knees and tried to settle his breathing. He was going to pass out if he didn't gain some control over his emotions. Before starting to walk, he searched ahead but still couldn't see the house. Finally, he stood up, oriented himself the best he could, and trudged forward, each step taking more effort than the last.

As Grant leaned into the wind, his mind began to wander. He was definitely concerned for Jaclyn's safety. But, he was also starting to feel angry. Why couldn't Jaclyn ever just let him in? Let him help her? Her independence had attracted him to her when they had first met, he was thrilled that she wasn't one of those overly-dramatic girls. But, her independence began to wear on him shortly after they got married. She always insisted on doing everything herself. It even irritated her if he opened her car door for her. He never understood her aversion to being helped. Her repulsion to being treated like she was valuable and loved. Growing up, Grant's mom had made sure that he knew how to treat a lady and insisted on it whenever she was around. Which was funny, because his dad had done no such thing. He had finally figured out, when he was an adult, that his mom wanted to teach him how to be a gentleman because his father wasn't going to do it. His father was overly demanding of his mom and treated her more like a servant, than a wife. Even as a small boy, he could see how much his dad's rudeness had hurt his mom, and he tried to fill that gap so she would feel loved. But, he was at a loss around Jaclyn. She wanted none of it. He had yet to figure out her love language. He even tried leaving her alone, but then she got even angrier. And now, he didn't know how to help her. There would be no right thing to do once he entered this house and encountered whatever was going on. All he knew was that he would do anything to make sure she was safe. And, if he had to be angry to fuel his mission, then so be it. They would work through it later when they were both safe. He decided that she could no longer call the shots. He was going to get her out of here and to safety no matter what he had to do.

Panting and sweating, he finally rounded a bend in the driveway and could see a faint outline of the front porch. There were no vehicles that he could see. Grant panicked. Where was Evin? Or whoever the hell he was? Had he left with Jaclyn? Before entering the house he walked the perimeter of the house, peeking in as many windows as possible. From what he could see, the inside of the home looked just like he had left it. He saw no evidence that anyone was even there. What if what's-his-name had taken Jaclyn somewhere else? What if he had already killed her? He quickly and quietly worked his way back to the front of the house, and shielding his eyes from the blowing snow, he looked in the garage window. There it was. Evin's black truck. So, he was here. Which also meant, Jaclyn had to be here, too. Grant bent over with his hand on his chest. He couldn't panic now. He had to stay in control. When his breathing was under control, he stood back up and looked in the window again. There was no movement, and the truck appeared empty.

He inched his way towards the front of the house. He ascended the stairs of the porch, trying to not make any noise. But, the sound of the snow crunching beneath his boots was deafening in this barren landscape. He stopped after each step, listening for sounds of anyone nearby. Nothing. Once on the landing, he shuffled his feet through the snow towards the front door. At the door, he took off his gloves and got a better grip on the ax. Then, before turning the doorknob, he listened for sirens. Nothing. Damn it! He needed backup now. The line of traffic he had encountered must be slowing down the police, too. But, if they were on a distress call, they should be more aggressive than he had been. Grant steadied himself then held the ax in this right hand and raised it to eye level. With his left hand, he turned the knob, but it didn't give. The door was locked. Shit! His keys were back in his truck. He put his gloves back on and, once again, circled the house, this time trying all the doors. Finally, the door into the garage twisted open in his hand. He made his way to the driver's door of Evin's truck and peeked in the window. But, he saw nothing out of the ordinary. He opened it slowly so he could inspect the inside. Sitting on the passenger seat was a copy of the contract they had both signed for the work he was doing for him. He climbed into the driver's seat then opened the middle console. Inside, he found Evin's wallet. Keeping an eye on the door to the house, he quickly leafed through the wallet. Everything in it identified this man as Evin Wolfe. The photos all matched his face. He continued to shuffle through a bunch of business cards and credit cards. Everything looked legit, but he knew this guy was a fake. Then a small school photo fell out of the wallet and hit the seat. He turned it over and stared in disbelief. It was Jaclyn. And she was about nine or ten years old. What the hell was going on? Had they really known each other since she was a child? He continued to look through the rest of the wallet's contents, not sure what he was hoping to find. Finally, he dropped the wallet on the seat and looked through the console. More receipts and lots of notes. Measurements and estimates. Then he saw a small piece of paper with their address on it. He knew where they lived? Had he been there? What was going on between these two? What if Jaclyn wasn't in danger at all? What if she was having an affair with this jerk? He was so confused. But, she was definitely afraid. He had never seen her more afraid. She tried to cover it up by being brash and secretive. But, she was afraid. He just knew it. But, he hadn't been able to figure out the who and the what of her fear. If she was having an affair, she wouldn't need a gun. This man was definitely a maniac, and he had his wife somewhere in this house. And he needed to get in there and save his wife.

Slowly, Grant climbed out of the cab and shut the door most of the way, but left it slightly ajar to avoid any noise. He made his way to the door that led into the kitchen, then stopped and listened, his ear against the thick wood door. He didn't hear a thing. He could feel beads of sweat dripping down the middle of his back. His knee ached. And he felt like he might throw up. He hated every bit of this. Growing up, he had no aspirations of being a police officer or fireman, as many of his childhood friends had dreamed of becoming. Those things that were predictable had always drawn him. He did not like anything that was unsafe or threatening. He enjoyed building, organizing, and mentoring others. Yet, here he was, acting out a living nightmare. He would give anything for this to all be a dream, or one of those shows where they jump out and tell you they had been filming you. But, he had a painful gut feeling that this was all real, and the danger on the other side of the door not for a young audience. Should he wait here until he heard the police arrive? What if Jaclyn was hurt or in trouble right now? If he waited, it could be too late. He leaned close to the door again and listened. Still nothing.

Finally, mustering as much courage as he could, Grant opened the door into the utility room. The room was dark except for the natural light coming from the nearby kitchen windows. He held the ax high and just listened. Nothing. Where could they be? If nothing was going on, what would his explanation be for the ax? At this moment, he felt terrible for jumping all over Jaclyn about her taking his gun. He was acting just as crazy. But, he decided that he didn't care what anyone said; he would rather be safe than sorry. He closed the door behind him then kept his back near the wall as he inched his way into the kitchen. He was dripping with sweat. He took his gloves and hat off and dropped them on the floor. Then, he put the ax down on the floor next to him and took off his coat. He needed to be free to defend himself if needed. He took a couple of steps sideways, his back still to the wall, but his boots made too much noise. He needed to surprise Evin, not the other way around. He bent down and untied his boots with one hand while holding the ax in the other. He slipped both boots off without a sound and stood back up, scanning what he could see of the kitchen and living room beyond. From where he stood, he could see all the way to the front door. And, on the floor near the front door, a pile of what seemed to be clothes met his eye. He sidestepped in that direction, careful to not turn his back to the large open room. As he inched his way towards the front door, he kept his gaze on the stairs leading to the basement. That would be where Jaclyn would have most likely encountered Evin since he should have been working when she arrived. Once he got closer to the front door, he finally dared to look down. The pile was Jaclyn's backpack, coat, hat, and gloves. She was here. Adrenalin hit his heart and doubled him over again. He placed his free hand on his chest and willed himself to calm down. He had to find her.

For several minutes, Grant stood frozen by the front door, unable to move. Then, suddenly, he heard the whir of a compressor kick on and the distinct ping of an air gun. He hit the ground out of pure instinct. The sounds were coming from downstairs. He listened, staying low to the ground. Evin was working. He must be nailing the soundproofing to the walls. Was Jaclyn with him? Had he hurt Jaclyn? He pulled himself up and slowly found his way to the top of the stairwell to the basement. He stood completely still, his back to the wall next to the opening so he couldn't be seen from below. The hammering continued. Whenever the compressor turned off, Grant strained to hear voices. But, all he could hear was the air gun continuing to shoot nails into the wall. When the compressor turned on again, Grant leaped at the chance of not being heard descending the steps. And with the ax raised, Grant cautiously took one step at a time into the cold basement. The large family room stood empty, the only light coming from the wall of windows on the far side. Slowly, he inched his way around the perimeter of the whole basement, checking every bedroom and bathroom for Jaclyn, but came up empty-handed. His heart was still pounding in his chest. The only doors left were those to the theater. And, he could hear the compressor working hard behind those doors. But still no voices. Where were the police? He strained to hear sirens or someone coming in the house upstairs. Anything. But, he heard nothing. His arm that was holding the ax began to shake. He was exhausted and pumped full of adrenalin. He decided not to rush into the theater. He heard no sounds of distress and maybe the police were almost here. Drawing some comfort from the sound of the nail gun, Grant set the ax down for a moment so he could wipe the palms of his hands on his jeans. He took a minute to rub the spasms out of his hands. The nail gun stopped. He grabbed the ax with a fresh grip and flattened his body against the wall outside the theater. He heard Evin shuffling things around, probably grabbing more soundproofing. After what seemed like an eternity, the compressor kicked back on and Evin continued working. Sweat dripped from Grant's face as he let out the breath he had been holding. Why was he being such a wimp? Why didn't he just walk in there and demand to know where Jaclyn was? This was his job site and Evin worked for him. Not the other way around. He turned the doorknob on the French doors leading into the theater. The compressor blocked out any noise he was making, so Evin did not turn when Grant first saw him. For several seconds, Grant simply watched Evin as he attached the sound barrier to the front wall. His work was extremely fast and precise. At least Grant's money was not being wasted. But, where was Jaclyn? As he was scanning the room for her, the compressor stopped. And at that same moment, Damien turned to grab more nails. Their eyes met. Evin smiled, then his gaze fell to the ax. He set the nail gun down and stood up tall, facing Grant.

"Well, hello, Grant! Nice of you to stop by. What the hell are you doing with an ax?"

Grant looked down at his white knuckles clenching the ax, then back at Evin. "Um...I went off the driveway near the highway and... um, tried to cut some branches loose to free my truck. I guess I forgot to put it back in my truck." Grant felt sick inside. He was wavering. He needed to take a stand. He needed to be the one in control, not Evin.

Evin chuckled at Grant's story. "Well, you could put it down now. There is no need for it here." He turned his back on Grant and loaded the gun with more nails.

Grant took his eyes off of Evin and surveyed the room once more, looking for Jaclyn. But, there was not one bit of evidence that she had made it down into the basement. He thought through all of his options and decided that he had very few. "No thanks. I think I will just hold it."

•   CHAPTER 17   •

Angela fumbled to end the call with Grant, shaken to her core. The phone eventually slipped out of her hand and hit the floor in the laundry room, cracking her screen. She cursed as she bent down to retrieve the phone, her hands shaking out of control. She had never heard Grant so worked up. He was definitely scared. She had been concerned about Jaclyn, but now, after talking to Grant, she was petrified. Jaclyn was really in trouble. This was the real deal, not just Jaclyn being elusive. Angela did her best to concentrate on the fact that Jason was probably almost to the Spindrift house. She knew he would do anything he could to help Grant find Jaclyn. He had said it himself when they had driven by their house and the girls' school. But, where was he right now? And, why had he not called her yet? Once she was able to still her hands enough to dial, she called 911, just like she told Grant she would. There was nothing wrong with over-reporting. Jaclyn needed as much help as she could get. The operator was kind and efficient, taking the information and reassuring Angela that an officer would be on the way immediately. This time, Angela carefully ended the call without dropping the phone. She felt calmer knowing that Jason and other backup officers were on their way. But, she still couldn't wrap her mind around Jaclyn getting herself involved in something so dangerous. Even if it was for her job. This had to be why Jaclyn had been avoiding her for the past week. Angela had to admit that she had been hurt by Jaclyn's recent behavior. But, all that mattered right now was that Jaclyn get back to safety. Angela was sure Jaclyn would share the details with her when this all blew over. At least she hoped that would be the case. But, the more she thought back over all their years of friendship, she had to admit that Jaclyn had always been pretty tight-lipped about her personal life. This wasn't something new. This avoidance. She would talk about the girls and superficial stuff, but not anything emotional. It was always Angela who did most of the sharing. Jaclyn had always been a great listener, and didn't seem to care about not sharing, but now Angela was questioning if Jaclyn would ever trust her with the details of what happened today. She hoped she would, given the fact that Angela had been wrestling with her kids half the day. Suddenly, screaming cut through the silence. It sounded like Anya.

Angela quickly ran to the living room where she found Anya laying on the floor crying, holding her foot, and Jenae peeking out from behind the recliner. She gently picked Anya up in her arms and sat on the couch trying to figure out the cause of her outburst. But, Anya wouldn't stop crying, no matter how hard Angela tried to calm her down. She sat with Anya in her lap and rocked back and forth, her arms wrapped tightly around the girl's tiny frame. She whispered calming words in her ear, over and over, reassuring her that it would all be okay. Angela was also keeping her eye on Jenae who had retreated even farther behind the chair. But, whenever Jenae would peek out, Angela would smile and motion with her hand for Jenae to come to see her. Finally, after several minutes, when Anya's crying subsided to involuntary sobs against Angela's chest, Jenae walked over to the couch and stood before Angela.

Angela gently grabbed one of Jenae's hands and looked her in the eyes. "Can you tell me what happened, sweet girl? It's okay. I'm sure it was an accident."

Jenae's lower lip began to quiver, and she started crying as she blurted out her confession. "It wasn't my fault! I just stepped on her fingers. They were in my way! It's her fault, not mine." Angela held Jenae's hand tightly and told her that even when it's an accident, it is always the right thing to do to apologize. Jenae burst into tears and screamed that she was sorry then ran back behind the recliner.

Anya watched Jenae run away then started screaming again. This time out of anger, not pain.

"Shh. It's okay, sweetie. Take a deep breath." Angela pried Anya off her chest and gripped her shoulders. "Listen, Anya, Jenae said she was sorry for stepping on your fingers."

Anya pushed back against Angela's arms and wriggled out of her embrace, kicking with all her might. "I no want sorry! I want mommy!"

Angela stood in shock and watched as Anya ran to her room continuing to scream. "Anya! Come back here!" She took a big breath and let out a long sigh as she turned to glance back down at Jenae, who was in the fetal position behind the recliner. How did Jaclyn do this every day? Ever since she had picked the girls up from school, they had been arguing, getting hurt, and crying.

Mandy was the only one who had tired quickly of trying to get along with her sisters and took it upon herself to go sit at the kitchen counter and color in her sketchpad. She appeared to be doing a pretty good job of ignoring all the commotion going on between Anya and Jenae. Mackenzie, however, was sitting on the other couch laughing and making funny faces at Jenae, who kept peeking out from behind the recliner. Soon, the two girls were laughing at each other while Anya was still screaming in her room.

Angela's frustration mounted to where she couldn't hold it in any longer. "Girls! That's enough! Mackenzie and Jenae, to your rooms now! Find a book and be quiet. I will let you know when you can come back out!"

Mandy turned and glared at Angela while she was yelling, but didn't say a word. Then she silently returned to her coloring. But, Mackenzie and Jenae both jumped at the sound of Angela's voice and took off running to their rooms, slamming their doors when they got there.

Angela walked down the hall to check on Anya. Anya lay face down in her little toddler bed kicking her mattress with her feet. Angela walked in the room and sat on the floor by her bed and rubbed her back. But, Anya kept screaming and kicking. Finally, Angela picked her up against her will and carried her back to the living room. She plopped her on the couch and tried to get her interested in a movie, but Anya wouldn't have any of it. She could hear Mackenzie and Jenae opening and closing their bedroom doors and giggling at each other, and it made her even madder. Anya fought her way off the couch and away from Angela, this time hiding under a blanket near the TV. Angela put her head in her hands and silently begged God for some help with these girls. She tried to have some compassion for the girls' fears. They didn't know what was going on with their mom and dad. Nothing had been normal since they had arrived home. She had to get their minds off of mom and dad not being here. And she had to not show how concerned she was. Which was going to be really difficult. Angela looked up and noticed that it was already dark outside. And, there had still been no word from Grant, Jaclyn, or Jason. Out of the corner of her eye, Angela caught Mandy looking at her from the kitchen. The girls had never seen Angela this frustrated before. She knew she had to get a grip and calm down or the girls were just going to act up even more.

Angela reached for her phone, Googled the local pizza place, and ordered a large pepperoni pizza and cheesy breadsticks online to be delivered. That should be enough for the girls. She wasn't hungry at all. Her stomach turned with the unknown. Why was this family falling apart right when her life was finally starting to look up? After placing the order, Angela tried calling Jason, but it went right to voicemail. Dare she call Grant or Jaclyn? What happened that neither one of them were checking with her about the girls? It was just weird. All of it. She put her phone down, leaned back and closed her eyes, trying to take advantage of the moments without someone crying.

But, within only a few minutes, Jenae had come running from her room and was tugging on Angela's sweatshirt. "I'm hungry!"

Angela opened her eyes, smiled, and took Jenae's innocent face in her hands. "I know, honey. Pepperoni pizza is on its way!"

Jenae smiled and gave Angela a big hug, then ran down the hall to tell Mackenzie. Angela breathed a sigh of relief. Finally, someone was happy.

"Mom doesn't like us having pizza all the time."

Angela turned and saw Mandy glaring at her, her arms crossed, her cheeks burning red with anger, and her bottom lip stuck out as far as she could in utter contempt. Angela attempted to reassure Mandy. "Mandy, it's just one night. It's okay."

Mandy yelled with all her might. "No, it's not! Daddy just bought us pizza Monday! Mom will be so mad!" Then she started to cry.

Angela started towards her, but Mandy jumped off her stool and ran to her room. "Well, I'm doing a great job as a parent," Angela whispered to no one. She returned to the couch and sat by herself, waiting for the pizza to be delivered. The girls were not happy, but at least all they were quiet for the moment. As much as Angela savored the quiet, the silence was painful. She couldn't help but worry. What was going on in Spindrift? The people she cared about the most in life, and possibly the future love of her life, were all in some sort of danger. She had never felt so helpless. But, isn't this what she had always been taught about faith? Faith is believing in the light when you are still standing in complete darkness. It is thanking God for life when sickness and death surround you. It is trusting God works even when those you love are falling apart and there is nothing you can do to help. How strong was her faith? Right this moment, she felt weak. Jaclyn had always seemed a little interested in Angela's faith, and Angela had always loved having deep talks about it with her. Jaclyn would intellectualize everything and Angela would stand firm on the simplicity of faith. The beauty of the mystery. But, there was never an explanation solid enough to convince Jaclyn a hundred percent, although she had admitted that Angela's faith was intriguing. That she could tell it was real. But, she still struggled to accept where Angela said it came from? It made no sense to her, except that her mom had had the same faith. Her mom had joy even when things went wrong. As a young girl, Jaclyn had told Angela that she spent so much time with her mom because she felt safe near her. She couldn't explain why, but Angela knew it was because of the peace Jaclyn felt near her mom. But, right this very minute, Angela feared there was no faith to be seen in her words or her actions. No peace for them to reach out to her for. It was always easy to spot the miracle of someone's faith in hindsight. Or, to watch someone go through a rough time and wonder how they were remaining so strong and peaceful. But, it was a different story to see faith at the moment. To recognize its power in the face of tragedy and fear and confusion.

Right this minute, she felt spiritually blind and helpless but knew she needed to take a stand for her friends. Especially the girls. The closest people she had to family. Why did it have to be so hard? As hard as she tried, she couldn't stop the tears from finally breaching her worried eyes and rolling down her face.

For several minutes, Angela allowed herself the emotional release of the tears, her head buried deeply in her hands. Then, she reached within herself and found the will to show herself to the girls as strong and confident. She walked to the kitchen and grabbed some tissues. She believed God was working in her life and the lives of her friends. But, she also believed they all lived in an imperfect world of men and women exercising their free will. It was a cosmic mess. But, today she needed to focus on the basics. God already won the battle for those who believe in him. Period. With a renewed sense of purpose, Angela returned to the living room to wait for the pizza. She turned on some music and sat alone, hoping it would draw the girls out of their rooms. But, it wasn't until the pizza arrived, nearly forty-five minutes later that the girls joined her again. But, finally, the pizza was on the table and all the girls were eating and laughing at each other's attempts to burp, even Mandy. Angela couldn't stomach the pizza, but she felt a little better sitting with the girls and listening to their laughter. Angela's phone had been quiet all evening. So, when she saw that the girls were all in good spirits, she walked into the laundry room and dialed 911 again.

"911 operator. What is your emergency?"

Angela kept her voice as low as she could. "I'm worried that some friends of mine are in trouble. I called a couple of hours ago, but I haven't heard from anyone."

"What is your name, Ma'am?"

"Angela Brixton."

"Where are your friends?"

"505 Highway 50 in Spindrift."

"Is anyone hurt?"

"I don't know! That's why I'm calling you!" Angela took a deep breath. She knew she was being rude, but she needed help and needed it now.

"Ma'am, we are trying to get your friends the help they need. Please stay calm. I see that we dispatched an officer to that location when you called last time. There is a pile-up near that part of the highway and the officer could not get through. Please hold while I check the officer's current situation."

"Thank you." Angela willed herself to be calm. Maybe their car was stuck and their phones were dead. Maybe they were all stranded at the Spindrift house for the night. The weather had continued to get worse every hour. She had no plans of driving to her house tonight, that's for sure.

"Ma'am, thank you for holding. The officer still cannot get through because of the pile-up, but they dispatched two patrol cars from Deerborn quite a while ago. Please hold on the line and I will check their location."

"Okay." Angela tried to be optimistic. Jaclyn, Grant, and Jason were all smart, level-headed people. They could handle hunkering down for the night because of the storm. And they were probably wishing they could check how the girls were doing and reassure them with their own voices. Angela liked to think they were at peace knowing she had the girls. Soon enough they would all be together again and laughing about their adventures.

"Ma'am, thank you again for holding. The officers from Deerborn are about halfway to the Spindrift address. They should be there soon."

"Thank you for checking. I appreciate it."

"It's an honor to help. Do you know what kind of danger your friends might be in? It would help the officers to know what to expect."

"I really don't. It has something to do with Jaclyn meeting someone for an interview. She's a journalist at the Cliff Creek Courier."

"So, maybe some possible argument? Or do you think it may lead to violence?"

"Again, I don't know. Her husband was on his way there to check up on her and he asked me to call 911. Maybe he knows more. I've tried calling all of them, but their phones must be dead."

"Okay, we will know more soon. Keep your phone nearby in case they call you."

"Will do. Thank you."

"You're welcome. Goodbye."

Angela stood still in the dark of the laundry room and listened to the girls chattering. Thank God they were finally getting along. Maybe she should have fed them earlier. What should she tell them about their parents? She felt way out of her league in this parenting role. Standing in the laundry room, she could hear the wind howling outside, and she shuddered with the chill and the horror of the unknown. Gusts of fear swept through her body and goosebumps raised in defense. Wrapping her arms around herself tightly, she held on to what was left of her sanity. If she could only go back to her phone call with Jaclyn earlier today. This time she would listen and not judge. Who was she, anyway, to think she knew what was going on in Jaclyn's life? They actually had very little in common except for their love of coffee and their strong-willed DNA. She knew nothing about the struggles of marriage or raising kids or being a journalist. Her clientele as a realtor was a dream compared to what Jaclyn had to put up with when trying to get someone to talk about a painful situation. She had been a fool pushing Jaclyn as she did. Maybe this could have all been avoided had she been able to just be Jaclyn's friend. The girls chattering brought Angela back to the present. She joined them at the table and tried her best to be upbeat. Pizza plates, crusts, and crumbs were all pushed back and the girls challenged Angela and Anya to the matching game. Anya climbed up on Angela's lap as the other girls set the pieces up in rows, face down on the table. For nearly forty-five minutes the girls were thinking only about their next move and catching Anya cheating. But, once Jenae won with the most matched pairs, Mackenzie demanded to know where her mom and dad were. She ran and got the home phone and called her mom, then her dad. Nothing. Both went right to voicemail. She threw the phone across the room and started to cry.

"Where is my mom? I want my mom!"

Angela tried to comfort Mackenzie, but then Anya started crying, too. Mandy watched with disgust. When Jenae tried to go get the phone Mackenzie had thrown, Mandy beat her to it and pushed her out of the way causing her to hit her head against the wall. A wailing symphony filled the room and Angela blew up.

"Stop it! All of you! Stop it, now!" Angela instantly regretted her outburst.

The girls stopped their crying and screaming, their attention drawn to Angela with fear and confusion.

Angela took a deep breath before continuing. "Please, girls, calm down. Everyone is okay. Your mom and dad will be home soon and we will all have a fun Thanksgiving tomorrow. I promise!" Even as the word promise rolled off Angela's tongue, she felt sick to her stomach.

How could she promise these girls something that she didn't know would even happen?

Mandy still looked mad but was the first to make her way to the couch and sit down. The other girls quietly followed suit. Angela tried a small smile in their direction, but the girls all looked at each other and then down in their laps.

Angela tried again. "Hey, girls. I'm so sorry I yelled." She looked at each one of their small faces, tear trails down all of their cheeks. "I hope you can forgive me." The girls didn't move. They looked at each other waiting for someone to take the lead. Mandy was usually the one who made the first move, but she sat completely still with her arms folded, leaving her sisters lost for what to do. Angela inhaled deeply, picturing optimism filling her soul and tried one more time. "Hey, I know, let's get comfy and watch a movie while we wait for your mom and dad. Okay?"

More out of shock at Angela's fit and weird change of attitude, than submission, the girls all agreed to get their pajamas on and watch a movie. They were definitely confused. Angela had always been the fun sitter, the one who brought small gifts and treats and let them do things their parents didn't let them do. But, not tonight. Anxiety had flooded the home from the moment they got home from school, and no one felt comfortable, especially Angela. While the girls were changing, Angela gathered all the blankets she could find and made each girl their own comfy bed in front of the fireplace. And, to avoid any further arguments, she chose the movie, one that she knew all the girls would like. There were no complaints. The girls all laid completely still as the movie started. Angela felt awful that the girls were worried about their parents. But, now they were also nervous about her behavior. She had blown it in more ways than one today. She couldn't wait for all of this to be just a bad memory.

The way the girls were acting was breaking Angela's heart, so, with one last ditch effort, she tried to win back their hearts. "Hey, girls, how about I go dish us up some popcorn and ice cream?"

Finally, their standoff crumbled and the girls all shouted with glee. Popcorn and ice cream had always been their favorite snack when Auntie Angela was babysitting. The normalcy of the offer brought smiles back to all of their faces. Angela breathed a sigh of relief, turned the volume up a bit, and retreated to the kitchen to get the treats. While the popcorn popped in the microwave, Angela stared out the kitchen window into the blizzard and said another prayer for her friends. Why hadn't anyone contacted her yet? Surely the police have arrived at the Spindrift home by now.

• CHAPTER 18 •

The cold from the cement seeped deeply into Jaclyn's body. She shivered as she attempted to loosen the duct tape from her mouth. The tape was giving up its grip as she scraped it across the rough clump of cement, but not yet enough to release the gag in her mouth. The skin on her cheek tore a little more each time. She could feel the warm blood on her face, but she didn't stop. She couldn't stop. She had to get free before Grant arrived. She needed to get the gun back. She needed to get back some control. But, the more she worked at the tape, the more exhausted she became. Her arms and legs ached and the skin around her mouth burned. She had to stop for a few minutes. Her head pounded and her lungs were burning with her effort. For a few moments, she allowed herself to rest. She knew how important it was that she didn't freak out and lose control of her senses. She willed her heart to slow and managed each breath. Her childhood defense mechanisms were finally paying off as an adult. When she felt more in control, she focused on listening. She could hear Damien moving things around in the theater. It sounded like boxes and tools. When she could hear him doing something at a distance, she could stay calm. But, every time there was silence her heart started beating faster. Her eyes stayed glued on the small door in the wall. She cursed her anxiety.

She needed to stay in complete control. Even if she was bound and gagged. Then, she heard a compressor kick in. Jaclyn lay still waiting to see if she could figure out what he was doing with it. After several minutes of him messing with something, it was finally clear when she heard the nail gun. He was going to fool Grant into thinking he was just working. But, what would he say about her car being abandoned on the driveway? He wouldn't get away with saying she wasn't here. And he had no idea that she had walked from the highway. Grant would catch him in the lie. He had to. But, she also needed to be able to get Grant's attention, otherwise, he wouldn't know where she was. To give her cheeks a break she rolled her body over. She painfully worked herself into a reclined seated position, her head off the ground and her feet in the air. Her stomach muscles burned as she held this position, searching the walls with her feet. She had to find something to tear the duct tape from her ankles. The wall to her left produced nothing. She pivoted and felt the other wall, her feet finally hitting something, possibly the end of a piece of rebar. Her stomach muscles ached as she laid back and started rubbing the tape around her ankles on the small defect in the wall. Her hands, clasped behind her back and also wrapped tightly with duct tape, crushed into the cement with each attempt to release her feet. But, she again didn't dare stop as long as the compressor and nail gun were covering up any noise she was making.

After setting and closing the door to the crawl space, Damien had gone to work on the soundproofing material while he waited for Grant. Then he paused and slowly stood. Thankfully, Angela had tipped him off on Grant's imminent arrival. Grant would expect to surprise Damien, but that would not happen now. Damien was confident that the odds were definitely in his favor. He was so close to his goal: One hundred thousand dollars. At least. Maybe more, if he could keep Jaclyn scared enough to keep sending it. Even if Jaclyn had to get it to him in installments, it would get him back to Canada and out of financial trouble. There was no question in his mind that he deserved the money after what Jaclyn had done to ruin his reputation over twenty years ago. He was sick of people not giving him the respect he deserved. As a young girl, Jaclyn had been like putty in his hands. She played into the fear he had created in her small world and had always been obedient and quiet. Until she couldn't control herself and caused her father, his boss, concern. He had been her dad's best employee. At least in his mind, he was. But, now Jaclyn was frustrating the hell out of him. Who did she think she was bringing a gun with her to meet him? That is the kind of disrespect he had never been able to handle. When people tried to threaten him, or act like they were better than him, it irritated him to no end. Damien had left home at only fifteen years old because he believed that his parents were pathetic cowards. They tried to parent him, but he was determined to make sure they were unsuccessful. By the age of twelve, police had arrested him four times, and he ran away so much that his parents would not even report him missing until he was gone at least a week. When they finally called the police, they would most often find him at a friend's house strung out on a variety of drugs. By fifteen, he just decided that it was best for all of them if they parted ways before someone got hurt. But, leaving home didn't solve his problems. In fact, they got worse. He constantly fought with friends he roomed with because everyone wanted to have some level of shared responsibilities. This is the reason he had left home. He didn't need anyone to parent him. He hated playing games with people. And that is exactly what Jaclyn was doing, playing games with him. She needed to be broken. Her wimp of a husband had allowed her to exercise her independence, and it pissed him off. Once she feared him again, like she did when she was a kid, he could control her. And he would control her all the way to the bank. During the past year, he had set up an offshore bank account under a non-profit extension of All's Quiet. He could easily get her money, and she would get a write-off. It was a win-win as far as he was concerned. But, today, it was imperative that he get rid of Grant. His plan would only work if Jaclyn acted alone, too afraid to not do what he asked of her. Once Grant left, he would make sure Jaclyn was ready to listen and then send her on her way. And, soon enough, Damien would be on his way back to Canada with a steady stream of money coming in. He was confident that Jaclyn would behave because he had yet to let her know that her girls' well being was at stake. He had already proven that just in the past few days. Frightening her oldest girl had been embarrassingly easy. And the younger ones would be a piece of cake, too. Those girls were his insurance that his plan of manipulating Jaclyn would work, and he could get back to living the life he knew he deserved. Damien reloaded the nail gun and started on a new section of soundproofing. The work was easy; he had always enjoyed working with his hands. It was mindless, allowing him time to plan his future.

Jaclyn flipped back over onto her stomach and rested her head on the cement. Her breathing was labored from working the tape against the wall. Every part of her body ached. She stretched out her fingers trying to get some circulation back and to ease the tingling, but they still felt heavy and numb. Every so often, the compressor would stop, even though she could still hear the ping of the nail gun, and she would listen for any sign that Grant was here. She had to get free to warn him that Damien had the gun. Whenever the compressor kicked on, she continued working on the tape over her mouth.

Then, there it was. She laid completely still listening. She heard Damien's voice, loud and commanding, but Grant's sounded far away and quiet. Was he scared? She couldn't make out anything that they were saying, so she rolled closer to the small door so she could hear better. Now, she could make out some words. She held her breath so she could listen more closely. She heard enough to know Grant didn't trust Damien. It was more the tone than the words.

"Okay, well, be careful so you don't hurt yourself with it." Damien laughed sarcastically.

Grant gripped the ax even tighter and, after searching the whole theater from where he stood, looked Grant directly in the eyes. "Where is Jaclyn?"

Damien laughed again. "Who? You hire girls, too?"

"My wife, Evin. Where is she?"

Damien set the nail gun down on the floor and stepped back towards the bar. "That sounds like a personal problem to me, Grant. Why would I know where your wife is?"

"Because her car is stuck in the driveway, down near the highway, and she isn't in it." Grant's jaws flexed with his anger.

"Hhhm? That's weird. She didn't come here looking for help. Maybe you should check the other houses nearby." Damien stared him down. Grant finally looked away.

A surge of adrenalin catapulted Jaclyn back to the wall. This time she got on her knees and found the small piece of rebar with her cheek and aggressively pulled the tape against the metal. She had to let Grant know she was here before he left.

After scanning the room again, Grant raised the ax to eye level and looked at Damien with disgust. "Why did you steal a dead man's identity?"

Damien quickly turned his head towards Grant. "Excuse me? What are you talking about?"

Grant cleared his throat and took a deep breath. "Your name is not Evin Wolfe. Evin Wolfe is dead. Twenty-two years dead. Who are you?"

Damien's cheeks flushed red with anger. "I think you must have me mixed up with someone else. I am most definitely Evin Wolfe. I'm sure there is another poor sucker named the same who is long dead, but I had nothing to do with it."

Grant didn't look away this time.

Damien postured his body threateningly and stared him down. "Grant, what's your problem, man? I thought you stopped by to check the work on the theater, not question my character. Quit freaking out! If you are having marriage proble...."

"Shut up! Just shut up!" Grant's face was bright red and he looked like he could have a stroke any minute. "You are my problem, asshole!" Grant raised the ax above his head. His heart was racing and he could feel himself slowly losing control. He bent forward a bit, without taking his eyes off of Damien, and worked hard to dial back his breathing before he passed out.

Damien jumped back behind the bar and replied with a calm, even voice. "Okay, Grant. You want to talk about your wife, let's do it." He knew he was about to blow his plan of keeping Jaclyn alone and under his control, and that he would have to include Grant in the plan to get his money, but he wasn't worried. Their girls would get him what he wanted. So, he continued. "Okay, Grant, I actually do know your wife. She single-handedly ruined my life and I will make sure that she pays for what she's done."

Grant stared at Damien, confused, but didn't say a word.

Damien smiled as he continued talking, revealing his version of Jaclyn's past. "Yeah, your sweet wife is a whore. Sorry to be the one to break that to you. She manipulated me into believing I was helping her and then she caused me to lose my job. It has taken me over twenty years of struggling, but I'm finally here to get what I have coming to me. The way I have it figured, she owes me at least a hundred thousand dollars, for pain and suffering, of course. I didn't want to involve you. You are definitely a wimp, but you seem like a nice enough guy. I guess you are kind of involved now. You could have listened and left me alone, but it really doesn't bother me a bit. And, actually, the more that I think about it, my plan may even go more smoothly if you are both involved."

Grant couldn't be more confused, and more freaked out. This guy was a psychopath. "What are you talking about? Where is Jaclyn?"

Damien rubbed his hand over his trimmed beard as he continued. "She's someplace safe. At least for now. And I promise that I will keep her safe as long as you are working on getting me my money."

Grant held the ax chest high and tried to unscramble everything Damien was saying. Over twenty years ago? Jaclyn was just a kid then. What was this maniac talking about? Jaclyn had said nothing about a crazy man in her life when she was a child. Did he have her confused with someone else? Was he on drugs and hallucinating?

Damien kept rambling on about his life over the past twenty years, all of it one hardship after another. And, all of it Jaclyn's fault. Not one bit of it made any sense to Grant. But, he kept his mouth shut, listening for any sign of Jaclyn's whereabouts.

Grant finally couldn't take waiting anymore and yelled. "Jaclyn?!" Then he listened, hoping he would hear something telling him which direction to look for her.

With Grant's outburst, Damien came unglued. "Listen, you son of a bitch, you can be quiet or you can join her. I think it is time that you get me the money. Until you do, you won't see Jaclyn. Are you ready to listen to your instructions?"

Grant kept straining to hear Jaclyn, but he heard nothing. He had to buy more time. He knew she was here somewhere in the house and he didn't want to leave without her. "Listen, you will have to help me figure out how to get you something I don't have. It is impossible for me to give you that kind of money."

Damien swore under his breath. "Oh, you have it all right. I've checked. All you need to do is take a loan out on the shares in your company stock."

This guy was nuts, but Grant knew that he needed to keep him talking. He needed to figure out where he had locked up Jaclyn. "But, they aren't all my shares. It's an employee-owned business. I just can't take other people's money."

Damien laughed at Grant's stupidity. "Sure you can. It's your company. Don't be some kind of saint, Grant."

"I'm not trying to be a saint, I just want to maintain my integrity." Grant took several side steps to the left side of the theater, hoping to hear something.

Damien watched him, unconcerned that he was moving around. He knew he was nowhere near his wife. "You think integrity is an asset, Grant?" Damien couldn't help but laugh.

"Actually, I built my business and my marriage on it. But, clearly, we don't see eye to eye on its importance."

Damien spit on the floor next to him. "That's an understatement. So, Grant, let me just be clear here. We will do things my way here, not yours. Do you want to see your wife again? And, how about your daughters? Your oldest, Mandy is it? She's a keeper. So beautiful and kind. We had a nice talk the other day at her school. She reminds me so...."

Grant's full attention fell on Damien again. "You sick bastard! Stay away from our girls!"

"Too late." Damien leaned on the bar and smiled at Grant. "You can't stop me, so you might as well join me. You want peace back in your life, just do what I ask you to do. It's simple."

Grant took several steps toward Damien then stopped when he saw the gun sitting on the bar by his hand. It was Grant's gun. Jaclyn was here. Somewhere. Was she hurt? His heart pounded in his chest and he started hyperventilating. He felt faint. He took a small step back and glared at Damien. Where were the police? He felt for his phone in the pocket of his coat, but it wasn't there. It must have fallen out in the snow.

"So, what do you think, Grant? Do we have a deal? Electronically this shouldn't take too long to complete." Damien stared at Grant, happy to see the sweat on Grant's forehead and the shaking in his hand. He had learned early in life what to look for in others to make sure they would stay submissive. He had also learned that he couldn't show any of those signs or he would give up his power. He came around the front of the bar, this time with the gun in his hand. As he waited for Grant's answer he leaned back on the bar and folded his arms.

"I don't have account numbers like that memorized." Grant kept trying to stall. "But, if I could call my accountant and explain that I wanted to move some money, she could help."

Damien looked at Grant for a long time trying to measure his sincerity. Unconvinced, he unfolded his arms and started playing with the gun. "Grant, come on, we don't need to involve anyone else in this transaction. I will keep Jaclyn with me while you go figure out your accounts. If you tell anyone or call the police, she dies. Go ahead, test me."

Sweat ran down Grant's face. He locked eyes with Damien and didn't look away. "First, I want to see that Jaclyn is okay. I want to talk to her before I go get you what you want."

"Grant, buddy, listen, I'm the one who calls the shots here, not you. Jaclyn is safe. But, only for now. If you don't get moving, you will need to look for a new wife."

Grant wrestled with what should be his next move. This guy was a mad man. Where were the police? He listened for both distant sirens and evidence of Jaclyn but heard neither.

"Seriously, if I could just see that she's okay, I will go get your money. I won't talk to her and I won't tell anyone. Please. I need to just see that she's alive." Grant hated that he was playing into this sociopath's narcissism, but he needed to see Jaclyn. He needed to know that he still had time to save her.

Damien laughed at Grant's pathetic plea. "I always knew Jaclyn would marry a wimp." He continued to laugh as he started waving the revolver around. "I will say it one more time, Grant; you may not see Jaclyn. Did you hear me? You may not see her!" He raised his voice, so he was sure that Jaclyn could hear every word. "She is safe. You will just have to trust me on that one. Once the money is in my account, she is all yours. I don't want the bitch. She's too much maintenance for me. So, leave. Now!"

Grant quickly stepped back as Damien raised the gun in his direction. "Okay, okay, relax, man. I will trust you. But, I need your account number first so I can transfer the money." He hated that his voice was shaking as much as his hands.

Damien's face turned bright red with frustration. "No, Grant, you listen to me! Go get your information and bring it back here. We will transfer it together, my laptop is in my truck. Now, hurry! And while you are at it, call Angela and let her know you and Jaclyn are okay, but snowed in for the night. She is with your kids. If you call the cops, Jaclyn dies. Period. I've disappeared before and I can definitely disappear again. They won't catch me. You will live the rest of your life suffering because of your stupidity. Now leave!"

What the hell? How does this maniac know Angela? Chills ran up his spine causing his whole body to shudder.

In the crawl space, Jaclyn worked feverishly trying to tear the tape from her mouth. Her stomach turned as she listened to Damien and Grant's conversation. Grant needed to leave. She wouldn't make it if he didn't get them help. But, she also needed him to know where she was. Blood poured from her face as she aggressively ripped the tape against the bar. Her knees ached, and she had no feeling in her hands and feet. Finally, with several panicked thrusts against the rough metal, the tape finally let go of the left side of her mouth. She continued to pull it back as she pushed at the gag with her tongue.

Grant saw no other choice but to go get what this creep wanted. He hated it, but at least it would buy him some time to think of a plan to get Jaclyn out alive. "Okay, okay. I will leave and get you what you want. But, listen to me. I will be back. And, once I give you my account numbers, I want Jaclyn. And do not lay a hand on her while I'm gone."

Damien shook his head back and forth. "That was always the deal, Grant. And, you listen to me. Watch your tone or you will get nothing in return for the account numbers. I'm the one calling the shots, not you. Don't forget that. Now, get the hell out of here!"

Jaclyn panicked that Grant was actually leaving and gouged her mouth on the rebar, finally ripping the whole gag out of her mouth. She screamed with every ounce of energy she had left. "Grant! Grant! I'm in here! Grant! Run! Get help!"

• CHAPTER 19 •

By the time the movie was half over, Mandy was the only one still awake. She had crawled up on the couch and was sitting next to Angela, her head tucked in the crook of Angela's arm.

"I'm scared." As Mandy whispered her confession, she hunkered down, pushing into Angela's side. Angela wrapped her blanket tightly around both of them and squeezed her with both of her arms.

"You are completely safe right here, sweet girl." Angela closed her eyes and pleaded with God for help to sound convincing. "Your mom and dad are also doing okay and they will be here when the storm lets up and the roads are clear again. Until then, we will just sit here together and stay warm by the fire."

Mandy burst into tears. "But, mommy isn't safe. She isn't safe! And it's my fault!"

Angela pulled Mandy even closer trying to quiet her down. "Shh, Mandy, don't wake up your sisters. What do you mean your mommy isn't safe? She is with your daddy and my good friend, Jason. They just can't drive in the stor...."

"Mommy isn't safe because that man in the scary black truck told me so." Mandy buried her head deeper into the blanket and Angela's side and started sobbing uncontrollably.

Angela's heart sped up. "What man, Mandy? And, where did you see this man? What exactly did he say to you?" She regretted asking so many questions but was blown away by Mandy's confession.

Mandy couldn't speak. Angela tried to wait patiently for an answer, but she needed to know what Mandy knew. She tried again. "Mandy, it's okay. You can tell me anything."

Mandy kept crying, then started choking on her tears. All Angela could do was hold her tightly and hope the other girls would keep sleeping.

"Shh, it's okay, Mandy, it's okay. You are safe and your mommy is safe. Shh." She hated promising anything, but she needed Mandy to talk. She needed to know what Mandy knew.

"She isn't safe!" Now, Mandy was mad because she didn't think Angela was listening to her. "She isn't safe. She isn't safe. And it's my fault." She put her head back down and wailed into the blanket.

Anya moaned and rolled over to face the other direction, but fell back to sleep. Angela grabbed the remote and turned the movie up a couple of notches, hoping the background noise would keep them all asleep. There was no sense in trying to get Mandy to talk until she could get her to calm down, so Angela leaned back and started rubbing Mandy's back. After a good ten minutes, Angela began to feel Mandy's body relaxing a little. Then her sobs became soft moans. Finally, Mandy lifted her head and looked at Angela.

"At school on Monday. This man, he scared me. He told me that my mommy needed to give him what he wants or she will die."

Angela stopped breathing. "What?! Did you tell your mom?" She regretted the words the second they came out of her mouth. This is why Mandy was so upset. Of course, she didn't tell her mom.

"No, I was too afraid. I just told her that he scared me." Mandy tried to bury her head in the blanket again, but Angela gently caught her by the shoulders, held her so they faced each other, and looked into her eyes.

"Did you know this man, honey? What did he look like?" She worked hard to keep her voice gentle and reassuring.

Mandy hesitated, but Angela rubbed her shoulders and looked with compassion into her eyes. "No, I didn't know him." Angela pulled her close and whispered to Mandy that she had been very brave.

Mandy interrupted. "But, he knew me."

Angela needed to look into Mandy's eyes again. What did she mean? She pushed her back again so they could look at one another.

Mandy looked away but continued. "He knew my name and said he knew my mom. He had a black jacket with his hood on, and he drove a huge black scary truck. He kind of had a beard and very scary eyes."

"Oh, honey, I'm so sorry he scared you. Did he give you his name?"

"No, But, he said he knew you, too."

Angela froze. Her heart pounded in her chest and she willed herself to speak calmly. "He did? What did he say about me?"

Mandy was feeling more comfortable talking about what happened and began to share freely. "He said you were a good friend and that you knew he was watching us. He said I couldn't tell anyone what he told me or mommy would die."

Angela kept seeking answers. "What did he tell you that he didn't want you to share with anyone?"

"I can't tell you! I can't tell anyone! I don't want mommy to die!" Mandy folded her arms and quit talking.

Angela couldn't help but think of Jason. He drove a big black truck and had promised to keep an eye on the girls and Jaclyn. It had to just be a bizarre coincidence.

Suddenly, Mandy pressed hard into Angela's chest and started weeping. "I shouldn't have told you anything, but I'm so scared. I don't want mommy to die. Now, mommy will die! And it's my fault!"

Angela's mind reeled with a million thoughts. She held Mandy tightly, at a loss for words. Why would Jason do such a thing? Was it even Jason? She held Mandy even more tightly and started to rock her back and forth, trying to calm herself down as well.

When Angela finally found her voice she asked Mandy one more time if there was anything else the man had said.

"Yes, but I don't want mommy to die." Mandy sounded so defeated.

"Okay, maybe I can guess. And if I guess right, you could just nod your head. If I'm wrong, then you can shake your head no. That way you aren't telling me and mommy will be safe. What do you think?"

Mandy looked skeptical but finally nodded her head.

"Okay, let's see. Did he tell you what he wanted from your mommy?"

Mandy sat completely still, staring at Angela. But, then slowly she began to nod her head just enough so Angela could notice.

"Good job, Mandy. You are doing great. Okay, did this man say he wanted some information that maybe she had from her job?"

Mandy shook her head no right away.

"Good! Did he say he wanted her to write something for him? Or cover some sort of story?"

Another no.

Angela was wracking her brain trying to figure out what someone could want from Jaclyn. "Did this man say he wanted money from your mom?"

Mandy's eyes widened, and she looked scared. She didn't move her head.

"It's okay, Mandy. Remember, you aren't telling me. You are just nodding your head yes or shaking it no. It's okay."

Mandy didn't blink as she nodded her head almost imperceptibly.

Money? This creep wanted money? For what? Angela was so confused. "Thank you, Mandy. Good job! Did he tell you how much money he wanted?"

She shook her head.

"You've done a wonderful job, honey. And you don't need to be afraid. You didn't tell me anything. Was that all he told you?"

Several tears trickled down Mandy's cheeks as she shook her head back and forth, keeping her eyes on Angela's.

"Should I keep guessing?" Angela hated to even ask. But Mandy nodded quickly. "Well, what goes with money? A car?"

No.

"Food?"

No.

"Jewelry?"

Mandy shook her head more and more aggressively each time Angela was wrong.

Finally, Mandy blurted it out. "He will take me! He wants me!"

Mandy buried her head again and started convulsing with heartbreaking sobs. Angela held her as tightly as possible. "Shh, Mandy, you are okay. Help me understand what you mean. He wants you to go with him?"

Mandy figured she had already blown it and through more tears, she finally shared what had been tormenting her for days. "He said if mommy didn't give him money, he would come and take me instead.

But, he said I couldn't tell anyone his plan or mommy would die. He said he would tell mommy what to do, and if she did it right, then he wouldn't need me."

Mandy collapsed against Angela and wept. She was spent. That was all there was, and it was terrifying. Angela was speechless. Angela was reeling with this news. She rubbed Mandy's back for a while without speaking. Then she again whispered to her that it would be okay. Her gut told her that was a lie, but she didn't know what else to say. This was bigger than any of them had thought.

Eventually, the weight of Mandy's confession crushed her spirit, and she began to get angry, too, yelling at Angela with her face buried deep in the blanket. "Where is mommy then? If everything was okay, then she would be here. Quit telling me that it's okay!" Mandy cried even harder. Her small body shook and her tears wet the blanket they both shared.

While Angela did her best to comfort Mandy, her heart pounded as she thought back on her dates with Jason. Jason fit Mandy's description. His dark neatly trimmed beard and piercing eyes had captivated her. But, she had also had to look away when he looked at her too long. It had felt like he was looking into her soul. She remembered blushing as he held her in his gaze. She had answered all his questions, even about Jaclyn and her family. Looking back she remembered almost being afraid not to answer him. His presence was sexy and alluring, yet almost commanding. Demanding. She had drunk too much and became too free, too loose, exposing herself and her friends to a man she hardly knew. Memories of their drive around town, first to Jaclyn and Grant's home and then the girls' school chilled her. Why had she trusted this man? She didn't even know his last name? Profiles on this website didn't show last names, and she didn't care to even ask him. How could she have been so stupid? If she called the local police station, would they be able to tell her if a Jason worked there? Her chest hurt as she tried to take some deep breaths. She needed to be strong for Mandy. And for Jaclyn. She had put this whole family in danger.

"Mandy, everything will be okay. You did the right thing by telling me. I will help your mommy. Did this man say anything else to you that would help us find him?"

Mandy buried her head even deeper into Angela's side. "No! I can't say anymore. Mommy is going to die!"

"Shh!" Angela held her closer to muffle her screams.

But, the other girls finally woke from their sleep anyway and stared at Mandy.

"I want mommy," Anya said sleepily.

"I know baby. Come on up here. It will be okay." Anya climbed up on the couch and snuggled into Angela's other side.

"No, it's not!" Mandy blurted out through tears and snot. "Mommy is going to die, and it's all my fault!"

Like the crescendo of a symphony, all four girls started crying at once and there was now no calming them down. Angela panicked as she frantically tried to calm everyone down. But, she was a mess, too, and they instinctively knew it. Finally, when her attempts to comfort the girls failed, Angela stood up and demanded silence. "Listen! Girls! Listen!"

The girls stopped crying, but they all looked scared.

"I will do what I can to help your mommy. And your daddy is with her helping her, too. They will come home. Maybe not tonight, but definitely tomorrow." Even as she said these words with exaggerated confidence, she knew she could be wrong. What if they never came home? How would she ever face the girls again? What if her stupidity is what ends up killing her best friend? She had to pull herself together. There were no definite answers. But, there was still hope. There had to still be hope. She needed to get a grip and at least be strong for the girls. For now. She could fall apart later. She couldn't even imagine the fear they were feeling. She found the remote and turned on the girls' favorite playlist of Disney princess music. The girls all looked up at her with wide eyes. Mandy looked most skeptical.

"Okay, this is what we will do." Angela enthusiastically laid out a simple plan for the girls where each one had a role to play in preparing for their mom and dad to come home. It may be in vain, but that didn't matter right now. What mattered most is that the girls stopped panicking. Even though it was almost nine-thirty at night, Angela turned on as many lights as possible. And, with a big smile, she told the girls that when her parents got home, they needed to be surprised with a big celebration.

"Tomorrow is Thanksgiving and we will celebrate being thankful that everyone is back together again. We will have the biggest party in the world's history!"

The girls all smiled at Angela's crazy hand gestures and animated voice. They wiped their tears and slowly moved toward all the craft supplies Angela was digging out of the hall cupboard. Before long, the three younger girls joined in the excitement and began to sing and dance along with the music. Angela's heart warmed at their innocence and resiliency. She longed for the same simple childlike faith. She felt like she was going to puke.

"Can I be the director for the party?" Mandy had quietly approached Angela, seeking courage with her eyes, not yet as excited as her sisters.

"Of course, you can! That is a great idea!" Angela smiled. "How about if everyone gives you their ideas and then you assign the tasks?"

Mandy gave Angela a big hug and then ran off towards her sisters, shouting orders.

Angela had to laugh at Mandy's first-born traits, for she was an only child and shared the same desire to be in control. Mandy finally smiled for the first time since Angela had picked her up. She ran to find her drawing pad in her room and returned announcing her plan of dividing the tasks among her younger siblings. She would review all the work before hanging it up. After only a few minutes, Mandy was singing along with her sisters and planning the celebration by faith.

Faith again. There it was. So simple, yet so powerful. Angela was still dumbfounded that she had blindly believed in faith almost her entire life, but couldn't really define it until now. But, this was it. This is what faith looked like and sounded like. Faith is what dries a traumatized girl's tears and turn her heart towards joy. Faith is every light on in the house and bright colors being turned into a celebration for what they could not yet see. What they could not yet guarantee would even come to pass. Faith is the music that filled the home with the telling of ancient stories: of damsels in distress, powerful giants, and evil queens, and the miracles that brought the dead back to life, the monster back to a prince, and the captive back to a free spirit. Angela's spirit also lifted, and she felt stronger than she had felt all day. But, not because they received good news. They still didn't know what was going on in Spindrift. But, in this place, right this minute, there was hope. Colorful, bright, musical hope. And it refreshed Angela's soul.

When the girls were in full party-planning mode, drawing pictures and making paper chains to hang around the living room, Angela quickly retreated to the laundry room. She held her phone in her hand, hesitant to call the police again, but knew she had new information that might help her friends. She looked up the local station number, instead of calling 911, and hit send. After the first ring, she hung up. She fell to her knees and failed to stop the flow of tears. For several minutes she choked back sobs and cried silently, not wanting to worry the girls any more than they already were. Finally, when she was able to gain control, she bowed her head and prayed. Her gut knew Jaclyn and Grant were in trouble and she was at fault. At least partially at fault. How quickly the beauty of faith had turned back to fear in the dark of the laundry room. She needed to trust, even in the dark.

"God, please protect my dear friends. Protect them from harm and return them to their girls. Stop this maniac in his tracks and restore order. I am so very weak and vulnerable and make stupid mistakes, but you restore and make whole again. You take whatever was intended for evil and use it for your good. Please, God, have mercy on us all. Amen." As Angela whispered her prayer, her breathing slowed, her crying subsided, and she felt renewed strength to do what she could to help bring this family back together again. She hit redial and waited.

"Cliff Creek Police Department, this is Janice, what can I do for you?"

"Hi, my name is Angela Brixton and I believe I have some information that could help the officers who are responding to a call about my friends being in danger."

Angela shared everything she knew about the interaction Mandy had had with the man at the school. When Angela was done, Janice repeated back everything she had said, making sure she had the correct information. Then Janice asked several more questions, but most Angela couldn't answer. No one had written down the license plate or even knew what state this man was from. Unless it was Jason. He had Canadian plates, but she still wanted to believe that it wasn't him. She desperately wanted to believe that. She only had a child's description of a man. But, she was becoming more and more convinced that it was the man she had just kissed last night.

Angela didn't want to admit it could be Jason, but she was tired of being the one who kept making mistakes. He would have to forgive her later if it ended up not being him and the police give him a hard time. She was sure they could laugh it off. "Janice, before I hang up, I may have one more detail. But, I'm not really sure."

"Please share everything you have, Ma'am. It's better to have too much information than not enough."

Angela hesitated, then closed her eyes and confessed. "First, I believe this guy is extremely dangerous. And second, it may be a coincidence, but Mandy's description fits a man I recently met online."

Angela explained that Jason had been very kind and attentive, but seemed very interested in her friend Jaclyn. She admitted to showing him where Jaclyn and Grant lived and where the girls attended school.

"I hope it is just a coincidence, but the similarities are frightening."

"It is always best to rule people out if we can. What is the name of this man you met?"

She was embarrassed that she only knew his first name, but she shared it, and that he had said that he was an undercover police officer in Cliff Creek.

"Well, that will be easy enough to check out. Jason, right?"

"Yes. Jason." Angela fought back tears of regret.

"Thank you, Ma'am. I will relay this information to the officers responding to the Spindrift residence, and to the undercover department. We should be able to have some answers soon."

"Thank you so much for your help. Will anyone call me with information when they have it?" Angela started to choke on her tears. "I am here with my friends' children. And, we are all concerned."

"Of course, Ma'am. I will ask an officer to call you when it is safe to do so."

Angela ended the call and started shaking. She again stood for a minute in the laundry room, her sanctuary in the storm, and focused on calming herself down. Her faith felt so weak. She was filled with so many doubts. Regret overwhelmed her. She had acted superior because of her faith, telling Jaclyn that it was easy believing in God. Today had been the most difficult day of her spiritual life. Today, the rubber hit the road, and she wasn't at all prepared. But, she was learning, and she was growing. She just had to keep believing that this was all going to turn out okay. And, if it didn't, then that would be the road they would all have to walk together. This world is a rough place to practice faith. She now saw with a new perspective, that it eats people up and spits them out and prayers don't change things instantly. And sometimes prayer doesn't seem to change things at all. But, if she truly believes all she had learned about God since she was a child, then she needed to continue to believe that God was working, even when what was happening around her didn't support it. After blowing her nose and psyching herself up to party-mode again, she returned to the kitchen where the girls had spread construction paper, markers, glue, and tape across every surface. Their work was soothing. Planning for a party. Such a beautiful, innocent act of faith.

She asked what she could do and Mandy put her to work right away. She wrote down loving phrases for the girls to copy and write on posters to put around the room. Then she cut strips out of construction paper and the girls glued them into a long colorful chain. Mandy and Angela hung up the artwork together, Angela handling everything that was too high for Mandy. The work helped pass the time, but Angela's fear involuntarily kept mounting with each passing minute. Why hadn't anyone called her yet?

• CHAPTER 20 •

"Grant! Grant! Run! Get help!" Jaclyn screamed as loud as she could, her voice was hoarse from the cold and the exertion of trying to get herself free in the damp crawl space.

Grant quickly scanned the room, trying to locate where Jaclyn's voice was coming from. Adrenalin pounded in his ears, making it difficult to home in on her exact location. But, he couldn't have been more relieved to hear her voice. She was alive. Damien, however, rolled his eyes at Jaclyn's outburst. Then he stared at Grant, posturing his body defensively, ready for a fight if needed. Grant noticed. They locked eyes, neither one wanting to look away first. Jaclyn was struggling to keep yelling. And Grant could tell she was crying. Somehow, he needed to reassure her that everything was going to be okay.

Grant looked directly at Damien but spoke directly to Jaclyn. "I'm here, Jack! I'm here! Keep talking so I can find you! I need to hear your voice."

Damien's steely gaze caused Grant to look away in fear. Instead, he looked toward Jaclyn's voice, but there was only a wall and a bar next to Damien. And, he knew that she couldn't be behind the bar by this maniac, her voice sounded too muffled and distant. She was in something or behind something. He just had to figure out what. There weren't too many places for her to hide in the basement. He had already searched the other rooms, closets, and bathrooms. Where could she be?

Damien came out from behind the bar and took a step closer to Grant, raising the gun and aiming it at Grant's head. Then he addressed Jaclyn, all the while glaring at Grant. "Shut up, Jaclyn! You are a stupid, stupid woman. You have grown into such an opinionated bitch. I miss the days when you did anything I asked you to do. If you are smart and care about this pathetic husband of yours, you will shut up!"

Grant's forehead creased with confusion. What the hell was this psychopath talking about?

Damien laughed, even though Jaclyn kept up her litany of pleas for help. "What's the matter, Grant? You don't enjoy hearing that you aren't the only man Jaclyn's been with?" Damien bent over with laughter, struggling to keep talking.

Grant's mind was reeling. What was going on? He didn't say a word, just kept searching for his wife. He knew better than to believe this crazed monster. This guy was sick, maybe even strung out on drugs. He needed to be careful and smart or they wouldn't get out of this alive.

Damien didn't like Grant's silence. He wanted a fight. "Grant, you need to shut up, too. Don't be a fool, man. We have a deal that makes sure everyone walks out of this alive. Don't listen to her. She's crazy. And, as you can tell, she's definitely alive. I don't know how you do it with her honestly. She is so annoying! Listen to her. She makes no sense. And all she does is...."

Grant finally spoke up, interrupting Damien's rant about Jaclyn. "Step aside and let me see Jaclyn. Right now!" He saw the displeasure in Damien's eyes and tried his hardest to soften his approach for Jaclyn's sake. "I promise I will get you your money. All I want to do is see her.

That will be the motivation I need to do exactly what you are asking me to do." Grant definitely spoke with more courage than he felt. His hands were shaking and sweat dripped down the sides of his face.

Damien shook his head in disbelief and let out a sarcastic chuckle. "I'm not a fool, Grant. Once you have what you want, I get nothing. She's alive. You've heard her. And, unfortunately, you keep hearing her." He turned his attention to Jaclyn, but without taking his eyes off of Grant. "Shut up, Jaclyn! You are not helping your husband. He will die if you don't shut up! Enough!"

But, Jaclyn refused to stop yelling, her protests muffled and distant. Damien shook his head, then rubbed his face with his free hand. He again focused on Grant. "Now, Grant, all you wanted to know was that she is alive. Done. She's alive and as crazy as ever. Now, be a smart husband and go get your account numbers. When you get back and we finalize the transaction, you can have the bitch. I have had it with listening to her. I will not do this much longer. I'm liking the idea of her being dead more and more every time she screams."

Grant didn't answer, and he didn't move. Instead, he looked away from the gun and continued to search for Jaclyn, his eyes finally landing on the small door behind the bar, leading to the crawl space. That had to be it. She was in the crawl space that Damien had asked about last week when Grant had shown him the theater. He looked Damien directly in the eyes and raised the ax.

"Open that crawl space door so I can talk to my wife before I go." Grant motioned towards the door with the ax.

"Talk to her through the door, you idiot. She can hear you." Damien didn't move a muscle and his formidable frame stood between Grant and the door.

Grant didn't let up. He wouldn't let up. He couldn't leave Jaclyn here with this lunatic. "I can't hear her. Open the door!"

Damien was running out of patience. "Listen, choir boy, you're not the one in charge here. In fact, you shouldn't be talking at all. You should walk out that door. The sooner you get me what I want, the sooner you can go home to your girls."

Grant stood his ground. He looked Damien straight in the eyes. All he could see was pure evil. He failed to hold back a shudder, his whole body shaking like a leaf.

Damien had always loved any evidence of fear in someone he was trying to dominate. "What's the matter, Grant? Scared?" Damien let out a belly laugh. "Grant, you're killing me, man!"

Grant didn't trust his voice. Instead, he risked taking a step forward, the ax in a position to hurt Damien.

Damien stopped laughing and looked Grant up and down. "That was a foolish move. Come on, Grant, I have nothing to lose. You do. My life ended when your wife went back on her word. I've been to hell and back since then. Everything in my life has sucked. I am not afraid to die, Grant. Are you?"

This time Grant refused to look at Damien, choosing instead to focus on the gun. He didn't answer.

"Okay, you have thirty seconds of grace, hotshot. Then I'm done with you. Jaclyn can get me what I want, especially if her girls' lives are at stake. Ready? Go!"

Jaclyn screamed for Grant to run. "Go, Grant! Go! Get help! I'm okay!"

Grant's eyes darted back and forth between the gun and the door. His stomach turned and his heart hurt. His hand holding the ax began to shake, and he adjusted it so he could hold it with both hands.

"Ten, nine, eight, seven...." Damien smiled as he counted down the remaining seconds.

"Get out of my way, you psychopath!" Grant charged toward Damien determined to reach the small door.

A shot rang out and Grant slumped to the floor only a few feet from Damien.

Jaclyn screamed and cursed. "No! What have you done? Let me out of here! Now!"

First, Damien made sure that Grant was not moving then he flew at the small door feet first, kicking it inward. He was out of control. His eyes were wild and an otherworldly growl escaped his lips. The wood of the small door splintered, showering Jaclyn who had rolled closer to the door so she could hear better.

"Shut up! Now! Or your girls are next!" Damien crawled halfway through the opening and glared at her with a demonic rage in his eyes.

She had rolled away from him as quickly as she could, then looked up. She saw, not a man, but an animal. A beast, dark and demonic. His eyes sat in the shadows of his face, illuminated by the room's light behind him, but they still attempted to penetrate her soul, to paralyze her will and render her powerless. But, the thought of submitting once again to this monster was repulsive. She felt nauseous at the thought. Then, out of the blue, an eerie calm came over her and she glared back. She looked directly into the dark cavern where his eyes hid and spoke evenly.

"No, Damien. I will not shut up. Not this time. Never. I'm done with being quiet. I'm done cowering from you. You are the one who needs to shut up. You are sick. You are a pervert. You need to be locked up. You robbed me of my innocence and threatened me until I was only a shell of a human being. My soul died when I was just ten years old.

It retreated so far within me I grew up believing I was unworthy of love. You killed my innocence and robbed me of all hope. But, I will no longer be quiet about it. I want to live. I want to heal. I want to learn how to love and be loved. And you will not stop me!"

Grant pushed his forehead into the floor and grimaced against the pain. He focused on catching his breath and trying to feel where the bullet hit him. He pleaded with God that it hadn't been a fatal shot. It hurt, but he had no problem breathing, and his heart was pounding rapidly against his rib cage, clearly working as it should be. When he felt more in control, he slowly lifted his head and saw a pool of blood forming under him. Then he felt pain that appeared to be coming from everywhere. He started to panic, but quickly laid his head back down and slowed his breathing. He knew that shock could be deadly. And so could losing too much blood. He needed to remain calm. With his head on the cool floor, he concentrated on Jaclyn yelling at the lunatic who shot him. He strained to hear her words, but his ears were still ringing from the gunshot. He had to figure out how badly he was hurt and if it was possible to help Jaclyn. The longer he laid there, the more he could feel the pain localized on the right side of his body. But, his legs seemed good. As his hearing gradually came back, he began to hear Jaclyn more clearly as she talked to this madman. He quieted his breathing as much as possible and then listened. She appeared calm. Weirdly calm. And in control.

Damien laughed then turned the gun on Jaclyn.

"Wow! This is what I get for everything I did for you when you were lonely and lost, not knowing how to grow up in this big, bad world? You were a pathetic child, Jaclyn. Afraid of your own shadow, with no hope of ever getting a man to be with you. Without my coaching, you wouldn't be where you are at today, and you know it. Although I do not understand why you settled for that wimp you married. He is worthless. I'm disappointed that you didn't find a real man like me. You had such potential, Jaclyn. You did. But, you just couldn't keep what we had to ourselves. You blew it. And now the day has come to pay for that mistake. I think some people call that karma. Now, shut up or you will be the next one bleeding out."

But, undeterred, Jaclyn continued to speak to Damien with increasing confidence.

"No, Damien. I will not shut up, ever again. And, our girls will not grow up like I did, abused and afraid. They are strong and smart and loved. I am, too, but it wasn't until now that I could see it. I see that my fears were unfounded. You are a coward, Damien. That's why you preyed on children. You don't deserve our money. You owe me! You owe me for robbing me of joy, for the distance I put between myself and my brother and dad so that they wouldn't get hurt, for the fear that damaged my marriage and kept me awake at night. Even when I thought you were dead, you haunted me. But, you will haunt me no more! Live or die, I will be free of the bondage of fear that you have used to keep me under your control."

This time, Grant could hear most of what Jaclyn was yelling and couldn't help the tears as he heard her anguish. He had had no idea what she had endured as a child. Why had she never confided in him? The fear she had felt all these years was eating her alive, and he hadn't even noticed. He had taken her attitude and crazy behaviors personally. He had been an idiot. But, that needed to stop right now. He needed to do whatever he could to rescue her. No matter what. He mustered as much energy as possible and yelled to her, "I'm okay, Jack! Help is coming! I love you!"

Jaclyn's words and Grant's response enraged Damien, and he screamed at both of them. "Enough! You are both going to die tonight if you don't shut up!" He didn't seem too worried about Grant and stayed laying half in and half out of the crawl space, facing Jaclyn. "Listen, lady, if you as much as utter one more word, I will have to get the money out of your daughters as they grow up because you and your gallant husband will be dead. I'm sure you both have pretty good life insurance policies that will take care of them after you die. So, what's it going to be, you or them who gets me what I deserve? It doesn't matter to me?"

Jaclyn kept moving her ankles, trying to break through the duct tape that bound them. She had weakened their grip by rubbing it against the rebar and she could feel that the tape had weakened. Finally, in the dark of crawl space, while Damien kept rambling about what people owed him, the tape gave way and her feet were free. But, she kept the release to herself for the moment.

"Now that I think about it, that's not a bad idea. I would rather wait and get to know them as they grow up." Damien was enjoying getting Jaclyn all riled up while he waited for Grant to bleed to death.

Jaclyn's voice remained even and calm. "You will not get within a mile of our daughters ever again. Your abuse stops today. In a matter of minutes, the police will take you to your new home. You are the one who will pay today, not me and my family. It's over, Damien. It's over."

Damien didn't believe that anyone was on their way, at least not for several more hours. "You and your husband are such fools. You think you can save yourselves. Neither one of you has a phone. How's that working for you? Fools! So, if you are done wasting your breath, I would like to talk about what happens now."

Jaclyn was curious about what he had in mind, especially since Grant was wounded and she couldn't go anywhere without people wondering what had happened to her face. His plan was ruined.

"Good. Finally, you are making a smart choice. Okay, well, you and your worthless husband are now unpresentable in public so we need to go about this a different way. No worries. I will still get what I want. But, I will need to not be here when someone eventually comes looking for you. They will piece it together that you hit your head when your car got stuck and then Grant surprised you and you accidentally shot him. End of story. All the evidence will line up. It's your gun, registered to you, not me. You fools set this up. It backfired on you. You two will suffer, not me."

Jaclyn couldn't help but let out a laugh. "Now you are the foolish one. No one will believe that story. You will be a suspect, especially if we let them know you were here. Your DNA is everywhere!"

"Of course it is!" Damien was furious at Jaclyn. "I have been working here for several days. As far as fingerprints, I have my work gloves on. You do think I'm stupid, don't you? Well, I'm not. It's time you respect me. Your very lives depend on it."

Jaclyn wasn't deterred. "We have our side of the story to tell, too. And, we will tell everything, just like it happened. You are not getting out of this, Damien. Not this time. Your glory days are over. The day has come for you to pay!"

Damien's pulse quickened. "How dare you speak to me like that! You will not be telling your side of the story. You will tell the story I tell you to tell. And if you choose to be foolish enough to alter that story even one little bit, I will grab your daughter Mandy and we will both disappear before you are even finished talking to the cops. I did it once, and I can do it again. They won't find me. I have a Plan B, Jaclyn. Do you?"

Jaclyn's heart sped up. This maniac was sick enough to do exactly what he said. She had to get her hands free, and she needed to get that gun. And why wasn't Grant saying anything? She prayed he wasn't dead. He couldn't be dead. They both needed to make it out of this alive. Their girls needed them.

"Not today, Damien. Not today!!" Jaclyn rolled onto her stomach so she could look Damien in the eyes. "You will have nothing to do with our daughters. There are police on their way and you will rot in jail. I will testify! I am no longer afraid to talk about the nightmare you drew me into as an innocent child. I will make sure that you will never taste freedom again!"

Damien laid down on his stomach and challenged Jaclyn's stare with his steely eyes. He started to laugh. He tried to talk, but couldn't stop laughing.

Jaclyn knew she needed to keep Damien talking until she could get free. She worked her hands behind her back, trying to stretch and tear the tape. She could feel her wrists swelling, making it even more difficult. "You are a psycho! None of this is funny. I hope you can still laugh when you are in jail, you sick bastard!"

"Hey, hey, hey, that's enough missy!" Damien stopped laughing. He was furious. He reached for Jaclyn's feet to drag her out of the crawl space.

Jaclyn wasn't going to give up without a fight. She kicked violently, Damien now aware that she had got her feet free.

"Whoa, bitch, whoa! Settle down. Let's come out of the crawl space and you can say your last goodbyes to your pansy husband."

Jaclyn stopped kicking and thought about the advantages of him helping her out of this dark dungeon. But, she knew it would be too risky. She couldn't let him lay a hand on her. He was stronger and she wouldn't have a chance against him with her hands still bound. When he reached for her feet again, she smashed the fingers on one of his hands. "Leave me alone, you freak! I'm not going anywhere with you. Grant can hear me from here. Grant! We will be okay. Hang in there. Don't leave me. I love you!"

Damien let out a belly laugh, rubbing his face with his hands. "You are unbelievable, Jaclyn. Everything you do has to be done the hard way. So stupid."

While Damien was focused on Jaclyn, Grant gradually pulled his body up off the ground, favoring his right arm and chest. He found the ax and gripped it in his good hand. Then, slowly he inched his way towards the bar until he was within a couple of feet of Damien's legs. Grant rested for a couple of minutes, listening to the verbal battle between Jaclyn and this maniac. Damien, was it? He was evil. Then Jaclyn started to scream for Damien to let go of her. Grant mustered every ounce of energy he had left, raised the ax with his good arm and brought it down right on the back of Damien's leg, the blade slicing deeply into his hamstring.

Damien screamed and rolled toward the opening, grasping his leg with the ax deeply embedded. Grant retreated as quickly as he could so Damien couldn't reach him.

Once free from his grip, Jaclyn was able to roll closer to Damien and kick the gun out of his hand. She moved her body towards the gun which had not gone very far. She attempted to get it close enough to grab with her hands behind her back. But, Damien released his leg, turned, and dragged himself over to Jaclyn. He pinned her to the floor with his whole body. His body shook and sweat poured from his forehead. Grant had hurt him somehow, but Jaclyn couldn't see in the low light. Suddenly, with a surge of determination, Damien raised his head up and grabbed Jaclyn's neck with both of his hands. He started choking her, and she resisted the best that she could. Her hands crushed beneath her by his weight. She attempted to move under his body, but couldn't get enough leverage to push him off. Her muscles burned and she couldn't get a deep breath. She spit in his face and screamed, but soon lost the air necessary to make any sound. Damien's strong hands constricted her airway and she could feel herself losing consciousness. Finally, her body involuntarily relaxed from the lack of oxygen and she whispered, "Grant, I'm sorry. I love you." Then everything went black.

• CHAPTER 21 •

After inspecting the two stranded vehicles near the driveway, the two officers who were called to the scene from Deerborn drove the rest of the way to the house and approached the front door with guns drawn. There was no response to their knocks and announcement of their arrival, so they cautiously entered through the unlocked front door. Once inside, they could easily identify the location of the dispute by the raised voices. But, not knowing if there were any weapons involved, they chose to quietly approach the scene as unnoticed as possible.

Descending the stairs with his gun drawn, the first officer caught sight of Grant lying in a pool of blood and gave the second officer behind him a head's up with a hand signal. Grant wasn't making any sound at the moment, but the officers could clearly hear the argument taking place in the crawl space behind the bar. As the first officer moved closer to the crawl space, he saw the ax embedded in Damien's leg and heard the low throaty moan of a woman in pain. He hurried even closer, held his gun with both hands, and tapped Damien's foot with his boot. "Freeze! Police!"

Damien ignored the officer and kept a firm grip on Jaclyn's neck, enjoying her unconscious state. "Not until I know this bitch is dead!"

With all the commotion, Grant came to and looked in the officer's direction. All he could muster was a raspy whisper. "My wife. Please, help my wife." The second officer had already requested an ambulance and was kneeling by Grant, gun raised in backup for his partner. While continuing to monitor the situation behind the bar, the officer attending Grant located the bullet wound in his right shoulder and began applying pressure to stop the bleeding.

The first officer demanded again that Damien come out of the crawl space with his hands up. But, this time, Damien didn't respond. The officer bent down and straddled Damien, holding the gun to his shoulder. "Release her now!"

Damien laughed and challenged the officer to kill him. "I have nothing to live for now, anyway. All I want to see before I die is this bitch dead! Go ahead, shoot me!"

The second officer had cut Grant's sweatshirt and instructed Grant to keep holding it to his wound with as much pressure as possible. He left Grant's side and approached the crawl space, shining a flashlight so they could both see Jaclyn. She was unconscious and pale. He nodded to the first officer to make a move. In one swift movement, the officer on top of Damien struck him in the head with the butt of his gun then grabbed him in a chokehold. Damien finally released Jaclyn as he passed out. Within seconds, the officer had Damien handcuffed. They pulled him from the crawlspace and the second officer crawled in to attend to Jaclyn. She was breathing very shallow, but she was alive. Together, they eased her out of the crawl space and laid her next to Grant.

Grant began crying. "Is she okay? Is she okay?"

"She's breathing. It's okay, the ambulance is arriving soon." The officer took over applying pressure to Grant's wound and monitoring

Jaclyn's breathing. His partner secured Damien at some distance from Grant and Jaclyn then radioed in that they had three in need of medical attention, one who had been apprehended.

Jaclyn's vision was blurry. She reached for her eyes to rub them, but someone grabbed her arms. She started screaming and thrashing, hitting at anything and everything. The person held on tighter and she fought even harder. The more she fought the clearer her vision became. Where was she? There were bright lights illuminating metal cabinets, equipment, and tubing. She squeezed her eyes shut and fought with all her might. Then someone poked her arm with a needle. She screamed one last time. Almost instantly, her breathing slowed and her body relaxed. She tried again to open her eyes, the lights still bright and painful. Then she heard Grant's voice.

"Jack, it's okay. Shh. It's okay. I'm right here."

Jaclyn groggily turned her head in the direction of Grant's voice and then she saw him. Tears flowed, her eyes releasing all the fear and anxiety she had held in for so long.

"Grant, I am so, so sorry." She struggled to weep, her body too relaxed to handle the intensity of what she was feeling.

"Shh. It's okay, Jack. I love you. We will be okay. It's all over. We are safe."

Jaclyn reached for Grant's hand and he found hers. Her tears slowed and she let herself be taken under by the drugs.

Over the next two hours, Jaclyn's wounds on her face were treated and Grant had a CT scan and was prepped for surgery. After being discharged, Jaclyn walked beside Grant's bed as it moved towards the operating room, her hand clinging to his. Tears streamed down her face as her heart struggled to feel both the joy of coming out of the confrontation with Damien alive and the overwhelming shame of causing the trauma they had endured that day. Despite Grant's injuries and new knowledge of Jaclyn's life, he smiled at Jaclyn as they moved down the bright hallway.

"I love you, Jack." Grant squeezed Jaclyn's hand.

Jaclyn looked away as more tears poured out of her tormented eyes. "Don't, Grant. You don't have to pretend that everything is okay. I know what you are thinking."

Grant continued to smile. "You do, huh? Well, then you know that I will always love you, no matter what. We will walk through this together. Damien is at fault here, Jack, not you. You were a child. He is a monster."

Jaclyn couldn't speak. She simply squeezed Grant's hand and continued to weep. The hope she had always worked hard to suppress was so strong that it battled against her shame to take control of her thoughts.

Outside of the double doors of the operating room, the nurse told Jaclyn she could go no farther with Grant. She assured her that the doctor would be out to talk with her as soon as he was finished removing the bullet from Grant's shoulder and repairing the damage it had caused.

Jaclyn bent close and kissed Grant. "I'm so, so sorry. I love you, Grant. I always have. I'm so sorry. I'm so sor...."

"Shh, Jack. You don't need to apologize. Listen, we are in this life together. We are a team. I love you, unconditionally."

Then Grant turned to the nurse. "Can I keep the bullet? I want it as a reminder of this day." He turned to face Jaclyn. "I want it to show you that I will always fight for you, Jack. I love you."

The nurse promised that she would ask the doctor about the bullet, then she pushed the button to open the double doors. As Grant's bed began to move, Jaclyn reluctantly let go of Grant's hand. She watched him as he moved into the operating room, the smile still on his face. How could he still love her?

Although she knew the police had already contacted Angela, Jaclyn needed to talk to her herself. She needed to apologize. She needed to know that her girls were okay. She sat in the empty waiting room and called Angela.

"Oh my God, Jaclyn! It's you. Are you okay? How's Grant? What happened? Where are...."

Jaclyn couldn't help but smile as her dearest friend became breathless with her care and concern. "Angela! Angela! We are okay. How are the girls?"

Angela took a deep breath to slow her words, but let the tears continue to flow down her cheeks. "They are good, precious friend. They are planning a party for you and Grant. A welcome home party." With her last words, a deep sob broke through, making it difficult to keep speaking.

Jaclyn could no longer hold back her tears, and for a moment there was only silence between them. But, it was a quiet moment of joy and celebration, each one of them smiling through their own relief. Finally, Jaclyn found her voice. "Thank you. Thank you so much. I'm so, so sorry."

Sniffing, Angela responded quickly. "Oh stop it, now. You know I would do anything for you. The girls are excited for you and Grant to come home. Will you be here soon?"

Jaclyn took a deep breath and explained their injuries, but not what caused them. She told Angela that Grant was in surgery and they would keep him for the night to make sure he was doing okay before discharging him. "Would you be able to spend the night with the girls?

I desperately want to see them, but right now I need to stay near Grant. He fought for me, Angela. He was willing to give his life to save me." And with this admission, Jaclyn wept uncontrollably.

Angela gave Jaclyn the time to weep while she silently thanked God for his protection of her dearest friends.

"Oh, God, I'm so sorry, Angela. I can't stop crying. I'm so sorry. I've just never felt this loved. It's so hard for me to accept it. I don't deserve Grant, or you. I have caused you both so much pain."

"Jaclyn, stop!" Angela paused. She knew she needed to be more gentle. "You've always been this loved, you've just refused to accept it. Our love is unconditional. And so is God's. It's okay, take it slowly. Stay with Grant. Be there for him tonight. Let yourself freely love him. The girls and I have a party to plan! Don't worry about a thing!"

Jaclyn smiled and inhaled deeply. "Okay. Thank you. Can you put me on speaker phone? I want to hear the girls' voices."

Angela put the call on speaker and called the girls over. When she announced that their mom was on the phone the girls all started screaming and talking at once.

Jaclyn tried to get a word in, but the girls all talked over her and each other. She finally just started laughing. When she could finally be heard, Jaclyn reassured the girls she and their dad were okay and coming home the next day.

"I can't wait to see you, girls! Thank you for being so good for Angela. I love you! Daddy loves you!" By this time, Jaclyn couldn't control the tears. She had spent several hours in the dark crawl space wondering if she would ever see the girls again. And here she was, alive and listening to her girls giggle and vie for her attention. And Damien was in custody. Just knowing where he was, and that he wasn't able to physically get to her, gave her some much-needed relief. She could finally relax a little. Maybe now she could move on. Maybe now she could learn to trust others. She whispered a genuine prayer that it would be so.

Angela knew Jaclyn had to be exhausted, and these girls would need to get some sleep before the big celebration tomorrow. "I love you, precious friend. I am praying for you both tonight. Try to get some rest. You are safe now."

Angela's words hit deep in Jaclyn's heart. Was she safe? Could she ever truly be safe? She was shocked that she felt resistant to Angela's words. Damien would soon be behind bars. About that much, she was sure. But, she didn't know for how long. And while he was locked up, could she truly feel safe? She couldn't ever remember a time when she had felt she could relax and enjoy life as it unfolded around her. Except when she had been near her mom. But, that memory was distant. It felt like a story she had once read, not a life she had once lived. She knew she was going to need some guidance as she navigated the path ahead of her. Grant now knew what she had gone through as a child. He now knew that she had kept this secret from him and had constantly lied about why she kept him at a distance. She had repeatedly convicted him as the reason for her apprehensions. Shame began to flood her soul, and she sank to the waiting room chair. She had forgotten that she was even on the phone with Angela until she finally heard her voice.

"Jaclyn, are you still there? Are you okay?"

"I'm fine. Listen, I need to go. Thank you for watching the girls."

Angela shuddered. Jaclyn's tone had taken a turn for the worse. "Jaclyn, what's wrong? Don't push me out again. It will be okay. I love you!"

"You won't when you know the reason behind the danger Grant and I faced today. It was all my fault, Angela. All my fault. Grant could have died and Damien could have hurt the girls." Jaclyn couldn't even cry now.

"Friend, quit beating yourself up. Rest. Be there for Grant now. Give yourself some grace. You faced the pit of hell today and you are still standing. You have a family who is going to walk through the days ahead with you because we all love you, without question. There is nothing you could ever do to change that."

Jaclyn felt a new twinge of hope amidst the shame and she allowed herself to tuck it away and treasure it. Maybe it would be okay. Maybe she and Grant could walk through her past together and find a new normal for their life together. He had heard her yelling at Damien and yet he still said he loved her before he went into surgery. She was so tired. She couldn't feel anymore tonight. "Thank you, friend. I needed to hear that. And I'm sure I will continue to need to hear it in the days ahead. Give all the girls a big kiss and a hug for me. I love you, friend."

"Love you, too. Call me in the morning so we know when to expect you. Should we come to pick you up?"

Jaclyn had another idea for how to get home. "I will call in the morning, but I have an idea for a ride and one more guest for Thanksgiving. Thank you for everything, Angela. I don't know how I will ever be able to repay you."

"That's just it. You can't." Angela laughed. "Now go relax and wait for Grant. Text me when he gets out of surgery so we know he's okay. Love you!"

"Love you, too." After hanging up, Jaclyn searched her contacts and hit send.

"Is everything okay, Jaclyn? It's the middle of the night!"

"Yes, Mark, everything is finally okay. Listen, would you like to join us for Thanksgiving dinner tomorrow?"

"Well, I was planning a full day of loneliness and working, but if you insist."

Jaclyn laughed freely. "Oh, Mark, you're a mess, aren't you?"

"Aren't we all, young lady? What should I bring?"

"I would be honored if you would bring me and Grant home from the hospital." Jaclyn explained the overall gist of their predicament with a promise of more details to follow soon.

"It would be my honor, young lady. Just call me when you are ready. I will pray for you both tonight."

"Thank you, Mark." She wanted to say more, but her throat constricted and she didn't trust that she could hold in the tears. "Talk to you in the morning."

"May God bless you with healing rest and unexplainable joy. You are deeply loved, my friend. Sleep well." And with that, Mark hung up.

Jaclyn couldn't even say goodbye. She hated the weakness she felt. She used to be able to put all emotions at bay with great ease, but now she seemed to have no control. She laid her head back on the chair and closed her eyes. The effects of the sedatives she had been given earlier were still lingering. She gave herself up to their pull and slipped into a light sleep.

In her dream, a warm, strong hand was gripping her shoulder. Jaclyn began to bat it away while trying to stand. She was disoriented and afraid. She tried to escape his grip and run, but he was too strong. Finally, she was able to open her eyes. A large masked man was grasping both of her shoulders. She screamed and fought with all her might.

"Whoa, it's okay, Mrs. Friedman. You are safe."

Jaclyn's heart pounded in her chest as she slowly regained consciousness. Finally, she could make out that the man restraining her was Grant's surgeon. He was gripping her shoulders, trying to avoid being slugged. Jaclyn quickly put her hands down. "I'm so, so sorry, doctor. I must have been dreaming."

The doctor made sure she wasn't going to become combative again, then released her arms. "No worries. And, I'm sure it wasn't a dream after all that you and your husband have been through today. More like a nightmare. It will take time to work through it all. Just take it slowly. I came to let you know that Grant is doing very well. The bullet hit the lateral portion of his upper arm resulting in a proximal humerus fracture along with retained bullet fragments in his subacromial space."

Jaclyn's look was one of confusion, and the doctor could tell. He chuckled, then tried to explain more clearly. "He's a lucky man. I was able to get the bullet out with no nerve damage, but it fractured his upper arm bone. It should all heal nicely. There are some fragments of the bullet in his arm, but they shouldn't cause any problems. I will want to see him in a week to check on his progress. The nurse will schedule an appointment with you."

"Thank God. And thank you." Jaclyn and the doctor shook hands, and she sat down again as he walked away.

Down the hallway, the doctor stopped and turned to face Jaclyn again. "Oh, Mrs. Friedman. Tell your husband I saved the bullet for him. It's not completely intact, but most of it is there. His nurse will give it to him when he gets to his room."

Jaclyn smiled and thanked the doctor. A souvenir from tragedy? It definitely had to be a guy thing like Grant said.

It wasn't long before a nurse came to get Jaclyn. She led her back to the recovery room where Grant was slowly coming out of the anesthesia. He looked so peaceful. And so broken. His arm and shoulder were bandaged and fitted with a sling and an IV slowly pushed fluids into his body. She sat next to the bed and reached for Grant's good hand. As she fit her hand into his, he gently engulfed her hand and squeezed. His warmth flooded Jaclyn's soul. She didn't hold back her tears as she looked up into his eyes that were working hard to focus. When his vision cleared, he smiled. She looked away, unable to face what she had done to him. She pulled her hand out of his and began to weep.

"I'm so sorry, Grant. I'm so sorry. This should have never happened to you. To us. To our family. I have been so stupid and stubborn. I'm so sorry." Jaclyn put her face in her hands, ashamed.

"Shh, Jack, come on now. We are a team. I'm pretty stubborn myself. And together we can't be beat."

Jaclyn still couldn't bring herself to look into Grant's empathetic eyes. She reached for a tissue and blew her nose, shaking her head in disagreement to his words.

"Okay, yes, you are stubborn. But, I'm crazy in love with you, stubbornness and all. And, Jack, I've always wanted to be shot and survive. It must be a guy thing." Grant couldn't help but laugh at his own words.

Jaclyn tried to resist, but his laugh was contagious and soon they were both unable to control themselves. But, pain interrupted Grant's joy. The nurse was watching and could see that Grant was becoming uncomfortable. She interrupted and gave Grant some morphine.

"We should have you up to your room shortly. Take it easy. The shoulder is a sensitive joint and does not like everything that has happened to it today." She checked Grant's bandages and entered the dose of morphine into the laptop in the corner of the room.

Jaclyn caught the nurse before she left the room. "Can I stay with my husband tonight?"

"Absolutely. There is a recliner in the room and you can order food along with his meals. It's always better for patients to have family nearby while they are here."

As the nurse left the room, Jaclyn hesitated, then told Grant she would be right back. When she caught up with the nurse down the hall, she called out to her. "Excuse me. One more question. The man who shot my husband. Is he here at this hospital?"

"Let me check for you. I doubt it. In cases like this, they will usually take the victims and the perpetrators to different hospitals." The nurse looked at the notes on Grant's chart and confirmed that that was the case. They had taken Damien to Community Hospital, a couple of miles from where they were at St. Maria's.

With her mind at ease, Jaclyn returned to Grant's bed to find him sleeping. The drugs were working.

Within the hour, they moved Grant to a room on the surgical floor for observation through the night. For about forty-five minutes Grant's room was a whirlwind of activity. A couple of nurses got him settled, checked his vitals, and made him as comfortable as possible. Jaclyn thanked the nurses for the pillow and blanket and she made herself comfortable in the recliner next to Grant's bed. As the last nurse left the room, she turned out the light. Grant reached out for Jaclyn's hand and for a few moments they connected without speaking. Then Grant whispered in the dark. "I love you, Jack."

"I love you, more." By the sound of Grant's breathing, Jaclyn could tell the drugs had already taken him under. She held his hand for a couple more minutes then placed it back on his bed. Then she laid back in the recliner and thanked God for protecting her and Grant. As she drifted off to sleep, she gave herself freely to a God she didn't fully know.

• CHAPTER 22 •

Jaclyn could hear voices in the distance, but she wasn't scared. She drifted in and out of consciousness. She knew where she was, but she imagined a different scene on the other side of her heavy eyelids. She pictured Mandy as the nurse laid her seconds-old body on her chest. Their heartbeats were synced, and Jaclyn felt more alive than she had felt for a long time. She could hear the soothing voice of the nurse as she took her vitals. Then she heard Grant talking to the nurse. She slowly began to resist the pull of sleep and fought to open her eyes. Her whole body hurt. As she opened her eyes, her blurred vision caught sight of Grant in the hospital bed. This wasn't Mandy's birth. What happened with Damien hadn't been a nightmare. It had really happened. An adrenaline surge flashed through her body and her vision cleared. Grant was smiling at her.

"How are you doing, Jack?"

Grant's smile melted Jaclyn's heart. "I'm okay." She smiled back. "How are you feeling?"

"Like I got shot." Grant tried to laugh, but the pain stopped him short.

"Take it easy, honey! It will take awhile before you feel back to yourself again. I'm so sorry you got involved in this mess. I feel horrible."

Grant reached out his hand, inviting Jaclyn to take it. "The day we got married I took on your mess as my own. And you took on mine. I'm just glad that now I know more about your mess."

"I'm so ashamed, Grant. I have always felt that it was all my fault. I thought since Damien had been reported dead that I could just move on with my life and not tell anyone about what happened. I have been so foolish."

Grant smiled until Jaclyn allowed herself to look at him. Then he smiled. "I love you, Jack. Mess and all."

Jaclyn took a deep breath and let out a long sigh. "I know. And I love you. But, being vulnerable is going to take me awhile to get used to."

"We have a lifetime together to work on it."

A knock on the open door turned both of their heads. It was Mark. The nurse waited for Mark to enter before leaving with a promise that the doctor would do rounds soon. Mark shook his head at the sight of Jaclyn and Grant.

"Thank God you two are alive." Mark shamelessly let tears run down his cheeks as he gave Jaclyn a tender fatherly hug. Then he shook Grant's good hand.

Mark's tears shocked Jaclyn. She was so used to him giving her a hard time. "Mark, I don't know what to say. This was all so unexpected. It's not every day that a madman comes after you."

"Nothing surprises me about your life, Scoop!" Mark let out a laugh and dried his tears. "You tend to walk into messes young lady."

Mark and Jaclyn laughed at this truth, but Grant just smiled, not wanting to aggravate his injury.

"You ain't kidding, Mark." Grant kept smiling and looked over at Jaclyn and winked.

Mark turned to Grant. "Well, what's the prognosis there, Champ?"

Grant explained the extent of his injuries to Mark in great detail, clearly proud of his survival. "I will be pretty limited at work for a while because I'm right-handed, but I can still supervise." Then he turned to Jaclyn. "Hey, Jack, grab the bullet off the nightstand.

Jaclyn grabbed the bullet, saved in a sealed plastic bag and handed it to Mark.

"Well, I'll be doggone. That's impressive. I'm just so thankful to see you both here, banged up, but still kicking." Then Mark turned his head toward Jaclyn. "While Grant is recuperating, you, young lady, need to stay away from the office for a few weeks. Maybe more."

"But, Mark, I have...."

Mark interrupted Jaclyn. "No, no, no. I will take your workload for a bit. I'm getting bored sitting in my office, anyway. I've been itching to write a story or two. You've just given me the opportunity to do so."

Jaclyn smiled. "Thank you, Mark. I really appreciate it, but I do better if I'm working. What I need right now is to get back to normal."

Mark shook his head. "No, what you and your daring husband there need to figure out is your new normal. When our daughter died, my wife, and I thought we could just keep living life the same way we had been and things would just get better. Guess what? It got worse. We were stupid trying to ignore what had happened. Please, don't do what we did. Take some time and talk. Get some professional help to put all this in perspective. And if I see that you are disobeying me, I'll make you take another week off." Mark tried to be stern with Jaclyn, but he couldn't help speak lovingly. She was like a daughter to him. A second chance.

Before Jaclyn could answer, the doctor knocked and quickly entered the room. "Well, if I knew there was a party going on in here, I would have been here sooner."

After shaking everyone's hand and introducing himself to Mark, he explained how the surgery went and what recovery would look like. "Did you get your bullet, Grant?"

Mark was still holding it in his hand. "Definitely a survival souvenir."

The doctor nodded in agreement as he listened to Grant's heart and lungs and checked the wound. "That it is. Everything is looking good, Grant. Take care and we should have you discharged within the next hour or so. Take it slowly and enjoy this Thanksgiving. You have much to be thankful for today."

"Thank you so much." Grant reached out and shook the doctor's hand again. "Happy Thanksgiving to you and your family."

When the doctor left the room, Mark put his hand on Jaclyn's shoulder and looked her directly in her eyes. "I love you like my own daughter. Please take care of yourself and your family. The story of your own life is the most important one you will ever tell." Mark gave Jaclyn a fatherly hug, then handed her a bag of clean clothes for both of them that he had picked up from Angela on the way to the hospital. "Now, I'm going to go get some coffee downstairs. Let me know when you two are ready to go."

Jaclyn sat back down in the recliner and smiled at Grant. Then they both laughed. "We are a mess! What are we going to tell the girls?"

Grant didn't hesitate. "We will tell them that we fought the bad guy together, and we won. That's what we tell them." He tried to puff out his chest in triumph but winced in pain.

"Hey, there, Captain America, take it easy." Jaclyn walked to Grant's bedside and bent down to kiss him. "Thank you for being my hero today."

Grant looked deeply into Jaclyn's eyes. "You are definitely worth fighting for."

Jaclyn let out a deep breath as she wiped at the tears that quickly formed and fell. "Well, that is what I need to learn how to accept. My whole life I've wanted someone to fight for me, but I believed no one would. I thought I had to fight for myself."

"I think we all need to do a little fighting for ourselves. But, the enemy wants us to be silent. That's the real madman. The murderer. The one who deceives us and destroys us. Silence. From now on, we fight the demon of silence together. Your pain is mine, and mine is yours. We are in this life together, Jack. For better or worse. It's time that we fight the battle on the same side." There wasn't one ounce of anger or bitterness in Grant's words and it caught Jaclyn off guard.

"But, how could you trust me now with all that I've put our family through? I don't deserve...."

"Stop, Jack. Just stop. None of us deserve anything. That's the painful truth. But, I'm learning that we've been freely given grace for our faults. We are loved unconditionally by a God I would like to get to know better. What do you say we get to know him better together?"

Jaclyn couldn't speak. Her mind filled quickly with the thought that her mom had poured her life out to God and all she got for it was death at an early age. Where was God when she stood with her dad and her brother in the cemetery afraid in the crowded loneliness?

Grant could tell Jaclyn was struggling with his words. "Hey, we have the rest of our lives to figure all of this out. Let's just focus on today. Angela tells me you bought food we just need to heat and serve."

Jaclyn couldn't help but laugh. "Yeah, I must have had some premonition we would need an easy day today."

"Well, as long as we are all together today, I don't care what we eat."

"Okay. You're right. We just need to get through today. I can't wait to see the girls."

Grant smiled. "Me, too."

***

The girls lined the couch on their knees watching for their mom and dad to get home. Anya leaned close and smashed her face against the window, quickly discovering she could make imprints of her face in the steam from her breath.

"Gross! Anya, stop doing that!" Mandy was disgusted by Anya's actions, and she was eager for her mom and dad to be home.

Anya screamed back and pushed Mandy, causing her to lose her balance and hit Jenae. In an instant, chaos erupted, all the girls yelling and shoving each other off the couch.

Angela lowered the flame on the burner, then ran to see what the girls were yelling about.

"Girls! Stop now!" She pulled Jenae and Mackenzie apart before anyone got seriously hurt. "Okay, we have no time for fighting. We've still got some work to do before mom and dad come home. I found some poster board in the craft closet. Mandy, can you tape several sheets together? Your mom and dad need a welcome home sign on the garage door when they arrive."

The girls jumped off the couch and ran to get supplies. While Mandy searched for the tape, the others got the two buckets of markers and crayons.

Angela went back to the kitchen with a smile spreading across her face. She couldn't wait for the girls to reunite with their parents. They all had so much to be thankful for today. Angela had been up before the sun with a hot cup of black coffee and her prayer journal. She noticed that it had been a while since she had written in it and was disappointed in herself. She had been so wrapped up in trying to find a man to date that she had stopped journaling. How could she had been so foolish? If she were to continue dating Jason, she couldn't ignore her time with God. She coveted their conversations: reading God's words spoken to her and journaling her responses back to God. Angela had taken advantage of this early morning's quiet and had read Psalm 18:16-19, "He reached down from heaven and rescued me; he drew me out of deep waters. He rescued me from my powerful enemies, from those who hated me and were too strong for me. They attacked me at a moment when I was in distress, but the Lord supported me. He led me to a place of safety; he rescued me because he delights in me." In response, she had written, "Your enormous love overwhelms my mind, but my heart cries out for more. Thank you, God, for seeing all of us through this dark night."

Then her thoughts turned to Jason. Why had he not called or texted her back last night? Had he been one of those who had rescued Jaclyn and Grant? She thought it may be too early to call, so she texted him. She hoped he was still planning to come for Thanksgiving dinner. Or, was he the one who had harassed Mandy? She needed to talk to him. She needed him to be a hero, not a monster. She had a lot to share with him.

When the girls were done with the sign, Angela helped them hang it on the garage door. The wind had subsided and the birds sang a chorus, rejoicing in the sun that was overtaking the clouds in the Cliff Creek Valley. It was cool, but the sun felt warm on her face. All the girls had written on the driveway with sidewalk chalk so Angela put Mandy in charge of making sure Anya didn't run off. She went back inside to check on the turkey. As she opened the front door, she heard her phone ringing in the kitchen. She hoped it was Jason. Breathless, she grabbed her phone and glanced at the caller ID before answering. It was Jaclyn. "Good morning, friend! How are you and Grant doing?"

Jaclyn sounded happy for the first time in a long time. "We are doing well. How are the girls?"

"Full of energy and creative ideas. I hope it's okay that they've practically redecorated your entire house."

Jaclyn chuckled. "I can't wait to see it. We should leave the hospital in about an hour. Mark, my boss at the Courier will drive us home and he's accepted our offer to stay for dinner."

"Wonderful! I will set another plate at the table. Speaking of guests, I haven't heard from Jason since last night. I'm hoping he is still planning to come as well."

Jaclyn held her breath and her heart pounded in her chest. She found a seat and took a deep breath.

"Jaclyn? Are you still there?"

Jaclyn knew she needed to tell Angela about who Jason really was, but she didn't know how.

"Jaclyn? Is everything okay?"

Finally, Jaclyn attempted to explain. "Angela, I have some bad news. Jason isn't who you think he is."

Angela gasped. "What?! What do you mean?"

Jaclyn took a deep steadying breath and continued. "Angela, Jason is the man who attacked Grant and me last night."

Angela burst into tears and slumped to the floor. "How can that be? He's a police officer. I called him to come to help you and Grant. He wanted to help. Didn't he come to help you?"

"It's not your fault, Angela. He's a liar and a monster. He did all this on purpose to get back at me. I will explain more in the days ahead. But, it's not your fault. It's okay now. He's in jail."

Angela's suspicions the night before were right. Jason had used her. He was the one who had scared Mandy at school. And she had given him everything he needed to get to Jaclyn and hurt her and Grant. "Jaclyn, I am so, so sorry. It is my fault. I showed him where you lived and where the girls went to school. I told him you were in danger in Spindrift and asked him to go check on you. It is my fault. I'm so sorry. I'm so sor...." Angela couldn't help but sob into the phone.

"Shh, Angela, shh. It's okay. Really. I know this man. I've known him since I was a child. He's pure evil. You didn't know what he was doing. Please, friend, trust me that it is okay. We are not upset with you. We are so very thankful for you. You are family. You have loved us and our children for years. Last night you were a true angel in our home, caring for the girls. We love you!"

Angela attempted a deep breath and a loud sob caught in her throat.

"I love you, Angela. You didn't know. You tried everything to help us. And you loved our girls. We can never repay you for that." Jaclyn quietly waited for Angela to get herself together.

"Thank you, friend. Thank you." Angela sniffed, then mustered as much energy as she could. "Okay! When can we expect you, because these girls are going crazy with anticipation?"

Jaclyn laughed. "I'm sure they are. The nurse is at the door now. We hope to be home within the hour. See you soon!"

Jaclyn hung up and stepped out of the way so the nurse could help Grant with his shirt and fit him with a sling. Stabs of regret hit her heart as Grant recoiled from the pain. The dam holding back her emotions had definitely broke, flooding her with decades of all that she had refused to feel. At moments in the last twelve hours, she had felt happier than she had ever felt in her life. Grant wasn't upset with her. He said he loved her unconditionally. They were injured and banged up, but they were alive. And so were their girls. But, at other moments, and without warning, she would suffocate on shame. While watching Grant struggle, Mark approached her from behind, gently placing his weathered hand on her shoulder.

"It will be okay, kiddo. Grant's a strong man. He's got this."

Jaclyn reached up and placed her hand on Mark's. "I know. It's just hard knowing I caused all this by being stubborn."

"You did what you knew you could do at the moment. We only learn and grow when we fail, Jaclyn. The times when the rains fall and the soil of our heart is turned up and scattered are the preparation for great things to come. When we are torn apart, we are desperately in need of God. And he does his best work in us when we have nothing left to do for ourselves. Believe me, I know." Jaclyn turned to look at Mark and caught him staring out the window, seeing past the trees into a past through which he had barely survived.

Jaclyn squeezed Mark's hand and their eyes connected. Mark enveloped Jaclyn in a big bear hug until Grant interrupted.

"I'm not sure what you two want to do, but I want to get out of here." All three of them laughed and agreed. Mark left to get the car and Jaclyn went into the bathroom to change into the clean clothes Mark had brought with him. She threw her dirty clothes in the garbage. She didn't want to bring anything from the day before back into their house. Today was a new day. A new life. It would take some work, but she knew for sure that she didn't want to go back to how their lives were before. She was more than willing to make some changes, no matter how difficult it may be.

When she came out of the bathroom, Grant was in a wheelchair dressed in gray sweats, a white T-shirt, and a blue zippered sweatshirt, with only his good arm through the sleeve and the other simply draped over his injured shoulder. "Am I presentable for Thanksgiving dinner?"

Grant's smile constantly disarmed her and butterflies filled her stomach. How could he be such a good sport? "Yes, you look quite dashing. It would honor me to attend Thanksgiving dinner with you."

She had walked over and assured the nurse she could push Grant to the car. But, the nurse walked behind the procession due to hospital protocol. Jaclyn, too, was also dressed in sweats and a sweatshirt, relieved to be out of her bloodstained clothes. As they walked out the main doors of the hospital, Mark met them and snapped a photo.

"Oh, Mark! Stop that. I look awful."

Mark shook his head. "No, you look triumphant. Believe me, one day you will thank me for this photo. When you are facing something difficult, you will look at this photo and know that you are strong and that God will see you through."

Jaclyn waved him away with her hand after setting the brakes on Grant's wheelchair. She squinted into the bright sun and breathed a sigh of relief. "Thank God the storm has finally passed."

Grant looked up at Jaclyn and smiled, then closed his eyes and soaked in some rays himself. "Yes, it has. And, I'm glad we will brave the storms yet to come together," Jaclyn was searching Grant's face when he opened his eyes and winked playfully.

"The sun may be shining, you two lovebirds, but it is cold. Let's get this show on the road." Mark jumped in the driver's seat and turned up the heat. Then Jaclyn and the nurse gingerly guided Grant into the back seat of Mark's car. Jaclyn climbed in back with Grant and teased Mark about being their chauffeur.

"Hey, as long as Grant's not in the firing line of the airbag, I don't care what you two do back there." Mark's belly laugh filled the car as they left the hospital parking lot.

From the end of the cul-de-sac, Jaclyn could see the sign on the garage and caught glimpses of the girls running to hide from them. Jaclyn couldn't hold back the tears and they took Grant by surprise.

"Hey, hey, hey. Jack, what's wrong?" He took her hand in his good one.

Jaclyn wiped at her tears and smiled. "I'm just happy, that's all." She looked directly at Grant. "I can't believe that just yesterday, less than twenty-four hours ago, I had no hope of ever seeing our girls again. And here I am, almost home. Here you are, alive and by my side."

Now Grant's face was wet with tears. Without speaking, he winked and squeezed Jaclyn's hand.

Once Mark pulled in the driveway, the girls couldn't help but peek their faces out from their hiding places and giggle. And once Mark and Jaclyn helped Grant out of the car, the girls could no longer hide and all came running at once. Mark quickly played defense, catching the youngest two in his arms so they wouldn't tackle Grant.

"Mom! Dad! Look at our sign! We made it all by ourselves. And, wait until you see what we did inside." Mandy hugged Jaclyn and smiled at Grant.

Anya laid her head on Mark's shoulder and weighed the scene in front of her. "What wrong, mommy? Daddy, you break your arm?"

Grant smiled and touched Anya's cheek with his free hand. "Well, I sort of broke my arm, but I'm going to be okay."

"And I just fell down and got some scrapes, but daddy and I are okay now. And we are so glad to be home with you!" Anya reached for Jaclyn, who took her into a big hug.

Just then, Angela yelled from the front step. "The food will not stay hot forever! And neither will the house if we keep this door open any longer." Relief clearly flooded Angela's face as she took in the sight of Jaclyn and Grant for herself.

Soon enough, all eight of them were seated together at the large pine dining room table, surrounded by colorful drawings, paper chains, and balloons.

Grant bent his head and held Jaclyn's hand. The others followed suit, with Jenae placing her hand on Grant's sling. "Thank you, God, for the miracle of us all being able to share this meal together today."

After several seconds of silence, Mackenzie opened her eyes and saw tears on her dad's cheeks. "Daddy? Wha...."

Mark gracefully interrupted. "God, may you continue to watch over and protect each one of us at this table. We are humbled by your love and your grace, and we are thankful. Bless this family, bless this food, and bless this party! In Jesus name, Amen."

• C H A P T E R   2 3 •

Two officers flanked the wheelchair as the nurse pushed Damien to the waiting patrol car. His time at Community Hospital had been short, just enough time to inspect the back of his right leg for arterial damage and stitch up the wound caused by the ax Grant had thrust into him.

"Slow down! What the hell are you doing? I'm in pain here!" Damien pulled at the handcuffs attached to each of his wrists and the armrests of the chair.

The armed officer to his left nudged Damien's shoulder. "That's enough. Keep your mouth shut. She's just doing her job."

At the curb, the nurse stepped back and one officer trained his gun at Damien while the other removed the handcuffs and placed them on both of his wrists.

Damien smiled at the lengths they were taking to make sure he didn't run. "Relax big guy, I'm not going anywhere. I can't even stand right now."

"Well, you need to stand so the nurse can take that chair back into the hospital, so get up." The officer reached out to steady Damien as he stood, but Damien twisted his upper body and knocked the officer's hand away.

"Don't touch me. I'm not a weak woman who can't do anything right. Give me some respect here!"

The officer took half a step back, prepared to catch Damien if needed. The second officer had put his gun back in his holster, but his hand was at the ready.

Damien winced at the pain caused by the bend to his leg as he clambered into the back seat of the patrol car. But, he didn't dare make a sound. He refused to accept defeat. He would get out of this. He had to get out of this. He still needed to make Jaclyn pay for ruining his life. Once he was in the patrol car, and the officer shut the door, Damien started thinking of ways to escape. He had hidden in plain sight for twenty-three years. He could surely escape from this podunk town. These police officers today were so full of themselves that all he had to do was play into their egos and he could easily trip them up. But he would have to wait until he got these handcuffs off. And, besides, Grant had come at him with an ax. He had to shoot him in self-defense. Even if he couldn't escape, he would plead his case in court and walk free. They had nothing concrete against him. It was a domestic dispute. And it was Grant's gun. All the weapons in the fight belonged to Jaclyn and Grant. Damien laughed out loud at the absurdity of the situation.

The driver looked in the rearview mirror and his partner turned to look at Damien. "Having fun back there?"

"Oh, you have no idea how funny this whole situation is. You are such fools. I can't believe you are wasting my time like this."

The officer driving scoffed at Damien. "Do I need to remind you that anything you say can, and will, be used against you? Everything you say is being recorded."

"It doesn't bother me. I'm the innocent one here. You've let the wrong people go. A child could have handled this whole thing better than you bozos."

The officers both decided that silence was the best way to handle Damien. They exited the parking lot and headed for the Jones County Detention Center.

It had taken several hours to book Damien and get him to his cell. By that time, he had been photographed, questioned, and asked to change into orange scrubs. He was exhausted. All he wanted to do was sleep. Then he would think of a way out of all of this. He needed to get back to Canada to regroup and reorganize. Jaclyn had money that he needed to move on, and he was still determined to get it.

Once in his cell, he laid on the thin mattress and tried to sleep. The noise of steel doors opening and closing and an annoying argument a few cells down irritated Damien to no end. He pulled the wasted pillow from under his head and placed it over his face, squeezing his arms against his ears. It didn't help. His stomach growled and his head throbbed. Why was he such a failure? He couldn't do anything right and it was slowly killing him. He beat his head through the pillow and whispered to himself, "You idiot. You stupid, no good, waste of human life." Damien hated that his mind was going there. The place in his mind he had lived as a child. His dad had been big and strong and mean. And he had hated Damien. Damien had been born premature and was always smaller than the rest of the kids. He was sick more than he was well. And, because of that, his dad teased him relentlessly. That is when his dad was home.

For most of Damien's childhood, his dad had been in prison. While his dad was gone, his mom would work three jobs, trying to feed and care for him and his younger sister. As early as when he was ten years old, Damien remembered yelling at his mom for how weak she was. She cried a lot and was often sick, but never stayed home from work. He was the one to determine if he and his sister would go to school. His mom had left instructions for him to feed his sister and walk her to school, but often that didn't happen. Some days he would tie his sister up with rope and eat in front of her, eating her portions, too. If she cried, he would slap her until she stopped. Once, he even found a lighter and burned the bottom of her feet. When the truant officer would come to the house, because they weren't at school, they would hide. He would cover his sister's mouth and threaten to kill her if she made a sound. Their mother must have received phone calls, but she didn't mention them to Damien. The older Damien got, the more afraid his mother became of him.

But, when his dad was released from prison, Damien would shrink within himself and not say a word at home. But, he had worked out. A lot. And stealing other kids' food at school. At about fourteen, he finally hit a growth spurt and by sixteen was an inch and a half taller than his dad and outweighed him by a good ten to fifteen pounds. Where his dad's weight was in his beer belly, Damien's was in his chest and shoulders. Damien knew that one day he would fight his dad. His rage against his demeaning remarks and beatings was building. He knew he could beat his dad in a fight. He was just waiting for the right opportunity. The only time his dad let up on him was when they would both degrade his mom. She was so weak. She never fought back or even stood up for herself. And Damien hated her for that. By this time, he hardly saw his sister. He knew she was doing drugs and sleeping around, often with some of his best friends, but he didn't care. She was weak, too. He knew he needed to get out of there to make himself any kind of life, but he couldn't ever keep a job long enough to save the money he needed.

An intense, throbbing pain was pulsing through Damien's leg, where the ax had cut deeply. But, it didn't even come close to the involuntary heart pain of childhood memories coming to his mind. He rolled over, attempting to relieve the pain in his leg and jostle the memories back into the abyss of indifference where Damien had kept them all these years. But, relief didn't come. He settled on his stomach and, in the semi-darkness of the cell, let a few tears soak into his pillow. The tears were from and for his young, inquisitive self who had once had dreams of being a scientist. Damien had cried rivers of tears into his pillow as a small boy, distracting his mind with possible ways to drown out the sound of his parents' fighting and beatings his mom endured without fighting back. He was determined to develop a way to tune out unwanted noise and by middle school had gone beyond his studies at school to learn myriad ways of controlling sound waves.

With a new identity and a fresh start in Canada after faking his death, Damien had wanted nothing more than to settle down and create a world that he could control. A world in which he would be happy. But, his intense need for respect eventually destroyed any relationship he attempted to make work. Finally, he started his own business and swore off all women, except those he could pay to be quiet. All women, except for Jaclyn. As a young, vulnerable girl, she had reminded Damien of his mother. And he hated her for that. His ability to manipulate her had fed a deep need he didn't fully understand. But, when she broke in front of her father and ruined what they had going, he vowed to make her pay one day. That day had now come and gone, and he was still the one paying for it. His tears stopped and the comfort of rage filled his deep breaths. Soon, he was asleep, rocked into fitful dreams between profound sadness and unfulfilled desires.

But, sleep didn't last long. Within what seemed like only minutes, the bright lights in the cell block were turned on and they gave orders to get up and make beds and wash up. At six-thirty a metal tray was slid into each cell and they gave them fifteen minutes to eat its contents. Damien was starving. His large frame was used to a lot of calories and he couldn't remember the last time he had eaten. He hobbled over to the tray and then sat against the wall to eat. The hot cereal had no taste, but the warmth and weight of it temporarily calmed the spasms in his stomach. And the thick horrid coffee had enough caffeine to jolt him awake.

Before long, the cell block was a din of metal trays being slid out of the cells and unpleasant conversations between inmates and guards. Damien couldn't take it anymore and started yelling a long list of expletives at anyone and everyone. A guard eventually came to his cell and rapped on the bars with his billy club, but Damien yelled even louder. His rant included demeaning remarks about the guard's mother, a woman he had obviously never met. The guard disappeared for a few minutes, but then returned with two more guards.

"All right, choir boy, step back so we can come in your cell." The guard waited for Damien to move to the back of the cell before putting the key in the lock. The other two guards kept their hands on their weapons.

Damien stopped yelling and started to laugh. "What's the matter, you scared of me? You should be."

The first guard demanded that Damien present his wrists so he could place the handcuffs on them. Damien did as he was told, but before the guard could get the handcuffs on, Damien swung an uppercut to the guard's chin and then attempted another swing.

Damien's head throbbed. And he felt a painful knot on the back of his hea. He tried to open his eyes, but they felt glued shut. The noise had stopped. It was quiet, except for the drumming inside his head. He reached for his eyes and rubbed them while he stretched his body long. Finally, he opened his eyes, pleased to find that the light was dim. He was alone. His cell was now a room, instead of bars. He had a bed, a sink, and a toilet. He laid his head back down and closed his eyes. His leg burned, the pain medicine's effects had worn off. This was it. He was done for. His resolve dwindled to nothing and his mind turned to ways he could end his life. Damien knew he wouldn't last in jail. He didn't have the patience.

And once again, Damien heard his dad's voice. He mouthed the words with barely a whisper as the phrases filled his head. "You will never amount to anything. You are the stupidest kid I know. You are worthless." He let the words flow out of his mouth for fear that his head would explode if he didn't. The longer he laid in his solitary cell, the more he was convinced that his life was over. He closed his eyes and let his memories take him.

Damien was seven years old and dressed in his best clothes. His mother had pressed his black dress pants, a white button-down shirt, and a white T-shirt. She had looked over his shoulder into the mirror with a big smile as she showed him how to tie his black tie. He smiled back, thrilled he was taking such a big step in life. His mom talked to God a lot, usually while she cleaned up after dinner, or after his dad had broken something in a fit of rage, then stormed out of the house to go to the bar. And now he was beginning classes to learn about God and to finally be able to eat the bread and drink the wine during the church service. He felt capable and proud. He would learn more about this God and how to talk to him. He desperately needed God to stop his dad from beating his mom, and him and his sister. His drunken rages were getting worse and Damien always feared that one day he would kill one or all of them. He had wanted his mom to tell his dad to leave, or call the police and have him arrested, but all she did was cry. And pray.

Damien only made it to a handful of classes and soon gave up trying to get there. His longing for God to intervene in his abusive home turned to anger at his mom for being so foolish to believe God would help them. By age ten, he had chosen to not believe in God. He would only get out of the mess he was growing up in by taking control and making it happen. When he was a few months shy of seventeen, he finally left home. He didn't say goodbye to anyone. He just left. For months, he slept on countless couches and in the back seat of cars people had foolishly left unlocked. His parents never came looking for him. He finally had the freedom he had always wanted.

But, where had it led him? Here, to this cell. To a dead end.

Damien heard a lock disengage. He opened his eyes and looked toward the door. A small panel lifted at the bottom of the door, just big enough for the tray of food to be pushed through into his cell. He must have fallen asleep again. He couldn't tell what time it was, but he knew, by the ache of his stomach cramping in hunger, that hours must have passed since he had eaten breakfast.

His leg was killing him and he screamed to no one. "I need something for pain, you idiots! This is abuse! Wait until you hear from my lawyer."

After he sat at the edge of the bed long enough to stop feeling light-headed, Damien reached for the tray by the door. His cell was about six feet by eight feet and, from his bed, the door was almost within reach. Once he had the tray, he leaned against the wall and stretched his leg straight on the bed, propping it up by a pillow so the deep cut wasn't touching anything. The tray was full of food and the smell melted away Damien's anger. He grabbed the spoon and shamelessly began to wolf down the mashed potatoes and turkey. When the cramps in his stomach subsided, he noticed a small envelope tucked under the plate. In between bites, he grabbed it and turned it over. "Happy Thanksgiving! You are loved."

Damien laughed out loud. "That's a joke," he said to no one.

He devoured the slice of pumpkin pie, then opened the envelope to see what other lies it contained.

"No matter what your life looks like right now, no matter how scuffed up and battered your emotions are, you are as valuable as you were the day God created you." Across the bottom of the card it read, "Thanksgiving dinner lovingly prepared by many who care at Cliff Creek Community Church.

Damien tried to concentrate on chewing the food so that he could suppress the tidal wave of sadness and longing that was beginning to breach his heart. His chest hurt and breathing was becoming more difficult. He stood up to relieve the distress, but he quickly doubled over from the pain. He screamed for help until his weeping silenced his cries. On the floor, he curled up into a ball, spasms of grief wracking his body and tormenting him with memories long buried. After almost an hour, Damien whispered with his last bit of energy, "God help me," and then he fell into a deep sleep.

• EPILOGUE •

Spring had finally come to Cliff Creek and Jaclyn couldn't be happier. The sun beat strong and warm on her face and shoulders as she focused on the scene in her viewfinder. Covering the third annual rescued animal reunion had been her idea.

When Jaclyn came back to work after a six-week leave of absence and requested to cover more human interest stories, Mark was shocked. Investigative journalism used to be a drug she needed to feel alive. But, things were clearly different now. Although she still occasionally agreed to an investigative piece, they had struck a deal that she would never step foot in a courtroom to cover it. Mark gladly took those stories and loved being back in the reporting game. In fact, he loved it so much, that he had demoted himself to assistant editor and helped hire a young go-getter from Denver to be the editor. This brought him more time in the field and more joy to his heart.

The trial had been extremely painful and had taken its toll on both Jaclyn and Grant, and their marriage. When the verdict was declared and Damien sent to prison for twenty-four years for first-degree assault and kidnapping, Jaclyn and the girls had taken a week to go visit her dad and brother in Denver. That same week, Grant flew to Omaha to spend some downtime with his friend Davis. He needed to clear his head and get some honest advice about moving forward. Grant had agreed to go to counseling with Jaclyn when he got back. He knew they needed some objective help to get their marriage back on the right track. But, he knew he also needed to vent. It hadn't been an easy pill to swallow that Jaclyn had lied so much to him. He knew she had been scared and didn't know what to do, but he needed to sort out his feelings about it. First with a friend, then definitely with a counselor. Jaclyn had been fully supportive of his trip to see Davis. She respected Davis and his wife and knew that Grant would be in good hands. And it also gave Jaclyn some much needed time with her dad.

When the news had come out about Damien, Jaclyn's dad had called and wept on the phone. He knew something had been off with Damien and it crushed him that he could not protect his young daughter. During their six-day visit, he didn't even go into the nursery to work. For once, he trusted that everything would be okay without him, and he stayed home to spoil his granddaughters as much as he could get away with during their visit. He had even given Jaclyn a ring. It had been her mother's wedding ring. A local jeweler had turned it into a Mother's ring. Her mother's diamond was set in a silver band with Mandy and Mackenzie's birthstones on one side of it and Jenae and Anya's on the other. Inside the band, he had the girls' names engraved and the citation for his wife's favorite verse, Ecclesiastes 4:12. Along with the ring, he had given Jaclyn a small card with the full verse, "Though one may be overpowered, two can defend themselves. A cord of three strands is not quickly broken."

"Your mother tried desperately to teach me this verse. She would always bring it up when we were having any sort of trouble. I can honestly say that I didn't get it, especially when the most important part of that verse to me died at such a young age." Jaclyn's dad explained that this verse had been the one the pastor had read to them at their wedding. He knew it meant that their marriage had been one between him and his wife and God. But, when she died, he tried to cut God out of his life, too.

"I just couldn't do it. God always reappeared somehow, some way. Sometimes through a friend, other times through a song or book. I just couldn't seem to get away from him. Your mother had been right, our commitment to God couldn't be broken. Just last fall I finally gave in and started attending church. It's been hard. But, good."

Jaclyn hugged her dad. "I can't get away from him either. He just keeps messing with me." She pulled back and met eyes with her dad. "Could we all go with you this Sunday?"

Her dad smiled, but couldn't say a word. Tears were streaming down his cheeks. Jaclyn embraced him again just as the girls ran in the front door.

He wiped his eyes, winked at Jaclyn, and made a proclamation. "Let's go get pizza!" The girls shouted with glee and ran out the door to the Jeep.

Jaclyn waited as her dad locked the front door, then they walked hand in hand to the car. The rest of their trip was wonderful. Jaclyn's brother and family came over a couple of the nights for dinner and on Saturday they had all visited the zoo. They left with a promise to visit again soon, and next time Grant would come, too.

Loud barking brought Jaclyn back to the present. She was done with her interviews and photos at the rescued animal reunion, but she couldn't leave just yet. Finally, her phone vibrated, and she smiled when she saw it was Grant.

"Hey, Grant. How are you?" Jaclyn stood facing the sun.

"Hey, Jack. I'm nervous and feel like I'm being led astray." They both laughed into the phone.

"Oh, come on now. Be brave. Are the girls with you?"

Grant parked the car and the girls all screamed with joy. "Does that answer your question?"

Jaclyn laughed. "Okay, okay, where are you parked? I will come to meet you."

Jaclyn walked towards the parking lot looking for Grant's truck. Before she saw them, she heard them, and simply followed the sound.

As she approached the truck, Grant grabbed Jaclyn's hand and gave her a kiss. She welcomed it and hugged him in return.

"Come on, you two! Enough! There are dogs waiting for us to rescue them." Mandy stood with her hands on her hips and a smile spreading across her face.

Grant put his hands in the air and feigned offense. "Dogs? Did you say dogs? No, no, no. Mom said A DOG. One. And that was a maybe. Like, let's go see if we connect with any of them."

Jaclyn brushed Grant off with a smile and a wave of her hand as she and the girls took off hand in hand for the area filled with dogs to still be rescued.

For nearly forty-five minutes, the girls played with the dogs and argued about which one they should adopt. Anya and Jenae had fought and Grant made them both take a time out with each other on a bench nearby.

"Girls, sit here until you can work it out. Then you can come to join us in looking again." Grant walked away but kept one eye on their progress.

Both girls folded their arms and refused to talk to each other.

Jaclyn joined Grant, and they stood amazed at their daughters' stubbornness. "They get it from you, you know."

Grant laughed. "Yep, that's what I was thinking."

They both laughed, knowing the girls' strong-willed nature had come from both of them. They had been doomed from birth. While they looked on, a shaggy brown dog with white paws walked over and place its head right between the girls on the bench. The girls looked at each other and smiled. They began to pet the dog together and the mutt's tail wagged with joy.

Grant shook his head. "I think our dog has found us."

Jaclyn couldn't be more in agreement. "Let's get Mandy and Mackenzie."

Grant yelled for the two older girls who had run off to meet some more dogs. Soon, they had all gathered around and the dog started showing off. First, she sat and offered her paw, then she rolled over and over in the grass. The girls clapped and cheered.

"Well, I think we've found our new family member. What do you think, girls?" Jaclyn could tell by the girls' interaction with the dog that it sold them. But, when they shouted yes in unison, it was a done deal.

"What are we going to name her?" Mandy was always a step ahead of everyone.

"Princess!"

"Buttercup!"

"Anastasia!"

"Potato!"

Jaclyn laughed but stepped into the conversation lovingly, but boldly. "What do you all think about naming her Hope?"

Miraculously, everyone agreed. So, Hope it was.

"Can we take her home now?" Mackenzie had already attached the pink leash they had bought that morning.

"Let's do it, girls." Grant signed the last bit of paperwork and they all headed to the parking lot.

Jaclyn stopped at her Jeep. "Okay, I will meet you all at home shortly. Auntie Angela and I are meeting for a quick cup of coffee. Should I invite her for dinner so she can meet Hope?"

The girls all shouted yes in unison.

Grant kissed Jaclyn goodbye. "See you soon, Jack. Love you!"

"Love you, too." Jaclyn waved goodbye and hopped in her Jeep.

Meeting weekly with Angela had kept her accountable to the hard work she was doing with her counselor. Life was good but still difficult. The demons from her past still taunted her, but there were no more secrets, no more lies. She was no longer a victim of the silence that had suffocated her spirit and just about killed her. And her husband. From now on, as painful as it could sometimes be, she would not keep quiet. She had learned that silence is not golden. And, in her case, it was almost deadly.

On the way to meet Angela, in the solitude of her car, Jaclyn spoke out loud to herself, like she was trying to do every day. "I have a voice and a calling to use it. What I have to say matters...a lot! I am worthy of love just as I am: scars, weaknesses, fears, and all. I now realize that no one protected me because they didn't know what was happening to me. I don't need to control situations, I simply need to ask for help."

She rolled down the window and let the crisp air play with her hair and fill her lungs. She finally had hope.

THE END

•   A C K N O W L E D G E M E N T S   •

Today, my life is as it should be. And I am thankful.

I am thankful for each and every moment leading up to this one. Both the good and the difficult, for they have all formed my heart into one that is daily getting better at giving and receiving love.

Although many of the details in this book are fiction, the heart of the story is real. Jaclyn's emotions are real. Her struggle is real. Her fear of reaching out to family and friends is real. I know, because they were real to me for almost two decades.

Thank you to my husband Dave. You've always supported me, even when you didn't understand me. And I am forever grateful.

Thank you to all of my favorite children (you know who you are). You have encouraged me and humored me. You are my biggest fans. I couldn't keep writing without any of you.

Thank you, friends. All of you. You feed my soul and give me perspective. And adult beverages when needed.

Thank you, God. You have ignited a passion within me to share a story of positive change and endless hope through my writing. And I'm loving every moment of it!

And I'm thankful for you, the reader. I pray your younger self receives hope from these pages and those still to be written.

Change For A Penny